PRAISE FOR *HEART ON A LEASH*

"*Heart on a Leash* had my heart from page one. . . . Whether you're a dog lover, cat lover, or romance lover, you're sure to fall head over heels for this book."

—Sarah Smith, author of *Simmer Down*

"A small-town romance that defies cliché. Complex family rivalries, swoon-worthy romance, and (of course!) adorable dogs make this a heart-melting love story."

—Michelle Hazen, author of *Breathe the Sky*

"A heartwarming contemporary romance that puts a new spin on the enemies-to-lovers trope, *Heart on a Leash* takes us on an insightful journey of falling in love without the support of family. Sexy and sensitive, the undeniable chemistry between the heroine and hero (and a pack of adorable huskies) drives the story to its charming conclusion—tail wags and HEA included."

—Samantha Vérant, author of *The Secret French Recipes of Sophie Valroux*

TITLES BY ALANNA MARTIN

....

PAWS AND PREJUDICE

———❤———

Alanna Martin

JOVE
New York

A JOVE BOOK
Published by Berkley
An imprint of Penguin Random House LLC
penguinrandomhouse.com

ISBN: 9780593198858

First Edition: June 2021

Printed in the United States of America
1 3 5 7 9 10 8 6 4 2

Book design by Alison Cnockaert

To my family, who made sure I always had a book.

1

KELSEY PORTER HAD always feared that the lies she told would one day come back to bite her in the ass. She'd just never expected the bite would come in the form of work she had no business doing for a man she wanted nothing to do with. But lies were cruel. They built on themselves— words turning into sentences and sentences into paragraphs, until Kelsey had written a novel of falsehoods about who she was and what she did for a living. So when her father volunteered her labor to Ian Roth, Kelsey was triply screwed.

One, she wasn't about to confess that her alleged work experience was a lie.

Two, she was already extremely busy.

Three, and perhaps most important, Ian was a jerk who didn't deserve what little free time she had.

Despite never having spoken to Ian, Kelsey was absolutely positive of number three. The man had shown zero interest in her dogs, and that spoke of a cold, unfeeling heart.

Kelsey had tried convincing her father she was too

busy to help Ian, but her reasoning had been brushed off as easily as the death glare she'd given him. That was no surprise. Kelsey's glare had a tendency to make people, particularly male people, want to pat her on the head and tell her how cute she was. Cherubic, even. Being taken seriously was hard when you were short. Add in her blond curls and blue eyes and it was damn near impossible. Her twin brother, Kevin, who shared her general appearance, at least had the advantage of being male. No one thought Kevin was cute when he scowled at them.

And no question, her father wouldn't have volunteered Kevin to do unpaid labor. That was the sort of BS demanded only of women. Her father hadn't cared one bit that Kelsey had deadlines to meet and a house she was renovating. Making Ian happy had been more important to him.

"You know I'm right," Kelsey said as she pointed out this last incontrovertible fact.

Josh had the good sense not to argue, which was why he was her favorite cousin. "You're probably right, yes. But try not to be so negative. Ian doesn't know your situation. It's not his fault."

So that was who the nagging *Be nice* voice in her head sounded like. She'd been telling it to shut up since her father had dropped this bomb on her yesterday, and Kelsey turned the full force of her glare on her cousin. It was a combination of displeased, dismissive, and disgusted that on another face might have been lethal. "Excuse me?"

Like her father had, Josh ignored the glare. Freaking men.

They had embarked on their semi-regular afternoon ritual, walking their combined six huskies around the park in downtown Helen. Kelsey had given Josh his three dogs when he moved here a couple of years ago, and they mingled with hers—Romeo, Juliet, and Puck—as they made a circuit around the park's perimeter.

What a difference a few weeks made. Helen hadn't entirely shut down for the winter yet, but the number of tourists had so rapidly declined, it was like someone had shut off a spigot. The park, just a couple of weeks ago, had been a maze to navigate with six dogs, but now it was an easy stroll. That was good, because the chillier weather made Kelsey want to keep a faster pace even as she delighted in the scent of the wet grass and salty bay water. Anything smelled better than the drywall compound she'd been inhaling all morning.

Well, almost anything. She was supposed to meet with Ian at his brewery in an hour, and Kelsey assumed the place would smell like beer. She hated beer. Even if she did have experience writing marketing materials, which she most certainly did *not*, she still would be the worst person in the world to help Ian.

"I'm not saying it was cool of your father to volunteer you," Josh said as he attempted to detangle a couple of leashes. "But how long can it take you to write some stuff for the brewery's website?"

"It's not only the website. It's also press releases, and a puff piece for the local paper. Maybe even a longer article to submit to some travel zines."

"And that." Josh winced, and Kelsey hoped it was dawning on him why she was being so negative.

Lies—spinning them for a living was called fiction. Living them was turning out to be a pain in the ass. Everyone in town, including Josh, believed Kelsey was a freelance writer, and they all had their own ideas as to what that meant. She'd never bothered to correct them, since it hadn't mattered. Until now.

Kelsey hadn't the faintest clue what the website work

might entail, but she did have an idea how much time it took to write for the *Helen Weekly Herald*, because she did it on occasion. It helped keep her cover and paid for the occasional new doggie toy, but she hated it. The only thing Kelsey enjoyed writing was novels. Steamy paranormal romance novels about a pack of husky shifters living in the Alaskan bush, to be 100 percent precise, because romance readers knew exactly what sort of stories they wanted, and Kelsey aimed to provide them for the ones who liked hers. It wasn't what she'd planned to do with her life, but she enjoyed it, was apparently good at it, and had gotten extremely lucky to be able to support herself with it.

And there was no way in hell she could tell anyone in Helen about it. Thank goodness for pen names.

"I don't know how long it'll take," Kelsey said after a moment of encouraging Romeo to get a move on. "My father's obsession with the brewery is going to drive me up a wall though."

Josh grinned. "Oh, come on. Your father volunteering you to do work for free is one thing, but the brewery is exciting. I can't wait until they open to the public."

"It's more people." Ian Roth might be Kelsey's nemesis, but he had a business partner, Micah, who'd moved to Helen with him. That was two more outsiders crowding a town that was already starting to split at its seams. "Besides, you know my father. He doesn't care about the brewery because he likes beer. He sold Ian the warehouse because he's all about *development*, and he's invested in its success because he thinks it'll drive even more development. Then he can make a killing selling off all the property he bought. If he had his way, he'd turn Helen into some sort of metropolis."

At least a metropolis by Alaskan standards, which basically meant pushing the town's population into the five-digit range and being big enough to support a Walmart or a Costco. Kelsey got the appeal of wanting more and closer shopping options, but it was bad enough that the local coffee shops now had to compete with a Starbucks and the town had erected two new traffic lights in the past three years. Granted, they were only truly necessary during the summer tourist season, but it irked.

Josh pulled a bag of trail mix out of his pocket and offered some to her. He'd just gotten off his shift at the hospital and was probably ready for dinner. "Need I remind you that I was one of the 'more people' when I moved here?"

Kelsey declined the offer of food with a shake of her head. Josh liked the healthy stuff—nuts and seeds. If she was eating trail mix, it had better be half sweets. "You're family. It's different."

They had this discussion whenever Josh chided her over her dislike of outsiders, which wasn't so much a dislike of outsiders at all. It was a dislike of Helen losing its small-town charm.

"I haven't even told you the worst of it," Kelsey said before they ended up rehashing that old argument.

"There's more?" Even Josh sounded wary now. But then, despite his original attempt to downplay her father's obnoxious behavior, Josh and her father weren't on speaking terms at the moment. Her cousin knew exactly what kind of crap Wallace Porter was capable of dishing out.

"Oh, there's more." Kelsey laughed, although there wasn't much about it that she found funny. Absurd was more like it. Her father's precise words had made her feel like she'd been dropped in the middle of a Regency-era novel. A day later, she could recall the culmination of his paternalistic speech with perfect clarity.

"We *founded* this town," her father had said. "Connections are important for maintaining our hold on our position, and think of the possibilities. Ian's family owns a very successful brewery in Florida. If Ian and Micah can replicate that success here, it would benefit us all for you to be a part of it. You'd be well taken care of too."

Yes, her father had had the gall to suggest that she might want to consider dating Ian or Micah for the sake of the family, *and* the nerve to suggest she might be happier with a man in her life. Kelsey laughed at the memory, because otherwise she'd scream.

No doubt her parents had been contemplating how to advantageously marry her off since the moment Kevin had gotten engaged and ruined their hopes of him increasing the family's status. Her mother just seemed pleased that her youngest son was happy, but her father was another story. Her was trying; Kelsey would give him that much, but only barely. But whether it was Kevin's fiancé's first name (Peter), his last name (Chung), or the fact that he was a poor graduate student (the disappointment!), Kevin's engagement had made life around the Porter nuclear family stressful.

The only thing that was helping smooth over the situation was the very reason that Josh and her father weren't on speaking terms—Josh was dating Taylor Lipin, and for a Porter, there was nothing more shocking and terrible than a Lipin. The Porter-Lipin feud had raged for over a century, and while Kelsey had enthusiastically embraced having enemies as a child, her adult self was starting to feel like the whole debacle was, in fact, childish.

Perhaps it had started during her time away from Helen while she was in college, or maybe it had everything to do with wanting Josh to be happy, but Kelsey had lately found herself dwelling more and more on the feud's downsides. As a state of mind, that was almost as heretical as dating a Lipin, so she kept her increasingly conflicted thoughts to herself and quietly supported Josh's uncharacteristic attempt at being the family rebel. She couldn't help herself. *Pride and Prejudice* had been a seminal novel in forming her ideas of romance, and thus there was no drama she loved more than a person horrifying their family in the name of love.

That was another truth that could only be dragged out of her under threat of someone torturing her dogs.

That said, it made perfect sense that her parents would currently be pinning their hopes for an engagement that would increase the family's status on her. Such was the burden of being the only daughter and living nearby. Kelsey was positive her older brother was not being subjected to the same expectations as she was. No one would expect Nate to move back to town and make a sacrifice for the family. She, on the other hand, had always been daddy's little warrior. Her father might not be happy that she refused to shun Josh, but until she indicated otherwise, he'd continue to assume that the six-year-old girl who "accidentally" spilled paint all over a Lipin boy's art project had grown into a woman who would flirt her way into a powerful alliance for the sake of the family.

Leaving out her thoughts about the feud, Kelsey relayed the gist of her father's ridiculous request to her cousin.

Josh laughed along with her. "Does your father even know you? What did you tell him?"

Kelsey sighed, because as much as she'd have liked to, she hadn't laughed in her father's face. "I didn't say much, but I did agree to this writing thing for the brewery, so I wonder if it wasn't some devious trick on his part—bring up something so outlandish that I'd agree to the less ridiculous ask."

"I'm not sure your father's that clever, but I was confused about why you were going along with being volunteered. That might explain it."

"Things are tense with my parents these days," Kelsey said, tugging on Puck's leash as the husky sniffed what must have been a particularly fragrant patch of grass. "If this helps, it seems worth it. It's strange being the family peacekeeper, but here I am."

That was one of the justifications she'd come up with. The others involved her real job. Namely, that writing stuff for the brewery kept up her cover, and her current book—the one under deadline—made her scream every time she thought about it. Kelsey hoped writing something completely different might give her some much-needed perspective on the book struggles.

For a moment, she was tempted to confess all of this to Josh. Yes, he was male and she'd had it up to her eyeballs with men, but he was one of the few people Kelsey trusted. On the other hand, the insignia for Helen Regional Hospital that was embroidered on Josh's jacket gave her pause. Josh would certainly keep her true vocation a secret, but how could she be sure her cousin the doctor wouldn't look down on her for writing romance? If he did, she'd be compelled to write him out of her already minuscule circle of trusted people

Josh raised the zipper on his jacket as the damp breeze picked up. "Well, since you are doing it, I recommend not letting your first impression of Ian completely color your opinion. He seemed nice enough to me."

Kelsey rolled her eyes. Josh could make excuses for Ian

all he wanted. That was just like Josh. Nate probably would too. But she was long past the point of making excuses for men acting like jerks. As far as she was concerned, Ian was an ass until proven otherwise. "He snubbed you and wasn't interested in petting our dogs. Who doesn't want to pet our dogs? They're adorable."

"Not everyone's a dog person, Kels."

"Exactly." Kelsey didn't trust anyone who wasn't, although to be fair, she didn't trust most people regardless. But not liking dogs, particularly her dogs, was a strike against someone. Her babies were sweet and friendly, even timid Romeo, who was every bit as distrustful as she was. All they wanted was to be loved and give love in return, and not reciprocating suggested certain things about a person's character that Kelsey couldn't abide.

Josh shrugged. "Maybe he's a cat person, or he has allergies."

"Your girlfriend has allergies, and she loves our dogs." Kelsey had probably put more weight on that point when reevaluating her previously negative opinion of Taylor Lipin than it deserved, but she figured she was at least consistent in how she judged character.

"Taylor is admittedly amazing."

Kelsey made a gagging noise that was entirely for Josh's benefit. While she would never say it in so many words, she was happy that he was happy. Josh undoubtedly knew it, but to admit it would be to give credence to all the times he'd called her a secret marshmallow. Which she was, but life had taught her the importance of hiding her gooey center under titanium skin.

Predictably, Josh ignored her attempt to goad him. Instead, he reached into a pocket and pulled out a pin with the letters *SHS* on it. "Since we're on the topic of outsiders,

I almost forgot. Someone left a pile of these along with some flyers at work. It seemed like something you'd appreciate, so I grabbed one for you."

Kelsey examined the pin more closely. Around the circumference were the words *Save Helen* and a website address. "Never heard of it."

"According to the flyer, the Save Helen Society is a group of concerned citizens who oppose the rapid increase in development and are trying to preserve the town culture and aesthetic." Josh shook his head. "I don't entirely disagree, but there are days when I'd sell my soul for a Target."

Kelsey let out a sharp laugh. "I do appreciate it. My father won't, but at the moment, that's an incentive to wear this thing. I'll look them up."

"I figured. Now try not to hold your father against Ian."

"Ugh. Fine. For you, and only because you gave me a free pin."

Sticking the pin on her jacket so she didn't lose it, Kelsey let her far more optimistic cousin try to convince her that Ian wasn't a jerk. By the time she pulled her SUV up to the brewery at the far end of town, she almost believed it could be possible. It wasn't much to look at from the outside. There wasn't even a sign yet, but the parking lot had recently been repaved, and the trash bin that had been sitting out for months was gone.

Kelsey parked and got the dogs out. She'd give Ian one more chance with them, and besides, she hated leaving them confined to the car, particularly when she didn't know how long she'd be.

Ian was supposed to be expecting her, but since the brewery wasn't open to the public yet, Kelsey assumed the polite thing to do was knock rather than barge in. A minute later she heard footsteps on the other side of the door, then it swung open. She'd seen Ian once, so she had just long enough to recognize that the tall guy in the doorway was him.

Then he slammed the door in her face.

2

◦━━━━━━━━◦

IAN RESTED HIS head against the doorframe, his pulse racing. He'd just slammed a door on Wallace Porter's daughter. That is, he was 90 percent certain the woman on the other side of the door was Wallace's daughter. He hadn't gotten a good enough look at her to notice a family resemblance, but no other women were supposed to be stopping by today.

No, he'd barely glanced at the woman, because his attention had immediately been drawn to the three dogs around her legs. Big dogs. Not huge dogs, but dogs that looked like they were of a size that could jump on you and tear out your throat.

Logic informed Ian that those dogs were unlikely to do any such thing, but his brain paid little heed to logic in the face of three large dogs. They had a wolfish look to them too. That probably meant they were huskies or part huskies, but it really didn't make a difference. He simply did not like large dogs of any breed.

Actually, Ian did not like any dogs, and to be fair, it was the dogs that had started it. He'd been three when one had jumped on him, and that was all he remembered—a large furry object zooming in for the kill and knocking him to the ground to feast. That the dog had probably not been trying to kill him in reality made no difference to the irrational part of his brain, which from that day forward considered all dogs to be furry killing machines. Even those little fluffy ones with the loud barks that everyone else thought were so cute.

Ian refused to be intimidated by those ankle biters, but the dogs this woman had were definitely potential throat biters. And they were not entering his brewery.

Shit. *Shit.* This was embarrassing on a personal level, not to mention problematic on a business one if that was in fact Wallace Porter's daughter on his stoop. He'd never have asked for writing help, but Wallace had assured him that his daughter did stuff like this all the time and wasn't busy, and Ian could really use the assistance.

The woman with the dogs banged once on the door, hard enough for it to vibrate and make Ian raise his head. "Um, hello?"

He thought he heard her add "What the hell?" under her breath, and he supposed he couldn't blame her. He'd acted like a first-class schmuck.

An excuse—that's what he needed. Ian's pulse had started lowering, but it rose again in desperation as he swept his gaze over the brewery's under-construction tasting room. He'd been installing shelves behind where the bar would eventually be, and a variety of tools—a drill, screws, a level, and more—were scattered about the area. If experience had taught him anything, it was that dogs could not contain their need to chase things. They smelled fear and charged it down. He would try to keep his distance, and they would home in on him like four-legged heat-seeking missiles. That meant a messy floor was a dangerous floor. Excuse found.

Ian cleared his throat. "Sorry. Are you Kelsey Porter?" That was the name of Wallace's daughter, right? He didn't need to do anything else embarrassing, like get it wrong.

"Yeah."

"Right, sorry again." Bracing himself, Ian cracked the door an inch. By keeping his focus on Kelsey's face, he could avoid seeing the dogs. It wasn't ideal—his nerves were quite aware of their presence—but it helped.

So did focusing on her face, because wow—Kelsey was cute. Her blond hair was pulled back, making it impossible to miss her big blue eyes and the couple of freckles that dotted her nose. She had the sort of face that sang of sunshine and innocence, but whispered that its owner was capable of much dirtier things in the bedroom.

That sort of perky cheerleader pretty had never been Ian's thing, but something about Kelsey told him he'd make an exception in her case. Possibly it was her lips, which made it clear that the perky cheerleader look was a lie. They were twisted in obvious annoyance with him.

Unfortunately, that was understandable, and the reminder kicked Ian out of his temporarily lustful state of mind. "You're welcome to come in, but you shouldn't bring the dogs. It's a construction zone in here."

Those big blue eyes narrowed at him, but they never quite met the threshold for being called icy. "Seriously?"

"Sorry." He was a broken record with this apologizing, but if he got rid of the dogs, it would be worth it.

Kelsey sighed in a far more dramatic fashion than Ian felt the situation deserved. "Fine. I'll take them back to the car."

Ian watched her turn away long enough to make sure she really was heading toward the unfamiliar SUV—and okay, also long enough to appreciate the way her ass looked in those jeans—then he ducked back inside. Time to make good on his not-quite lie.

Quickly, he scattered a few screws around the floor and took a broom to the pile of sawdust he'd so meticulously swept up a couple of hours ago. For good measure, he also carried the circular saw from the back room into the main room and set it on top of the sawhorses sitting in the corner. In a few seconds, he'd uncleaned the room and made it hazardous to energetic animals.

Two steps forward, one step backward. That seemed typical for how getting the brewery off the ground was going. He and Micah had run into more roadblocks than any reasonable person could have expected. Sure, there were the normal *It takes how long to ship that to Alaska?* kinds of delays. But there were also delays that Ian could ascribe no other reasoning to than malice.

He'd just finished wiping his dusty hands off on his jeans when he heard Kelsey's footsteps on the stairs. Crisis averted. Barely.

"You can come on in."

"Thanks." For someone who looked so sweet, she could pack an impressive amount of bitter into one syllable. Kelsey reminded Ian of that coffee stout he'd once made that was too cloying on the initial taste and a bit like drinking diesel fuel in the aftertaste. Not every recipe that was good in theory worked in practice. Not on the first try, anyway.

On the note of second tries, Ian held out his hand and introduced himself. Kelsey's skin was pleasantly cool, and he had to fight the urge to clasp her hand more tightly. If he had to guess, she was nearly a foot shorter than him, and that difference in size made her hand fit perfectly in his. He rather liked the thought of that too much, so he pushed it as far into the back of his mind as he could. It wasn't too difficult when Kelsey continued to scowl at him.

"Sorry about slamming the door on you," Ian said, trying once more to smooth away her expression. "I was worried the dogs might dart inside and hurt their paws."

If anything, Kelsey's scowl deepened. "My dogs are very well behaved. They don't dart. If I told them to stay, they would."

Okay then. Given the way she glared, Ian was doubly glad he'd made her keep the dogs outside. She'd probably have told them to go for his jugular.

He'd make one more attempt, since he didn't like getting off on the wrong foot with someone. "Good to know for the future. Can I get you a drink?"

"I'd rather you get to the point. I don't like leaving my dogs in the car for too long."

Fine. That seemed fair, and besides, he could take a hint.

Ian started to ask another—to the point—question, and that's when he saw the pin attached to Kelsey's jacket. Before her dogs and before her face (or ass), that's what he should have noticed. That pin likely explained so much about her attitude. Although the Save Helen Society had been a thorn in his side for months, it was only recently that Ian had discovered the group had a name as well as a mission.

Ironically, he didn't even disagree with their mission. Like dogs, the Save Helen Society was fine in theory, but in practice it was a massive pain in his backside. Part of what Ian loved about this town were its size and unique charms, and he didn't want it overrun with chain stores and restaurants or bland housing developments either. But while that might be the SHS's ostensible goal, it seemed like they'd taken their ire beyond it and were aiming it at any and all outsiders—him and the brewery included.

For no reason, Ian had had perfectly put together permits denied or simply held up at city hall until contractors became unavailable. Zoning issues that should have been completely straightforward had been questioned, forcing him and Micah to petition for them. And they'd been outright told by people on the town council that Helen was no place for a brewery.

The first time a permit had been "misplaced," Ian had assumed it was a mistake. The fourth time, he assumed it was one person with an anti-alcohol agenda. It was only after meeting the mayor's mother herself that Ian learned she'd been spearheading a group—the SHS—to protest any and all new development.

Well, screw that. Everything he and Micah had done was entirely legal, and no matter what a small band of xenophobic townspeople thought, most of Helen was clearly excited about the brewery. And Ian was excited to open it.

He was also determined to make it a success, and far past the point of believing he could make this process go more easily by being nice to the zealots. Even if the zealot in front of him was supposed to be helping him and happened to look damn good in a pair of tight jeans. Kelsey Porter had made her feelings abundantly clear in one pouty-lipped scowl.

Ian motioned to the pin. "You a member?"

Kelsey seemed confused for a second as her eyes dropped to her chest. "Oh, that. I'm not much of a joiner, but I appreciate the sentiment. This town is getting too big, too many new people moving in. No offense."

Oy. Her tone clearly intended offense. How was he supposed to trust her to do a write-up of the brewery? What had Wallace been thinking?

God, he wished Micah were here to deal with this crap. All Ian wanted to do was brew and sell some beer. Micah was the people person, the sales guy. He could fake a smile and sincerity like no one's business, whereas Ian usually had no trouble getting along with people, so he didn't need to try. Everything about Kelsey, however, was putting him on edge. Blame it on her dogs, maybe. That had made him twitchy to begin with. Toss in that her sweet face was having an unwelcome impact on his lower body while at the same time he wanted to kick her pert ass out the door for interfering with the one goal he had in life, and yeah. He was on edge.

Since he didn't feel like lying and pretending no offense had been taken, Ian didn't bother to fake a smile. Small talk was over, if it had ever begun. He had to get Kelsey out of here so he could get back to work. Neither she nor the SHS was going to get in his way.

"So what do I need to do for you? Besides get out of town, that is?"

Kelsey raised an eyebrow. "I didn't suggest it."

"Your pin did the talking."

"You sound defensive."

"When one side goes on the offensive, being defensive is smart."

Kelsey's face lit up in an expression that Ian might have considered cute under other circumstances. "You know, usually I have to open my mouth before people call me offensive. What a good little pin this is." She stroked it. "I've leveled up if I can hurt someone's feelings without saying a word."

Ian grabbed one of the screws sitting on his makeshift plywood table and spun it around to keep his hands busy. It was either that or start futzing with the drill, and that seemed kind of violent. "I don't recall suggesting my feelings were hurt. I promise you, they're not. The brewery is opening for business, even if the tasting room isn't completed and the website is unfinished. I feel very good about that, actually, and we're not going anywhere."

That froze Kelsey's cruel smile in place. "I'm sure. So about the website?"

"Never mind. I'll handle it." Writing something as short as a five-paragraph About section would cost him hours of stress, but he'd do it. Too bad Micah hated writing even more than he did.

"I can do it." Kelsey crossed her arms. "I told my father I would. I just need you to give me information and to tell me what exactly you want it to say."

He wondered if he could actually trust her, but Ian supposed nothing would be posted without him reading it, so it wasn't much of a risk. "My family's brewery has a short History-slash-About section on their site. I want to include something like that on ours."

"Your family down in Florida?"

Wallace must have told her where he was from. "Yeah. My aunt and uncle started it. I worked for them."

"Explain to me why anyone who lived in Florida would want to move here?"

It was a fair question and certainly not the first time he'd heard it, though maybe the first time he'd heard it asked so disdainfully. But the answer was complicated, and there was no way he was about to share it with Kelsey.

Before he could decide what sort of nonanswer to give her, she kept going. "Tell me it's not because you have some obsession with a book or something."

He could have choked on the bland answer he'd been settling on. The dogs, the SHS pin, and now this. It was like she knew exactly what pressure points to poke to cause him pain.

Yes, he did love *The Call of the Wild*, or at least the illustrated children's version of it his mother used to read to him before she died. Was it ironic because of his dog issues? Sure. But Ian associated the story with warmth and love and everything exciting. It had been instrumental in him begging his grandparents to take him to Alaska when he was younger, and that trip had cemented his love of the untamed, snowy north.

Knowing Kelsey would scoff at him for it increased Ian's frustration with her a thousandfold.

The screw's sharp edges dug into his fingers, but hopefully the pain kept those thoughts off his face. "I'd visited Helen before, and when my family discussed opening another brewery, someplace as far from Florida as possible sounded perfect."

There was some truth to that, more than Kelsey deserved, but he'd have to explain for the website regardless, so this didn't feel like he was giving up any secrets. The fact that his aunt and uncle had been skeptical of letting him open the brewery in Helen wasn't something that would be going in any PR materials. They'd been thinking of another location in Florida or, at the very farthest, Boston, which was at least on the East Coast. Ian was certain their reasoning had been that it would be easier for them to help out that way if needed. His brewery and their brewery had different names, and he was fully in charge of this brewery's recipes and production, but financially, the two businesses were linked. If he screwed up and couldn't pay off the loans, he'd cost his aunt and uncle a lot of money and possibly hurt their brand's reputation.

"I grew up in Massachusetts," Ian added. "I'm familiar with the concept of cold, so don't worry about finding me frozen like a Popsicle one day."

Kelsey's lips twitched in a manner Ian couldn't decipher. "I wasn't worried."

"I'm shocked." He glared at her, daring her to throw another punch.

She glared back.

The staring contest that followed probably only lasted a second, but it felt to Ian like an eternity as he debated whether it was worth being the one to break it so he could get back to work. It should have been an easy call. Who got into staring contests as an adult? But Kelsey was absolutely infuriating, and that she looked hot while being so was doubly infuriating.

Ian had no clue what malicious thoughts were running through her faux-perky head, but Kelsey broke out of the moment at the same time he did, and they talked over each other.

"Is there anything—"

"I need to go."

Relief swept through Ian. "Okay. How will I send you the brewery information?"

She shrugged. "I'll look at what's on your family brewery's site and email you questions."

Email sounded good to him. The less time spent with Kelsey and her dogs, the better.

3

◦————————◦

A LIGHT RAIN had started to fall while she'd
unintentionally—and then very intentionally—attempted
to goad Ian, but Kelsey didn't rush her steps back to the
car. She stood in the drizzle, breathing slowly as though
she could exhale the conversation. In college, she'd tried
meditation for a while to help with stress, but she'd never
mastered the art of clearing her mind. The best she could
do was turn her focus elsewhere, and *elsewhere* typically
involved words. If she could distill whatever was bothering her into a single word, she could better grapple with
the problem.

For Ian, the word she chose was *insufferable*. Kelsey
liked that word for both its Austen-ish feel and the sound
it made it, which reminded her of *suffocate*. Right now,
she also liked the idea of smothering Ian with a pillow.

That much accomplished, Kelsey climbed into her car
before she got any wetter. Rain was a part of life in Helen,
especially in the fall. Kelsey would have greatly preferred
it to snow as much as the tourists who swarmed the city
every summer assumed it did. Instead, it snowed half as

much but rained twice as much. She was used to it, but she'd never liked it.

Ian, however, she'd tried to like—or, at the very least, she'd tried to tolerate him. She couldn't help it if he made that impossible. Not letting her dogs into the brewery had been annoying, but she could almost have overlooked that when she saw the mess in the room. After all, Ian was right when he said he had no way of knowing how well trained her babies were. If she were being fair, he'd made the right call from his perspective.

Kelsey did not feel like being fair though. Ian already had three strikes against him before she'd officially met him today. He was part of the town overdevelopment problem, he'd previously been rude to her dogs and to Josh, and her parents—really her father—expected her to like him, or pretend to for the sake of the family. And then today he'd . . . What?

She fumbled with that question as Romeo climbed onto her from the passenger seat and licked her face, but the husky's kisses didn't entirely wipe away her frown as she pondered this last point. "Down, boy. It's only been five minutes since you last saw me."

Poor Romeo and his attachment issues. She'd adopted him four years ago, and he still got stressed if she left him alone. Kelsey had hoped his siblings would ease his anxiety, and they did, but only to a degree. Some dogs, like some people, were just less resilient than others. Juliet and Puck had been rescues, too, but they'd settled down with relative ease. Winning Romeo's trust was much more difficult, but once you had it, he got stressed when you weren't around.

"Go on. Get in back with the others." Kelsey patted Romeo on the butt, and the husky climbed into the back seat, swatting her face with his tail as he did.

Males. Even the dogs had it in for her.

Which brought her back to the topic of Ian and the word *insufferable*. There had to be something about him to make that particular word leap out of her subconscious.

Yes, he'd challenged her. Ian had proved he wasn't about to take hits from the SHS without fighting back, but normally that was something Kelsey could respect. It might even have made her like him a bit, despite him being an enemy. Yet she did not feel any more kindly disposed to Ian than she had this morning. She felt less.

It was the Popsicle comment. Dear God. She figured it out as she put the SUV into reverse. For a second, after he'd joked about the cold, she'd had the very intense image of licking the man like a Popsicle. Of sucking on—

Hell no. Kelsey smashed down the accelerator, trying to banish the idea from her brain with pure acceleration.

She wouldn't pretend that he wasn't attractive. Kelsey didn't remember him being so hot when Josh had pointed him out a couple of months ago, but she hadn't been paying much attention then. Today, though, there was no denying it. He was tall, which she could take or leave, being short herself, and he had one of those genial, friendly faces that made her think of puppies. But Ian was clearly no puppy. He was very adult and very much a man, with honey-colored eyes and sandy hair and cheekbones that looked like they could slice a woman's tongue if she kissed his face.

Which she was totally not imagining doing.

The jeans and sweatshirt he'd been wearing had been faded and stained with paint, and they had not detracted one bit from the pretty package. If anything, they balanced out his kind features with just enough edge to suggest he held depths, and they could make a woman question what sorts of muscles were hidden beneath them.

Which she was totally not wondering about.

His appearance was simply annoying, that's what it was. Annoying because she resented being pressured into helping Ian, and because she resented the suggestion that she might want to be romantically interested in him. As a result, she hadn't wanted to like him—and she didn't. She also hadn't wanted to find him attractive—but she did.

Whether or not any of this was Ian's fault didn't make a difference. The end result was that he was insufferable. Leaving quickly with a plan to email him questions had been the only smart choice, even though it would take more of her time and make the whole task more difficult. But she could handle difficult. She simply didn't want to handle *Ian*.

Or, well, part of her did, and that was the problem.

Grumbling to herself, Kelsey pulled her SUV into the lot by Lucky Hardware. This was one place in town that didn't have competition from any of those chain stores yet. Kelsey wondered what the Lukavich family, who'd owned it for generations, thought about her father's plans for expanding Helen. They were Porter people through and through, but she didn't see how expansion could be anything but bad for their business.

"Sorry, guys. You're going to have to wait in the car a little longer," she told the dogs. Disappointed faces stared at her from behind the windows as Kelsey shut the door.

Whether it was drywall compound, sawdust, or paint stripper, Kelsey was getting sick of the stink of home renovation, and Lucky Hardware blended all those smells, along with other indefinable construction odors, into something that could give her nightmares. She supposed it wasn't the store's fault that it smelled like its products, but for the dogs' sakes and her own, she rushed down the aisles to grab more drywall compound and keep the visit quick.

Maggie, daughter of the current generation of owners and a friend from high school, was behind the register reading a book when Kelsey plopped her tub down. She sneaked a glance at the cover and was surprised to discover it was a romance. It wasn't an author Kelsey was familiar with, but she recognized the cover and the name.

That was interesting. Everyone's reading taste—or lack thereof—was a point of interest to her for obvious reasons, but she hadn't known Maggie's extended to romance. Her paranoia about her job being exposed kept her from talking about books with people in real life. Online, where people knew her under her pen name, was another story, but even online Kelsey hid most of her life to protect her privacy.

Of course, she didn't talk to Maggie that often anyway, but hers was one of the few friendships from high school that Kelsey had maintained, and that was because Maggie had proven herself to be an actual friend.

That was yet another problem caused by the feud. Starting in kindergarten, classes had been divided between Porters and Lipins, and to have one of those magical last names meant you were the center of the schoolyard universe. Those were the days when the ability to play nasty pranks on the Lipins without being punished for it— hell, being *rewarded* for it—had been fun. But the fun had lessened with age as the pranks had grown nastier, and eventually Kelsey had realized the popularity was as superficial as her joy. For her own sanity, she'd needed to figure out which people genuinely liked her and which ones only called her a friend because they thought she and her family could do something for her. She and Kevin had worked together devising tricks to get people to expose themselves, and the results had often been disappointing.

Maggie, however, had passed every one of Kelsey's and Kevin's tests. Still, even with friends, there were degrees of trust involved, and Kelsey didn't trust anyone more than absolutely necessary. At the moment, *absolutely necessary* did not cover revealing a shared love for the romance genre.

With Josh, Kelsey worried he might look down on her if he knew. With Maggie, the reason for keeping silent was different. Maggie wouldn't mean to be careless if Kelsey told her anything, but normal people didn't watch their every word. The last thing Kelsey needed was for news that she wrote romance to spread to the Lipins. It didn't matter that romance was the biggest-selling genre, or that the (mostly) women who read it were smart, discerning readers, or even that many of the best romance books were wickedly feminist. Like so many fans of the genre, Kelsey could defend its merits to her dying breath, but that wasn't the point. The point was she didn't want to *have to*, and the Lipins would surely make her. All the negative stereotypes about romance readers and writers would be used as ammunition against her and her family, and no doubt some Lipin would coordinate an online attack on her books. It certainly wouldn't be the first time either family had tried to ruin someone's career or reputation.

For those reasons alone, Kelsey figured she had a familial duty to hide her true career. With the feud, any worries about nasty small-town gossip had to be taken to the most extreme conclusion. It was simply another reason she was starting to find the feud less entertaining and more exhausting. And at times like this, Kelsey reminded herself that she was lucky to enjoy being a hermit and that was why she surrounded herself with dogs. Dogs were way better than people.

Maggie must have been engrossed in her book, because

it took another second before she glanced up, and she jumped slightly in her seat. "Kels, oh my God! I'm sorry. I didn't make you wait too long, did I? I heard someone set something down, but it didn't quite fully penetrate my brain."

"Interesting word choice, given your reading material."

Maggie grinned. "As a matter of fact, I was just getting to the good part."

"Well, geez, I feel bad about interrupting."

"You should." She ran the drywall compound over the scanner with sigh. "Living through fiction is about the only way I'm getting any these days."

"You and me both." Although in her case, that was by choice. Kelsey hadn't slept with a guy since Anthony, her evil college ex, six years ago. Still, it wasn't like she missed sex. The stuff she wrote and read was way better than anything she'd experienced with Anthony, which was one of several reasons she hadn't gone looking for it.

Honestly, Kelsey would take book boyfriends any day over having to deal with real-life men. Judging by the comments she often got from her readers, she wasn't alone in that.

"Pathetic," Maggie said. "There's something wrong with the world when men aren't falling at our feet."

Kelsey made a sympathetic noise as she swiped her credit card. Maggie wasn't entirely wrong. She was cute, and in a fairer world, she wouldn't be wanting for dates. Herself, on the other hand—she'd had her share of her parents, aunts and uncles, grandparents—you name it— setting her up with guys. She might not have had sex in many years, but she'd suffered through her fill of terrible first dates, mostly to make her family happy. Not one of the guys had ever warranted a second.

"I wouldn't have time if they did," Kelsey said. "So I suppose that's okay."

"Because the house is under construction?" Maggie nodded toward the drywall compound.

"It's mostly the walls left, but yeah. Between that and work, I'm swamped. And get this." Kelsey waved her credit card around in agitation. "My father kindly volunteered me to help out the brewery guys by writing for their website. Like I have nothing else to do."

At the mention of the brewery, Maggie's face lit up. "Oh, there could be worse things. I mean, yes, that's crappy of your father to volunteer you. But have you met them yet?" She fanned herself.

"Seriously?"

"What? I told you—I'm in a slump. But even if I wasn't . . ." Maggie fanned herself again. "They've both been in here a lot, especially Ian, because they're doing most of the renovation themselves. They brighten up my shifts."

Kelsey rolled her eyes. "I've met Ian. He's good-looking, I suppose."

She supposed. Like she hadn't been chewing this fact over and trying to spit it out for the past ten minutes.

"And nice and funny."

"And full of himself and naive."

Maggie frowned and shot Kelsey a disbelieving expression. "I've seen no evidence of either."

"That's because you haven't had a long enough conversation with him." Part of her recognized this was ridiculous. Odds were that Maggie had actually had longer conversations with Ian, simply by shooting the shit while he was in the store. But her meeting with him today felt like it had lasted a lifetime.

"Uh-huh." Maggie pretended to smack Kelsey with her book. "Once a cynic, always a cynic."

"Are you a cynic if you're right?"

"Something only a cynic would ask. Wait—I just had a

depressing thought." Maggie dropped the book and leaned over the counter. "Do you think Ian and Micah are together, like in more ways than only the brewery?"

Kelsey laughed at her friend's distraught face. While she most definitely did not want the town to keep expanding, she had to admit there was something limiting about the current dating pool. It didn't affect her, since she didn't care, but she could see why Maggie might be sad if she learned that the two new men in town weren't available.

She considered the possibility more as she put her wallet away. "My father doesn't seem to think they're a couple, but then, given his initial reaction to my brother's engagement, he might not be the best judge. All the signs could be there, and he'd probably miss them."

And wouldn't that be fantastic? There would be no chance her parents could try setting her up with Ian or Micah, and no opportunity for her to cave and allow it.

"I'll let you know if I hear anything new," Kelsey promised.

Conscious of her poor dogs, who'd had to spend way too much time in a car already, she said goodbye to Maggie and drove home. But the question of whether Ian and Micah were a couple lingered in her mind. First, Kelsey told herself that it was because, if true, it removed one source of potential stress. Then a better reason occurred to her.

It was because the possibility had made her bring up her brother, and thinking about Kevin made her think about his friend Parker. A couple of months ago, Parker had been partially responsible for the rift that currently plagued her immediate family and the guilt Kelsey felt about the situation. That was because Parker, acting on her father's idea, had launched an offensive against the Lipins by salting the wine the Lipins served guests at their luxury hotel.

It had been a bad move. Involving guests at the hotel violated an unspoken rule of the feud, which was that outsiders were never targeted. Her father's suggestion and Parker's action had pissed off Kelsey to no end. But there was a useful idea in that terrible one—sabotage.

What if she could sabotage the brewery? She didn't want anyone to get hurt; she only wanted to make Ian and Micah decide that Helen was the wrong place to open their business. And yeah, maybe it was a way to make Ian a little less smug too. Being insufferable practically demanded being punched, metaphorically if no other way.

She could take a cue straight from Parker and put something in their beer. Parker had supposedly used salt, but the possibilities were endless. Orange juice? Chili powder? It didn't much matter what it was. If she could keep ruining batches of beer before they could bottle it, how long would it be before Ian and Micah decided opening Northern Charm Brewing in Helen had been a mistake?

Of course, since she didn't know anything about beer (perhaps it was brewed in vats that would be hard to tamper with), then she could always pick a lock and leave a door open in the winter. The local wildlife would love a nice, warm place to hang out, and Kelsey would love to see Mr. Florida and his business partner try figuring out what to do when a moose parked itself inside their building. (Answer: back away slowly, especially if the moose had been drinking.)

It would be so satisfying to be the one who convinced the men to leave. Likely it wouldn't ruin the whole business, right? All she needed was to drive them out of town and force them to open it somewhere else.

"What do you think?" Kelsey asked as she let the dogs inside the house. "Should we sabotage the brewery?"

Three sets of blue and brown eyes just stared at her. Their ears were perked with interest, but something in their faces admonished her.

Right. Because they were huskies and would therefore probably love Ian if he let them.

"Look, it's not like he's ever been anything but rude to you. You don't have to like him." She stuck her hands on her hips, and that finally got Juliet to bark at her.

Kelsey groaned. "You just want dinner, don't you? Fine. Be that way, but stop trying to make me feel guilty. I'm allowed to fantasize."

She was, after all, good at that, and sabotaging the brewery was a far safer fantasy than any that involved Ian's Popsicle.

4

SILENCE GREETED IAN as he opened the door to the rental house he was sharing with Micah, and that could only mean one thing: his best friend hadn't gotten back from his trip to Anchorage yet. They'd lived together on and off since first sharing a dorm room in college, and Micah's inability to tolerate quiet was something Ian had learned to adjust to. He didn't really like it, but since neither of them could draw much of a salary from the brewery yet, sharing a place temporarily had seemed like a smart option. For a year, he could put up with Micah's need to have music streaming or the TV blaring the entire time he was awake.

Ian prided himself on being the kind of guy who could put up with a lot and get along with anyone, which was why his interaction with Kelsey earlier continued to burn him like a paper cut. Even after she'd left, he hadn't been able to get her out of his head. He didn't want to blame the fixation on her tight jeans, but it would be dishonest to claim the animosity was because she was the first person he hadn't gotten along with in Helen. Not when the entire Save Helen Society had it in for his business.

The other SHS members he'd met hadn't been so openly hostile though. Maybe that was the difference. They also weren't supposed to be *helping* him.

There—he liked that explanation. The reason Kelsey was distracting was because the arrangement was awkward. If he were more superstitious, Ian would say having her work on the brewery website was a bad sign, but he wasn't the superstitious one. That was Micah.

Of course, that didn't stop Ian from staring thoughtfully at the hamsa Micah had hung on their living room wall. Ian had given him a good ribbing about that, but his friend had insisted they could use all the help they could get, and that was undeniable. They had their work cut out for them, even without an irritatingly hot blond getting in his face. Besides, Ian didn't mind having one attractive decoration hanging on their otherwise bare walls.

With a sigh, Ian set the salmon he'd bought on the way home in the fridge, then showered and changed out of his sawdust-coated clothes. Two texts waited for him when he got out. One was from Micah, letting him know he was half an hour away in case Ian would be so kind as to make dinner even though it wasn't his night to cook. The other was from his sister, who was still living in Naples, Florida, asking him to call.

Ian didn't bother responding to Micah's message, since his friend should be driving, not texting. But Isabel's message was surprising. Ian called her back as he contemplated what to do with the salmon. He had the basics of cooking down fine. His bubbe wouldn't have permitted anything else. But he wasn't the world's most adventurous cook, and after a while, even he got bored with himself. Tonight did not feel like an adventuring kind of night though. He had no problem doing the cooking, but he was too irritated by Kelsey to think clearly enough to make a big effort. Fortunately, salmon under the broiler was about as easy as it got. After several months of living in Helen, where the salmon was relatively cheap and plentiful, Ian could practically cook it in his sleep.

His sister picked up on the second ring. "That was fast."

"Yeah, well, you called while I was in the shower. What's up, Iz?"

His sister hated being called that, and Ian could practically feel her glaring at him from five thousand miles away. "Not much, but my spidey sense was tingling. I thought I'd better check in with you."

In light of the day's events, he had to admit that Isabel's "tingling" was an odd coincidence. "Not much going on here either. In fact, life up here gets pretty boring. You sure you want to join me?"

He was only ever half joking when he teased Isabel about her plans to move to Helen after she finished school. His sister was something of a wild child who'd only gotten her life together in the past few years. Given their screwed-up family situation when they were young, Ian understood why she'd acted out, even if he'd taken the opposite approach. But as much as he'd like her closer, he wasn't sure how well Isabel would adapt to small-town Helen life. And after his dealings with Kelsey today, he was even more apprehensive of anyone else he cared about moving here.

"I'm starting to think you don't actually want me to move closer." Isabel's tone was teasing, but Ian winced at the suggestion. Being left behind was a theme in their lives, and as such, it wasn't a thought he wanted to cross her mind.

"What brother wouldn't want his bratty younger sister cramping his style? I just feel compelled to keep reminding you that life is different around here. We're very much outsiders."

"Something did happen today, didn't it?"

Ian gave a disbelieving glance at his phone, which was totally missed by his sister, seeing as it wasn't a video call. Since she was so psychic, however, he assumed she got the gist. "Nothing important. I had a run-in with one of the Save Helen Society people I told you about."

A run-in with her and her dogs, but he didn't see a reason to mention the dogs. Isabel was aware of his feelings about them.

His sister snorted. "Well, ignore them."

"Of course I'm ignoring them." He was trying to, anyway. Kelsey's smug smile and tight jeans were putting up a decent fight in his head.

"Good. I can ignore them, too, when I finally make it up there. I'm very good at ignoring annoying people. So good, actually, that I forgot to mention what came in the mail yesterday."

Ian got out a bag of potatoes and set them on the counter with a thud before realizing Isabel was waiting for him to ask something. "What?"

"A birthday card. I was going to make you guess, but I figured the odds weren't good."

"That's because your birthday was two months ago."

"Exactly."

Ian started to ask who it was from, then he realized the answer and why Isabel hadn't volunteered the information. She'd expected him to figure it out because there was only one person who would send a card two months late, if he bothered to send one at all.

Their father.

Ian's grip hardened around the potato in his hand, and he forced his fingers to unclench. "Why?"

He asked partly to himself and partly to the universe, but he wasn't entirely sure of the question. Why had their father forgotten Isabel's twenty-fourth birthday? Why had the man taken the time to send her a card two months late when he couldn't bother to do anything else for her?

Why did he continue to pop in and out of their lives at the most random times, like an unrelenting zit?

Isabel, unaware that the question hadn't been directed at her, gave Ian the only answer he was likely to get. "Who knows? It's kind of hilarious."

Although Ian was glad she'd finally reached a point in her life where she could find humor in the situation, he couldn't. Especially not after the reminder he'd gotten today from Kelsey of what he was up against to get the brewery running successfully. His father was out there just waiting for the brewery to fail so he could swoop in and say *I knew it*.

Ian would not let that happen, even if it meant taking on half the town. He didn't only have some of his aunt and uncle's money invested in Northern Charm Brewing—he had too much of his life invested.

He talked to Isabel for a few more minutes while he started the potatoes baking and got the challah out of the freezer. If he'd been living alone, Ian wouldn't have taken the time to mark Shabbat, but Micah's family had always done it and therefore so did his friend. Since there was no place to buy challah in Helen, Ian contributed by baking the bread. His bubbe's recipe was easy, but the end result looked impressive, so Ian kept that secret to himself.

Micah opened the door about ten minutes after Ian had gotten off the phone with his sister, looking exhausted but triumphant as he spread his arms wide. "All of it. You can thank me now."

"All of it? Really?" Despite his own less than stellar day, that news perked Ian up immediately. His father could shove his dire warning about his children never amounting to anything straight up his absentee ass.

Micah tossed his jacket on the sofa. "Every drop of our next two batches is sold. Am I not amazing?"

"Are you not the guy who brewed it? Oh wait, no, actually, you're not."

"But I am the guy who schlepped it all around the state to line up buyers. Did you want to do that part?"

"Nope." Ian just wanted to make the beer. It was the creative part of the job that he liked. The selling of it and the dealing with numbers parts were best left to the guy who was good with both people and numbers. "Celebratory beer?" Ian pulled one that wasn't their own from the fridge and held it out.

Micah grabbed it, nodding. "Thanks. Been on the road way too much today. Appreciate you making dinner. Is that salmon?"

"Of course it's salmon." Ian was positive the day would come when he got sick of salmon, but given how expensive normal groceries were, he was not looking forward to it.

"Of course." Micah laughed into his beer and looked wistfully at the challah. "You know, since I was on the road so much, I had time to think. And I think we should expand the brewery to include a bagel and bread bakery to go along with the beer. I mean, look at this loaf. It's beautiful. You have skills that are being seriously underused."

"You are joking, right?"

Micah dropped onto a chair. "Completely serious. What's the point in having so much salmon around if you don't have good bagels to eat it with? We could call ourselves Breads and Brews."

"No."

"The Yeast Men."

Ian shook his head, starting to wish he'd begun drinking earlier. "That's horrible."

Micah conceded with a shrug. "Okay, this is my favorite though—The Yeast We Can Do."

"This is why I named the brewery, and hell no." He stuck the salmon in the oven and put the bread that had started this entire bizarre conversation on top of the warm stove to speed up the defrosting process. "Besides, we have enough issues with this town as it is without starting yet another business. Case in point—I met Wallace's daughter today."

Quickly, he filled Micah in on the status of the website writing and Kelsey.

As Ian should have guessed, Micah focused on the important question. "Is she cute?"

"I don't know. I was too busy staring at the SHS pin she was wearing." Great. So he was lying to his best friend, but saying he'd been distracted by her large dogs did not sit well with his ego. And for some reason, admitting Kelsey was cute bugged him. The enemy should not be cute, and her scowling lips should not have any effect on his groin. "I'm not sure we can trust anything she writes."

"Oh, relax. I'm sure it's fine. Remember—I sold us out of our entire inventory before it's even ready. We're in good shape."

That was true, and Ian relaxed slightly. They would be fine. With the skills he'd learned from his aunt and uncle, and with Micah's gift for sales, they would make this venture work. So never mind Kelsey. As his sister could attest, he'd endured far worse than this town had thrown at him.

5

◦———————◦

SOMEONE DID NOT want her to write. He rested his head on Kelsey's knees and stared up at her with hopeful brown eyes as if to say, *How dare you ignore me for that glowing screen when I'm so much cuter?*

"Mama has a job to do," Kelsey said to Puck, although she wasn't sure why she bothered. She was emphatically not making any worthwhile progress.

The husky's ears perked up, probably because he'd sensed he'd won the battle for her attention.

Groaning, Kelsey rubbed the top of his head. The bright yellow she'd painted her office walls glowed in the afternoon light, a cheerful and energetic color, which was why she'd chosen it in the hope it might rub off on her work. Except she was feeling neither cheerful nor energetic at the moment, and her work (or lack thereof) was reflecting that.

"Get your ball." She pointed to the chewed-up tennis ball in the corner, and Puck scampered over to it, paws skidding on the hardwood floor in his haste.

There were a few reasons Kelsey had opted to adopt

older rescue dogs. One was that she felt a kinship with them. She didn't believe in reincarnation, but she considered herself to be an old soul kind of person. Dogs that had been there and seen that fit her style. Older dogs were also generally less likely to be adopted by others, and although she kept her bleeding heart well hidden, Kelsey understood what it was like to be less wanted, and she empathized.

But the reason she'd have given to anyone who asked why she adopted older dogs was that they were less energetic and demanding than younger ones. Alas, Puck had never gotten that memo. Not only was he a good ten pounds smaller than his siblings, he acted a good five years younger. Basically, he was a fully adult male husky stuck in a teen husky's body with a puppy husky's brain. Kelsey would never play favorites among her dogs, but she adored him for it.

Just not so much when she was supposed to be working.

Puck dropped the ball at her feet, and Kelsey obligingly tossed it into her narrow upstairs hallway. The wannabe puppy vanished after it like a supercharged snowball. Puck even fit his name. With pure white fur except for patches of brown around his feet, there was something fey about his appearance.

Her phone barked (a recording of Romeo's voice) with the arrival of a text while Puck chased the ball. Grumbling, Kelsey picked it up, since it wasn't like she was doing anything else productive. She should just give up. Clearly she wasn't going to finish her current chapter today.

The message was from her friend Emily to their college friend group chat. I hate to do this to you guys, but can we postpone our girls' outing for a few more weeks? Some idiot broke her foot last night.

Assuming the *some idiot* was none other than Emily herself, Kelsey snickered. Moving the date for their annual get-together, which was supposed to be next weekend, would actually be fantastic. This weekend already marked the beginning of September, making it unofficially fall, and she still had summer tasks to accomplish.

Her maternal grandparents in Wasilla had put aside some furniture for her, and she'd promised them she'd get it soon. That had been two months ago. Her grandparents wanted it gone before the winter so they could put their car in the garage, and Kelsey wanted the furniture in her mostly empty house. (Being able to afford her own place had negated being able to afford furnishing said place. Irony.) The problem was she needed help moving the furniture, and the two men she'd normally depend on for help—Kevin and Josh—had gotten caught up in relationship nonsense over the summer. All of that should be settling down by now though, so she'd just have to bully or bribe one of them into helping next weekend. No problem.

Sure, Kelsey wrote back to Emily. Name the date. It wasn't as if her book deadline was going to creep any closer regardless of when she took a weekend off, and maybe this way she could knock out whatever crap she was supposed to write for Ian's brewery before she left.

Ugh. Ian. He wasn't helping her concentration either. She'd taken time yesterday to look up his family's brewery website and email him a bunch of questions. In all, this task she'd been volunteered for had taken her about two hours, and she hadn't written a word yet.

Some of that was her own fault. After she'd discovered a family photo on the About page with a younger-looking Ian, she'd gone poking around the rest of the site. That had eventually led her to a page called The Brewmaster's Blog, and even though Kelsey didn't care for beer, she'd mindlessly read a few posts until she'd found the one announcing the opening of their sister brewery in Helen. That post contained another photo of Ian, this time wearing a T-shirt with the name of the brewery on it. A tight T-shirt. One that made it clear that her assumptions about the body he'd been hiding under his sweatshirt on Friday were not at all wrong.

Kelsey had closed the website at that point, but the memory had remained as she typed out her list of questions for him, and it remained today when she was supposed to be writing about a guy who did not look at all like Ian. That was infuriating. She had an excellent imagination, but instead of picturing a rugged mountain man with brown hair and a barely trimmed beard, she kept picturing a tall, muscled beermaker with sandy hair and a puppylike expression.

By the time the girls' weekend arrived, she was really going to need that vacation—just her and her three closest friends in a secluded cabin with alcohol, junk food, and no internet access. The place belonged to Emily's parents and was totally off the grid, powered by a generator and heated by a woodstove. Some people might call it a setup for a horror movie, but as long as it didn't get too cold too quickly, Kelsey called it exactly the sort of break from reality that might keep her sane. There would be no family breathing down her neck, no feud to deal with, and definitely no men.

No hiding or lying either. Emily, Lauren, and Amy were the only three people among her circle of family and friends who knew about her writing.

Sometimes that made Kelsey nervous. What was that saying about how two could keep a secret if one of them was dead? But the three of them had been there during the incident that had set Kelsey down this path. They knew what a dickhead her ex Anthony had turned out to be and why she'd switched from dabbling in writing young adult stories to trying her hand at something steamier. They'd encouraged her, commiserated with her, and celebrated with her along the way. The idea that she should keep her pen name a secret from them had never occurred to Kelsey, just as the possibility that she would end up writing romance as a career hadn't. Life had simply happened, and by then it was too late.

Puck barked at her, and Kelsey realized she was ignoring him. She promptly tossed his ball again. "Go get it!"

Puck charged down the ball, and oh, why couldn't humans be as easily entertained as dogs? For that matter, why couldn't they be as loyal and as friendly? If Anthony had been any one of those things, she might not be in the position she was today.

"Insufferable," she muttered out loud, saving her file. But no, that wasn't the correct word for Anthony. That word was more like *asshole*. Whatever Ian's faults—and she was certain there were many beyond ruining her little town—he hadn't earned that word from her yet. He would remain insufferable, however, for as long as he continued to occupy space in her brain that she needed for other endeavors.

On that thought, since she wasn't writing the words she wanted to write, she might as well check if he'd responded to her email.

Lo and behold, he had. Kelsey was about to award him some minor redemption for promptness, but then she read what he'd sent back. "Nope. Still insufferable."

Puck dropped his ball at her feet and cocked his head.

"He gave me one-sentence responses to everything," Kelsey explained. "There's nowhere near enough for me to work with if he wants something more than a terse, bor-

ing summary for the website. For a press release, it's fine,
I suppose. But for an entire newspaper article, or an About
page that's worth clicking on? Forget it."

A lifetime of assuming the worst about people's intentions made Kelsey wonder whether Ian had responded the
way he did on purpose. To annoy her. Obviously, he had
to know how rich and detailed the information on the
Florida brewery's website was; he was the one who'd
brought it up. Had he expected her to just plagiarize some
of it, substituting his half-assed answers in where appropriate? But even that didn't make sense. How the brewery
had come to be opened in Florida had nothing to do with
why Helen had been selected as the site for Northern
Charm. Ian's *We were looking for an adventure in a new
state* did not explain why that state had to be Alaska.

The husky whined in a questioning sort of way, so
Kelsey picked up the ball again and waved it around in her
agitation. "See? This is like me holding the ball up here
where you can't get it, making you think I'm going to
throw it and play with you, but really just being insuffer-
ably rude because I'm not."

Now that Puck was as displeased as she was, he jumped
up, trying to catch the ball, and Kelsey sighed. She'd
trained her babies (as best she could at their age) to not
jump, but this was her fault. She tossed the ball back into
the hallway for him.

"He's even making me be mean to you when he's not
around."

Almost as bad, Ian was making her email him again,
because damn it—if he was going to intentionally piss her
off by not taking her questions seriously, she was going to
piss him off by rejecting his answers.

Truly, she was a glutton for punishment. The smarter
choice, and the passive-aggressive one, would be to use

Ian's responses to write the press release plus something short and boring for the website, as well as a note that she was unable to produce a newspaper article with what he'd given her. But anything she wrote with the scraps he'd tossed her way would reflect poorly on her skills, and besides, Kelsey never liked to take the passive-aggressive option when the active-aggressive one was available.

So nope. She'd suck it up and deal with the man face-to-face one more time in an attempt write something she wasn't embarrassed by. She was no coward. She wasn't afraid of Ian getting stuck in her head.

Which was convenient, since he was already there.

Then, to make herself feel better, she'd see if her father had a key to the brewery. For sabotage fantasies, that was. This time, she'd go into the meeting with him better prepared for dealing with the aftermath.

6

AS LUCK WOULD have it, Kelsey pulled into a parking spot by the Espresso Express at the same time as Ian was getting out of his truck. A second guy with long, dark hair pulled back into a ponytail followed Ian from the vehicle. That had to be Ian's business partner, Micah. Kelsey wasn't expecting him to be at the meeting, but she wouldn't be sorry about it if he was more forthcoming than Ian.

That said, she also wasn't exactly thrilled. If Micah did turn out to be like Ian, the meeting would be doubly troublesome.

Ian must have pointed her out, because Micah crossed the short distance between their vehicles, holding out a hand. "Micah Bauman. You're Kelsey Porter? Nice to meet you."

She wondered what Ian had told Micah about her. She'd assumed it was something along the lines of her being *that bitch with the SHS pin*, which made this cheerful introduction highly suspicious. "Nice to meet you."

Kelsey shook Micah's hand and . . . nothing. No nerves in her hand woke up, no images flitted through her mind about licking him like a Popsicle. Interesting. Her body's lack of reaction certainly had nothing to do with Micah being unattractive. He was, in a square-jawed kind of way, something like a rock star crossed with a lumberjack. But no part of her body, from her toes to her brain, gave a damn.

"Oh, look. Puppies!" Micah waved through her SUV's cracked-open rear window at her dogs. Since Kelsey didn't intend this meeting to last more than fifteen minutes, she'd brought them along so they could go walking afterward. Helen had a few tiny parks interspersed among the residential streets, but the main park with all its winding paths was a couple of blocks from the coffee shop.

Juliet and Puck vied for space to greet Micah while Kelsey looked on amused. Ian, she couldn't help but note, hadn't come closer. He was leaning against his truck with his arms crossed. Still insufferable. Still rude to her dogs.

Still annoyingly eye-catching, despite wearing a heavy fleece today. The ends of his hair lifted slightly in the wind. He rubbed at the layer of similarly colored scruff on his jaw with one hand and raised his other an inch in greeting. The bare minimum of politeness.

Kelsey mimicked the gesture rather than make an effort to goad him.

Kudos to Micah for being friendly. Apparently he was unlike his business partner in multiple ways, and therefore more deserving of her attention.

She introduced her dogs, including Romeo, who was cautiously observing Micah from afar. "I can't take too long, since I brought them to go on a walk."

"No problem." Micah glanced in Ian's direction. "I'm sure we can wrap this up quickly."

Five minutes later, Kelsey brought her caffè mocha to the table Ian and Micah had claimed. The Espresso Express didn't cater to sit-down business, so while there were a half dozen or so scuffed tables around the counter, they were small and packed together. In retrospect, suggesting they meet at Starbucks might have been better, but then, Kelsey hadn't been expecting Micah to join them. So really it was Ian's fault they were going to be cramped.

With three mugs of coffee on the table, there wasn't a lot of space to set up her laptop. Kelsey slid her chair over to get the best possible angle, causing her knee to bump Ian's leg. He didn't react, but she wasn't so sure she was able to hide her own expression, which was problematic, since she also wasn't sure what it was. She didn't want to touch Ian, but the jolt she'd felt had suggested she had nerve endings in her knee that she'd been previously unaware of that could cause crackling sensations in her torso.

Kelsey decided the smoothest way to play off whatever had happened was to pretend it hadn't.

"We brought you something," Ian said as she opened her laptop. They were the first words he'd spoken to her, and he set a six-pack on the table. "We didn't exactly get off to the best start last time, so . . ."

Given the way he trailed off, Kelsey wondered if Micah had forced him to do this.

She spun the closest bottle around to read the Northern Charm Brewing label, but that was all she got from it. Ales versus stouts versus IPAs meant nothing to her. She felt bad about that, since at least one of these men was trying to be a decent guy, but it just showed why she was absolutely the wrong person to help them.

"Er, thanks. But I don't actually like beer." She made an apologetic face and slid the bottles back toward Ian.

Ian cast a glance at Micah as if to say, *Told you so*, confirming to Kelsey that this hadn't been his idea. "Of course you don't. No beer, no outsiders. Is there anything you do like, besides dogs?"

Oh, good. They were back to snark. She could handle that much better than she could handle knee jolts.

Kelsey pretended to contemplate. "Small towns? Look, you don't have to take any of this personally, you know."

"How am I supposed to not take it personally when you support people who are intentionally making my life and livelihood difficult?" Ian motioned toward the SHS pin that she'd never bothered to take off her jacket, and his stupid leg pressed into her knee.

Kelsey could have told him she'd forgotten about the pin and that she'd never gotten around to looking into the group, but it was more satisfying to let him believe the worst of her. She reached for her own coffee, giving her the excuse to shift in her seat. Tall people were always taking up too much space. She would now officially hold Ian's height against him, just because. "How about because I'm here, helping you?"

"Are you though?"

Was he serious? "Yes, and for free, I might remind you." Her father deserved a good ass-kicking for that, but he'd never get it, unfortunately.

"All right, kids." Micah held up a hand between them. "Let's focus and calm down. Kelsey, we appreciate your help."

Uh-huh. Possibly one of them did, but as much fun as it might be to continue trading jabs with Ian, she didn't have time for it. Especially not with her dogs sitting in the car. "Can I just get some answers to my questions. Real answers instead of the equivalent of manly grunts?"

Micah chuckled and tried to hide it behind his coffee mug.

Ian scowled. "I don't understand what additional information you need."

"Have you even read your aunt and uncle's website? If

you want me to write something similar, I need a similar level of detail. Obviously. Who are you both? Where did you come from? Why did you open the brewery in Helen? Where did you learn the business?"

And why did her freaking knee tingle when it brushed Ian's leg? If she was going to get all tingly over a guy— and frankly, she'd rather not—couldn't it be for the rock-star-slash-lumberjack who liked her dogs and wasn't completely insufferable?

Those last couple of questions were between her and the universe, though, and it was just as well. She had enough questions for the men as it was.

Ian rubbed the thin layer of stubble on his cheeks in obvious frustration. "Like I said in the email, I'm origi-nally from the Boston area. I moved to Florida to live with my grandparents when I was twelve and went to work for my aunt and uncle at their brewery after college."

"Yeah, I got that. Those are the *what* answers. No one gives a shit about the *what*. *What* is boring. It's the *why* that makes a story. That's what gets people interested."

Ian sipped his coffee thoughtfully. "Why? I like beer. *Obviously.*"

If it wouldn't have ruined her laptop, Kelsey would have tossed the remains of her mocha at him. For a sec-ond, she'd almost thought she'd gotten through to him. Instead, she closed her eyes in frustration. Freaking men.

Freaking insufferable Ian. Even if she did drink beer, a six-pack would not have been enough to thank her for her time and patience.

Micah started to say something, but Ian cut him off, setting down his mug with so much force that coffee sloshed over the sides. "The whys aren't that interesting. Can't you make something up if you want to?"

Oh, she was tempted to make something up, but she

was pretty damn sure Ian wouldn't like what she wrote. It might entertain her enough that she didn't dream about suffocating him though.

Micah might have read some of those thoughts on her face, because he raised his hands a second time. "Your life isn't that boring, my friend. How about this? Why don't I take a look at the questions Kelsey sent, and at your answers, and I can fill in the blanks?"

Ian gave his friend an unreadable look but finally nodded. "Okay. Fine."

Kelsey shrugged. "Whatever works."

Despite not wanting to write something for them in the first place, she'd always intended to do a decent job. But that was only because of her pride, since the newspaper piece would bear her name. But maybe she could sit down with Micah—and just Micah—sometime to talk about the article.

Micah was not insufferable, even though he was still an outsider. He was friendly to her dogs. He seemed to appreciate her help. Talking to Micah would likely be much more productive and perfectly boring.

For some reason, that greatly disappointed her.

A FEW MINUTES later, Kelsey transferred the rest of her coffee into a thermos and left. Finally able to stretch out his legs, Ian did so as he cupped what was left of his drink. There were only a couple of other people in the coffee shop, but it had felt alarmingly claustrophobic when Kelsey had been sitting across from him.

That had nothing to do with the overall tight space or dark wood decor and everything to do with him being exceptionally aware of her presence. Her leg under the table, where if he wasn't careful, he brushed up against it.

Her face peering out over her laptop screen, emphasizing how small the space between them was. Her hand mere inches away when she reached for her coffee. Sitting down, Kelsey had seemed a lot larger than she really was. Ian wasn't sure if it was because she took up her share of the table, or because she was taking up too much space in his head.

There were likely dozens of people in the SHS. It shouldn't bug him so much that Kelsey was one of them, and yet it did. Because of that, Ian had thought responding to her emailed questions quickly had been the best option. Get it over with and he wouldn't have to run into her again. Obviously he'd done a fantastic job of misjudging that play.

"You see what I mean?" he said to Micah as Kelsey disappeared through the door. "She's not very personable."

Micah shifted his chair, also taking the opportunity to spread out. "I don't know. She seemed friendly until you started arguing with her."

"I didn't argue."

"Whatever you want to call it, you started it. Which is interesting." Micah tapped his fingers against his mug.

Ian narrowed his eyes. "What does that mean?"

"It means you're not usually the kind to start shit with people."

"Call it what you want, but I'm not the one who started anything." He lowered his voice even though the coffee shop was noisy with the sound of the grinder in the background. "The SHS started it, and you saw her pin. That means she started it by association."

"I did see the pin. I also saw her, and you were holding out on me. She's cute."

More like hot, especially when she did that kind of sneering thing at him. Ian wasn't even entirely sure she was aware that she did it, and he had no idea why it activated the dirty thoughts portion of his brain. But damned if he hadn't been fighting alarming thoughts about her mouth during this entire failed conversation.

The lower half of his body stirred as he recalled them. "I didn't say she wasn't."

"But you didn't say she was. That, combined with you starting shit, is what's so interesting."

Ian rubbed his face in his hands, grimacing, and not only because he needed to shave. "If you want me to admit that I find her attractive, then fine. I find her attractive. I think lots of people probably would."

Micah chuckled quietly, as he'd been prone to do too much of this afternoon. "Agreed. She'd got a kind of sweet-and-sour thing going on. It's deceptive."

Sour wasn't the word Ian would have chosen, although he wasn't sure what was. He tried to think of one to counter Micah, though, because he didn't like that his friend's interest in Kelsey was making him as grouchy as Kelsey herself could. Eventually he gave up and finished his coffee. Not discussing Kelsey further was probably the best choice for his peace of mind.

"She also has a great ass," Micah added after a moment.

"Are we done?" He wasn't sure if he was asking about the coffee or Kelsey, or if it mattered.

Micah drained the rest of his mug. "Yup. Because we have more work to do."

"You mean Kelsey's questions? I'm finished. That was you volunteering, not me."

"Not the questions. I mean our sign." Grimacing, Micah held out his phone. "We just got an email from the town saying they're denying our proposed design for not meeting their guidelines."

Ian stared, but Micah gave off no suggestion of this being a bad joke. And of course it wasn't. No doubt the

Save Helen Society had struck again. That was why it didn't matter how hot Kelsey was. The SHS was a menace, and Ian was ready to hit someone.

"Doesn't meet the guidelines?" He attempted to keep his voice down as he gathered his and Micah's empty mugs. "Yes, it does."

"No, it met the guidelines they originally gave us, which are not the same guidelines they've attached to this email. They either changed them or gave us the wrong information before."

"Or they're giving us the wrong information now to screw with us."

"Or that." Micah shrugged. "Luckily I hadn't ordered the sign yet."

"There's nothing lucky about any of this." Ian carried their mugs over to the dirty dishes spot at the serving counter, trying to hide his bad mood in case anyone was watching.

He couldn't shake the feeling that he and Micah stood out everywhere they went in town these days. They were the newcomers, the outsiders who'd pissed off a sizable percent of the town without realizing it. During the summer months when tourists flooded Helen, he'd felt comfortably anonymous most of the time. But as August had given way to September and the raging stream of tourists had slowed to a steady trickle, that comfort had drained away too. It was becoming ever clearer to Ian who the locals were and who was just visiting, and yet he was neither. Not really. Not yet. And unless a local was wearing one of those bright yellow SHS pins, it was impossible to determine what they thought of him and his business. Excitement? Or resentment?

It could just be that he had an overactive imagination and the paranoia to go with it, and in truth nobody spared him a second glace. It was easier to assume that was correct after a beer or two. Then he could hear his bubbe's voice in his head, reminding him that of course he was paranoid— he was Jewish. Paranoia was called being smart.

After a couple of beers, that joke seemed funnier too.

Ian set down the mugs and turned back toward Micah, who was staring at his phone, brow furrowed. Should they go back to work at the brewery, or head to the town offices to appeal their sign? He should probably read the email himself before reaching a decision, but he was so tired of this crap. Still, Ian pulled out his phone to check. He was not submitting to any of this town's BS without a fight, and to fight well, he needed all the information. No matter how infuriating.

Across from him, the shop door opened with a jingle, and Ian glanced up as a familiar face entered. Tasha Mc-Cleod noticed him at the same time, and her lips pressed together in something that was almost but not quite a smile. Ian wasn't sure what to make of that. He and Tasha weren't exactly friends, but Tasha worked for the town. Since he and Micah had lost innumerable hours of their lives on the other side of her desk at the town hall, he'd probably spent more time talking to her than most other people in Helen.

Then Ian saw the SHS pin on her jacket, and that explained everything. When Kelsey had walked into the brewery on Friday wearing one, it was only the second pin Ian had seen. Three days later they appeared to be everywhere, spreading like a virus.

"Et tu, Tasha?" he asked, mostly to himself.

Tasha didn't catch the question, and she forced her mouth into a more normal smile. "Hey, how's the brewery going?"

He should lie, be polite and pleasant. He told himself

Tasha didn't deserve his bad mood, since allegedly she wasn't the one making his life miserable. But the pin made it hard for Ian to believe that.

"The brewery would be going better if you and your friends weren't trying to sabotage it," Ian said, gesturing at her pin.

He glanced toward Micah again. There was no way his friend couldn't hear their conversation, but he was keeping his head down. The jerk.

Tasha's smile wavered. "No one is trying to sabotage anything. Forms just need to be filled out correctly. As for the pin, containing development is a priority of the mayor's. It's nothing personal."

"It's starting to feel very personal."

"I'm sorry you think that way." But she stumbled a bit on the words, and her phone rang. "It's the day care. I need to take this."

Ian nodded and headed back toward Micah. Saved by the ringtone. There was no point prolonging that conversation anyway.

Micah tossed on his jacket, and they left in silence. Ian no longer felt like discussing the sign problem somewhere with an audience, and that meant waiting until they were back in his truck.

"So the whiny town clerk has a pin too," Micah said as Ian started the engine. "Figures."

"She's not whiny. There's enough we can kvetch about without making stuff up."

"I disagree. She has one of those nasally voices that makes everything she says sound like she's whining." Micah pretended to shudder. "Why defend her when she's wearing an SHS pin?"

Ian wasn't sure. He backed out of the parking spot, making the executive decision to head toward the brewery rather than the town hall. It was late in the afternoon. If they were going to fight the sign issue in person, it was probably best to wait until tomorrow morning.

"Kelsey was wearing an SHS pin too," he pointed out, "and you didn't seem to have an issue with her."

"I like Kelsey."

"You like Kelsey's ass."

"I can like more than one thing about a person."

Ian shook his head. "What else is there to like about Kelsey?"

"For starters? The way you get all tense whenever her name comes up."

"I do not." He made himself loosen his grip on the wheel, and he didn't need to take his eyes off the road to figure out Micah had noticed. "I'm tense because of the sign problem."

Micah exhaled something between a groan and a sigh. "We'll deal with the town tomorrow. Tonight I'm going to need a drink."

"Conveniently, we happen to have some alcohol." Ian pulled into the brewery's lot. The bare spot over the door where their sign was supposed to hang looked extra empty, and instead of parking in front, Ian pulled around to the back so he didn't have to see it.

"Drinking our beer reminds me too much of work." Micah slipped off his seat belt.

Ian jumped out of the truck, wishing he'd bought more coffee to take with him. There was so much to do, never mind the sign taking up more of his time. "Fine. We can drink someone else's beer, but I've got to get that inventory list finished, and those new tanks need to be—"

"No." Micah held up a hand to cut him off. "We're stopping at dinnertime. We don't have to work late every night."

"I can't let this stuff sit."

"Yes, you can, my friend." Micah took the keys from Ian's hand and opened the back door. "Sign issue notwithstanding, everything is on schedule. We are in good shape, and no matter how hard you work or how many more batches of beer you want to start, you can't make the current ones brew faster. So relax a little before you give yourself an ulcer."

Ian blinked as the industrial-strength lights overhead turned on. How were there still so many boxes to unpack? Why was the bottling equipment in such disarray? Was there something off about the smell in the air? What if a batch had gone bad? What if he was going to fail?

He inhaled more deeply, breathing in the scent of alcohol, hops, and other fermenting grains that weren't entirely beer yet. At least not beer he'd want anyone to drink.

"That's right. Breathe it in and relax." Micah handed him back the keys. "Look at it this way—we should be out and about more, frequenting the places around town that we want to become our customers. Make them see us. Make them like us. Make them want to buy our products. That's good business."

Ian couldn't argue with the logic of that, although it felt like a convenient excuse to take a break. One he would regret later if the business went under.

He ran a hand over the stainless steel tank closest to him and told himself that Micah was right. If he was acting like this, he probably *did* need a drink.

Unfortunately, going out wasn't as simple as Micah was making it out to be either. "Yeah, yeah. But do we go to a Porter place or a Lipin place?"

As ridiculous as the question was, the last few months had taught Ian it was taken very seriously. A feud had overtaken the town decades ago. Ian didn't know what had caused it, but for some reason, people had never gotten over it. The only upside Ian could find for being considered an outsider was that no one expected him and Micah to pick sides, at least not yet. He hadn't figured out whether Kelsey helping the brewery would change that, but he sure could imagine Kelsey being the type of person to enjoy a feud. Picking fights seemed like her hobby, and she probably thrived on the animosity. He had practically felt it radiating off her today. It made her more . . . interesting. That was unfortunate, but Ian told himself it was only because hers was a mindset he would never understand.

But Kelsey's *interesting* shortcomings aside, Ian hoped her help wouldn't drag the brewery into the morass. If he had his way, they would never get involved in it. Not every business did. There was only one supermarket, one hardware store, and now one brewery, which suggested they should be positioned to remain neutral.

As for the other businesses, Ian was still learning about their affiliations, so to be safe, when he went out, he made sure not to show favoritism to any one bar or restaurant. It was an additional hassle in a town that seemed to thrive on creating hassles for him, and one more piece of evidence that there was definitely something in the water around here that drove people to irrationality. Ian fervently hoped it wasn't as contagious as those damn SHS pins so he wouldn't catch it.

7

MICAH HAD SENT his responses to her questions yesterday, but Kelsey had been in no mood to look at his answers. His email sat in her in-box, contributing to her pile of electronic guilt. In fairness, her Should Be Working On pile was massive, and she was adept at ignoring it. Why should the brewery work be treated any differently? She'd get around to it when her irritation with Ian simmered down.

Because eventually that would have to happen. It had to. It just couldn't while the memory of him looking so damn smug played through her mind. Smug and sexy and insufferable and insolent. No, wait. Her list of words for him was expanding, but *sexy* was not supposed to be on it. Damn it.

Procrastination via running errands, rather than working on the brewery piece, was also supposed to have prevented Ian-related thoughts from intruding on her time. So much for that.

Kelsey paused on the steps outside the post office to zip her fleece higher. It wasn't raining yet, but she swore she could smell rain in the air, and she hoped she could get a good walk in before it actually started. Maybe a walk would clear Ian from her mind.

A mail truck pulled down the narrow, alley-like street, and Kelsey waited for it to pass before crossing. She'd just stepped onto the sidewalk when the library door opened in front of her and out popped the last person she wanted to run into.

Kelsey pursed her lips and prayed Ian wouldn't notice her. *Smug.* She focused on the word to keep from focusing on the man, but there was truly nothing smug about the way Ian walked down the path toward her.

She told herself there was nothing sexy about it either. He was wearing jeans and a green jacket, and it was a totally workmanlike combination. It was the sort of thing any guy in this weather, in this town, might wear. Same with his hair. It was a boring color, a common one. There was nothing special about it. Nor about his face. Perfect cheekbones were overrated.

"Kelsey." Ian gave a slight wave.

She startled and her heart landed somewhere around her throat. Shit. Had she been staring?

She'd definitely been staring. Here was hoping the stare was more of a glare. "Hi."

"Hi." Ian's brow, which really was just another forehead and also not exciting, furrowed. "Why are you looking at me like that?"

What kind of stare had been giving him if it wasn't a glare? And why hadn't she brought her dogs with her? Maybe Ian would have snubbed her then. "Like what?"

His brow lines deepened. "I don't know. Like you're suspicious of me or something."

Suspicion was totally not what had been running through her head, but she wasn't about to let the excuse Ian handed her go to waste. "You're walking out of the library."

"So?"

"That suggests you might read. Seemed suspect." Ouch. That was meaner than she'd intended, but it was the first relatively logical bit of snark that came to mind.

Ian seemed to take it in stride, or perhaps he'd learned what to expect from her. "I'm actually a man of many talents, reading among them. In fact, I was finally getting my library card. I hope that's okay with you."

Anyone who got a library card was more than okay with her, but it wasn't like she was going to admit that. Once again, though, Kelsey had to appreciate that Ian would return her snark volley for volley. "You don't need my permission to read a book, although I reserve the right to judge your choices."

"That doesn't surprise me. Do I lose points for fiction versus nonfiction? Are certain genres worth more or less? What about length—does it count?"

She couldn't repress a smirk. "Length always counts."

"Spoken like a woman."

Sure, *he* looked physically pained saying the words, but *she* was currently the one imagining the length of his "book." Unfair.

"Length is not as important as quality though," Kelsey added hastily, trying to purge the image of a naked Ian from her brain.

"I'm sure Hemingway is relieved."

Whoa. Ian could make literature jokes? She was impressed despite herself, and that did nothing to banish those images, which had morphed into a naked Ian reading in bed. "Don't worry. I'm not going to ask to see your books."

His lip quirked. "Believe me, I have no reason to worry if you did."

"Spoken like every overconfident man."

Ian's lips twitched a second time, and he stuffed his

hands into his pockets as though attempting to become physically and emotionally more standoffish. "Anyway, glad I have your permission to use the library. Seeing as everyone around here wants to make me jump through a million hoops to do anything, I was expecting a blood sacrifice would be required to get my card."

Kelsey almost laughed at that. "Don't you think you're being a little dramatic?"

"Dramatic? No, not me." He pointed toward the town hall, which was next to the post office. "How about the town changing the guidelines for what is and isn't permitted on signage *after* we had our sign designed to meet them but *before* approving it, all apparently done at the behest of the SHS."

Surprised, Kelsey chewed that over for a second. "That does seem—"

"Dramatically directed at us?"

"I was going to say unfair and possibly shady." Of course, the town was run by Lipins. The mayor was a Lipin, and Lipins dominated the town committees. Shady could be expected. Ian's problem was that he didn't know he shouldn't expect better of the family.

On the other hand, this was the sort of petty shit they'd usually only pull on her family. It was odd that they'd treat Ian and Micah in a similar way. For some reason, Kelsey had expected better of them. More professionalism maybe.

It also reminded her that she was long past due to delve into what the Save Helen Society was about. It really could be just a group of citizens concerned about over-development. That was generally a more Lipin-affiliated attitude, but Kelsey knew she wasn't the only Porter quietly worried. It could also be something the mayor had cooked up to generate support for his positions, however. Kelsey's fingers flexed with the urge to remove the SHS pin, but she wasn't about to do it in front of Ian, especially because the group might truly be benign.

"Nice of you to admit it." Ian seemed to shrink an inch with exhaustion.

It wasn't exactly sexy, but it wasn't insufferable either, and for a painfully long second, Kelsey almost felt bad for him. Somewhere deep inside, her determination to dislike Ian Roth cracked ever so slightly. She knew what petty Lipin BS was like, but more—she knew what that kind of exhaustion with life felt like. She'd been feeling it more and more over the last several months.

This was another reason she tried to avoid humans. As soon as she felt the slightest bit of sympathy for someone, it was so damn hard to keep up her ice queen exterior.

"Honestly, I don't know much about the SHS or why they might be directing their ire toward you," Kelsey admitted. "I just don't want Helen to turn into a glorified strip mall. I like it as it is."

Ian took a moment to respond, forcing her to wonder what was going through his head. Possibly she'd shocked him by not saying something sarcastic. She'd kind of shocked herself. "I like it as it is too. It's one of the reasons I moved here."

"Which makes you part of the problem."

That brought a faint sardonic smile to his face, which Kelsey took to mean he couldn't argue the point. "I'm only one person."

"That's the thing." Her restless fingers brushed the SHS pin, and Kelsey curled her hands into fists to keep herself under control. Then, because that looked more confrontational than she was feeling, she shoved her hands into her pockets. "Everyone is only one person. It's when you add one plus one plus one, et cetera, that you start running into problems."

The smile on Ian's face broadened a touch, eliciting a dimple on his left cheek. How had she not noticed it before? Had she never actually seen him smile? She should say something mean to make it go away before the dimple exerted more sympathy from her. That could destroy her determined dislike.

Ian shrugged in defeat. "Fair enough. If you can admit that the sign thing might be shady, I can admit you have a point. In theory, I agree with the SHS's goals."

Kelsey's cheeks twitched, and she caught herself before she could join him in a smile—or, worse, before she let out a victory cry and punched the air. Ian's admission was nothing to celebrate. She wanted to dislike him on principle, and a reasonable Ian—an Ian who also had a library card, made Hemingway jokes, and had a goddamn dimple—was a hard Ian to dislike. She should leave. Now.

"Well, I'm glad we had this conversation," Kelsey said. "I'll be in touch about the website soon."

"Me too. Actually, Kelsey?" Ian called out to her as she turned away, and Kelsey cringed with her back to him.

"Yeah?" She turned around.

"About the website. I still want to compensate you for your help. The beer was just a token, but I want to pay you whatever your going rate is for projects like this."

Now he was really messing with her head. Not to mention that she didn't have a going rate. Also not to mention that her father would probably be upset if she accepted payment when her labor was supposedly his generosity. She should have ignored Ian when he'd acknowledged her existence. That was how puppies got to you. All you had to do was look at them and suddenly you couldn't dislike them.

Kelsey cleared her throat as a proxy for the brain she couldn't seem to clear of Ian. "That's okay, really."

"Honestly, it's not. It was nice of your father to suggest you could help, but I don't want to take advantage of your time."

Oh, so Ian could see that her father volunteering her was a dick move, but her own father couldn't? Why did he have to be like this? It was so much harder to dislike him if he insisted on compensating her for her work.

"I don't need money for it." Kelsey forced the words out, debating whether it would be too strange if she sprinted toward her car.

Ian frowned as though working through a problem, and he took a step closer. "All right, if you don't want money, and you don't want beer, something else? Your father mentioned you're renovating your house. Anything I can do to help? I'm pretty handy and good at moving heavy objects."

Handy and good at moving heavy objects—that reminded her of the picture she'd seen of him on his family brewery's website. The one where his arms and chest made it clear he was, in fact, capable of moving heavy objects.

The wind was suddenly drying out her lips, and Kelsey wet them. "Is that from all the time spent lifting kegs of beer?"

"Something like that." He seemed amused, and she hoped her face wasn't making questionable expressions again.

Kelsey hesitated. Her hopes of moving furniture this weekend had been dashed yesterday. Josh had to work his ER shift, and Kevin and Peter had appointments to tour a couple of venues for their wedding location. At this rate, she was going to have to move the furniture by herself, unless . . .

No. Asking Ian to drive to Wasilla with her and lift furniture was out of the question. It would take an entire day, and it wouldn't be easy. It was too much compensation for what she was doing for him. Not to mention that the drive alone would be about five or six hours round trip. That much time in his company was too much temptation.

Ian noticed her hesitation though. "So?"

Damn it. Ian had put the images of him being all manly and lifting stuff for her into her head, and now she was stuck with them. He also seemed to honestly want to compensate her, and that was pushing him ever closer to likable. She was going to suggest this plan.

She was weak.

She also wanted the furniture.

Also, she was weak.

Kelsey kicked a loose stone down the sidewalk. "How do you feel about road trips?"

IT WAS IMPOSSIBLE to be stressed while being loved by a puppy. Such was Kelsey's philosophy, and since she was stressed, and since her own babies were no longer puppies, she'd sought one out specifically for his therapeutic services.

Neptune was her brother Kevin's dog, and although he was getting bigger, he retained his distinctly puppyish features. And distinctly puppyish attitude. Her dogs had grown weary of Neptune's shenanigans after a few minutes in his company, so Kelsey sat on the floor of Kevin and Peter's house and let the relatively small bundle of black-and-white fur pounce all over her, giving her dogs a break from his attention. It took only a minute for her blood pressure to return to normal.

"You didn't come here to visit me, did you?" her brother asked, strolling into his living room. "Just the puppy."

"Look at that face! Look at those bright blue eyes."

Kelsey grabbed Neptune before he could get away and rubbed her forehead against his head.

On the couch, Peter chuckled into his laptop. "I think you need a new dog, Kels."

"I think she needs to get laid," said Nate through the video chat program Kevin had started. "She's acting hormonal."

Kelsey raised a middle finger in her older brother's direction and hoped he could see it from the computer screen's angle. Technology was often a poor substitute for face-to-face interaction, but without it, they'd hardly ever see Nate.

To his point, though, she didn't need anything, despite what the men might think. She was quite capable of taking care of that sort of business on her own. She had her book boyfriends for emotional fulfilment, and Mr. Happy—her vibrator—for those more physical urges. But Nate's unfortunate comment did bring to mind Ian, and the puppylike way he'd gotten under skin today. And now she was feeling stressed again. It was bad enough that she'd been forced to acknowledge Ian was good-looking. She did not need to begin equating him with sex, too, although that conversation by the library was making it a challenge.

"Actually, did you know men's hormones fluctuate more on a daily basis than women's do?" Peter asked. "If anything, women are calm and steady compared to men."

"How do you know that?" Kevin asked, plopping down on the couch. "You research fish, not people."

Peter merely shook his head. "I have three sisters. I made it a point to learn these things in school. It's called survival."

"I knew I liked you," Kelsey said. She tapped the floor, and her dogs ran over to her. "You're a smart man. Pay attention, brothers. You might learn something."

Nate scoffed and stuffed a bite of pizza in his mouth.

"I'm a college dropout. Can't I just continue to be out-classed?" Kevin sat up abruptly. "Neptune, no! Drop it." The puppy had started chewing one of his shoes. "Still, Kels, how long has it been since you spared a guy a second look?"

If *spared a guy a second look* was a euphemism for getting laid, six years. Not that she was about to tell her brother that. And not that she cared. As she'd told Maggie, she didn't have the time, and she didn't have the interest.

If *spared a guy a second look* was taken more literally, well, it was more like six hours. Hence the need for puppy therapy. Kelsey wanted Ian out of her brain, but that didn't seem likely, given he'd agreed to her ridiculous request for help moving furniture.

"Change of topic," she said as Neptune, having abandoned Kevin's shoe, jumped on her lap. "What do you know about the Save Helen Society? Who's behind it?"

Their website had contained scant clues as to the latter question. Based on her conversation with Ian, Kelsey had become convinced it was someone with sympathetic ears at the town hall, and the lack of information on the group's website only made her more suspicious.

"I only know what it says on their website," Kevin said, after giving Nate a brief rundown of the group. "As to who's behind it, I'm pretty sure it's Theresa Lipin."

"Theresa Lipin?" Kelsey heard herself squeak, and it wasn't only because Neptune had decided chewing on her arm was an acceptable substitute for her brother's shoes. "Are you sure? How do you know?"

"I'm not positive, but that's what I've heard. You might learn things, too, if you left your house more often and talked to people."

"I don't like people." Kelsey swore internally. She

should have known it was the Lipins from the beginning. Even if it wasn't the mayor himself using the group to drum up support for his antidevelopment agenda, Theresa Lipin was his mother. She was also the grandmother of Josh's girlfriend, and that raised a whole new question. "Josh better not have known that when he gave me the pin."

Kevin's eyebrows shot up. "He gave you an SHS pin? I don't know. Can't picture Josh tricking you into supporting a Lipin cause."

He hadn't tricked her, precisely. She did support the cause, and it annoyed the crap out of her that her interests aligned with those of the Lipins in this case. "You're right. Josh is too much of a cinnamon roll to do that to me on purpose."

"Too much of a what?" Peter had been pretending to read whatever was on his computer, but he shot Kelsey a bewildered expression.

"Too nice," she explained, not bothering with a longer definition. "I wonder what the Lipins have against the new brewery."

"The Lipins are against everything that's good and pure and true." Even Kevin couldn't keep a straight face as he said it. "Who else could be against beer?"

"They do make good beer," Peter said, abandoning all pretense of working.

"Very good." Kevin nodded.

"Wait, since when does Helen have a brewery?" Nate asked.

Kelsey stretched out better on the floor. Neptune was exhausting himself, and he was taking her along with him. "You've had their beer?" she asked, ignoring Nate's question. "If I'd known you liked it, I'd have taken the beer the guys offered me for you."

That might not have prevented Ian from offering to pay her for her work, but who knew? Maybe she could have avoided the day's awkward conversation and prevented those frustrating cracks in her dislike.

Peter let out a whimper, and Kevin actually bounded off the couch. "You passed up free good beer? How could you?"

"Quite easily."

"Now I'm never going to help you get that furniture," Kevin said.

Kelsey snorted. "Good thing I've arranged for alternate assistance, then. Ian and possibly Micah are doing it, since I can't count on family anymore."

She expected a snarky comment from Kevin in response to her friendly jab, but he gave her a surprised look. "You're letting them help? Taking them to our grandparents'?"

Taking them to her grandparents' house was unfortunately unavoidable, but she was desperate for the assistance. That was the lie she was telling herself, anyway. It felt a lot better than saying she was weak.

"They owe me for the work I'm doing for them. Seemed fair." She kept her voice nonchalant, but her stomach squirmed when she thought about the long drive and longer day ahead of her with Ian for company.

But hopefully not just Ian. He'd said he'd get Micah to help as well, which seemed like way more muscle than necessary, but having the rock star lumberjack around might be best for her sanity.

"Neptune, leave Juliet alone." Kevin swooped in and picked up the puppy, who'd grown bored of Kelsey and had started using her dog as his chew toy again.

"She's fine," Kelsey said. Juliet merely looked exasperated with the little one. Kelsey could relate, although she was thinking of someone significantly larger.

Her brother struggled to hold on to the squirming husky as he paced. "Make sure Dad doesn't find out about all this time you're spending with the guys if you don't want to make his week. I think he's given up on me or Nate *carrying on the family legacy* and is counting on you to provide him some heirs."

Kevin's tone suggested he thought as much of the family legacy nonsense as she did, but he and her older brother got to laugh at it. Because of course they did. Kevin was right. No one was putting pressure on them. As the girl child, all that shit was dumped on her.

Kelsey closed her eyes and groaned. At least it sounded like her twin wasn't going to blab about it. The last thing she wanted was for her parents to increase their meddling into her (lack of a) love life.

No, make that the second to last thing. The absolute last thing she wanted was a love life—period.

Again, it wasn't Ian's or Micah's fault her father was acting like a pest, but she had a hard time not resenting them for it. But maybe that resentment wasn't a bad thing. She could use it to patch some of the cracks Ian had made in her walls today. She could plaster over her brief moment of empathy. Cover it up and bury it. It might make the trip less pleasant, but that seemed like a small price to pay for her ability to keep an eye on the big picture.

8

◦————————◦

IAN WAS GOING to kill Micah. When he'd suggested the two of them could help Kelsey with the furniture on Friday, he'd done so because he'd known Micah was also available. He'd even made sure their plans would get them back home before sundown so it wouldn't interfere with Shabbat—not because he cared, but because Micah would. So it was extremely convenient that his friend just happened to set up a meeting with a potential buyer for Friday morning that couldn't possibly be moved.

"If nothing else, you could have had the decency to pretend you had a meeting *before* I scheduled a time with Kelsey," Ian said, filling his thermos with coffee. "That way I could have asked to leave later instead of trying to accommodate you."

Unlike him, Micah was not dressed yet. Because unlike him, Micah was a lying liar.

His friend stuck a bagel in the toaster as though nothing was wrong. "I'm not pretending. I do have a meeting."

"Which you set up after I told you I'd volunteered us."

"That's an unfounded accusation."

Ian held out a hand. "Okay, let me see your phone so I can make it a founded one."

Unsurprisingly, no phone appeared in his upturned palm. "Relax. You're going to have a fun road trip."

"The point isn't to have fun. It's to repay Kelsey for her time."

He'd always intended to offer her payment and would have done so at their first meeting, but she'd shown up with that SHS pin and a bad attitude (not to mention three large dogs), and he'd completely forgotten. Offering her beer later had been just what he'd said at the time—a token gift. It certainly wasn't payment.

So when Kelsey had reminded Ian that she was helping them for free, Ian had decided he couldn't forget again. And when she'd acted almost human the other day, it had seemed like a good time to do it.

Although simply writing her a check would have been easier, Ian had gotten the sense that wouldn't have gone over well with Wallace. Since he didn't know what the dynamic was between father and daughter, or what Kelsey thought of her father suggesting her writing services, he'd followed her lead.

Now he was regretting that. Micah would have provided a buffer on this trip. Without his friend, it would be him and Kelsey trading barbs all day.

Or worse—him and Kelsey not trading barbs. If they were getting along, and if he believed Kelsey didn't personally have it in for him or the brewery, then Ian wasn't sure how he'd survive the car ride. In that situation, Kelsey would become not an enemy but . . . something. What exactly, Ian wasn't sure, but it included being an extremely attractive woman who he was trapped in a car with for six hours.

Once upon a time, that might have been the kind of situation Ian looked forward to, but that time had vanished many years ago. He had too much work to do to indulge in anything as frivolous as dating. The brewery had to come first, and in his experience, women didn't like knowing they couldn't be his top priority. Not that anyone liked it, he supposed, but it ruled out even casual relationships.

Of course, it was still Kelsey who was provoking these thoughts, and the words *dating* and *relationship* were therefore irrelevant. The world was full of pretty faces, and those attached to ugly personalities held no appeal. It was yet to be seen whether he and Kelsey could spend more than five minutes alone together without blood being spilled.

An SUV hauling a small trailer pulled up in front of the house, and suddenly a new concern popped into Ian's head, one he should have been worrying about far more than Kelsey's sweet eyes or bitter attitude. Her dogs. There was no way he could get in the vehicle with them. None. Just thinking about it had his hands sweating and his heart pumping so fast as to make the coffee pointless.

He'd need an excuse. Something he could toss out at the last second that would sound plausible. Micah would back him up, but Ian hated putting his friend in a position where he'd have to lie.

Ian had been looking out the window, and he ducked back into the living room, feeling like a fool. Here he was, a twenty-eight-year-old man who couldn't get into an SUV with dogs. He knew it wasn't impossible to get over his issue, but it was so far down on his list of priorities that he had never bothered to deal with it. Most of the time it didn't even come up. He could handle dogs in public as long as they didn't get too close; it was dogs in confined spaces that were another story.

"You okay?" Micah noticed him pacing, and he stopped adding cream cheese to his bagel.

Cringing, Ian motioned toward the window. "Does she have the dogs?"

"Oh." Understanding dawned on his friend's face. He dropped his knife and peered out the window. "I don't see any. Need me to run interference?"

Ian took a calming breath that wasn't particularly effective. Then another. "Only if it turns out she does have them."

"I'll cover for you. No worries."

The way Micah had his back—never blinking, never missing a beat—should have been reassuring, but it only made Ian feel more ridiculous and embarrassed. "Thanks."

"She's coming up the path." Micah shoved Ian toward the hallway that led to the bedrooms. "Hide. You can't be standing around looking healthy if I need to tell her you've been vomiting all morning."

"That's what you're going with—vomit?" Ian shook his head and darted into his bedroom.

"You prefer I tell her you've had the shits all night?"

His blood pressure was already through the roof, so it wasn't like Micah could make it worse, but his friend was sure trying. "How can you manage to be an asshole while simultaneously helping?"

"Not being an asshole," Micah said, his mouth full of bagel. "I'm doing you a favor by lying for your pathetic ass. It's a mitzvah. Now hide."

Ian ducked into the room as he heard the door open.

"Hey, Kelsey," he heard Micah say.

"Hi." Kelsey sounded surprised and suspicious, probably because Micah was in plaid pajama pants rather than road trip attire. "Are you guys coming with?"

"Actually, I can't go. Got a meeting this morning. Are your dogs out there though? Can I say hi?"

Ian rolled his eyes. Micah was so subtle.

"No," Kelsey said. "I need the space in the car. Is Ian coming?"

In the bedroom, Ian let out a long breath, and his hand uncurled around the door knob.

"Yes, I'm coming!" he yelled. He took one more breath, then returned to the living room before Micah could start making up stories about his digestive system for laughs. "Let's do this."

Kelsey stood in the doorway, looking ready to move furniture. Her hair was pulled up again, and she wore a heavy flannel shirt over a pair of beat-up jeans and some solid-looking work boots. Strangely, the shapeless, made-for-heavy-labor outfit didn't detract from her appearance. She could do nothing about that cherubic face, but for once her outward look matched the tough, take-no-shit attitude that lurked inside. Ian wasn't sure if it was the alignment between her inside and outside that made her seem more appealing at the moment, or if he'd finally spent enough time in Alaska to begin appreciating the local dress code.

Either way, he found himself hoping for more snark on the drive, because flannel had never been such a turn-on.

"HAVE YOU BEEN to Wasilla before?" Kelsey asked as she pulled the SUV onto the highway heading north.

Ian sipped his coffee, watching the paw print charm dangling from her rearview mirror swing back and forth. "No. Micah's been hitting the road, not me. I've been to Anchorage and Juneau, and a couple of smaller towns between, but that's about it. All I know about Wasilla is that it's where—".

"Don't say it." Kelsey held up her right hand. "That's all anyone in the rest of the country knows about Wasilla."

Ian fought down a laugh. "Fine. Is it bigger than Helen?"

"Yes, much bigger. We're growing, but we're not that big yet."

"Not even in the summer?" He was only partially joking.

Kelsey sucked on her bottom lip, which had the unfortunate effect of drawing Ian's attention toward her mouth. He'd never been fascinated by lips before, but Kelsey's were always pink and pouty in a way that stirred the lower half of his body.

Ian turned his gaze back to the road, willing his cock to behave. Kelsey was starting to be a whole lot of firsts for him.

"Helen's population goes up in the summer by a third maybe?" Kelsey said, oblivious to his thoughts and sarcasm. "Enough to be annoying, but still not nearly as big as Wasilla."

"But also necessary."

She sighed. "Yeah, necessary. I know. My brother's sightseeing business relies on tourism. It's not the tourist expansion that bugs me except when I'm trying to find a parking spot. It's the people who come and *stay*, who develop open land, who open chains or franchises that threaten our local businesses—that's who."

Ian cupped his hands around his thermos, even though the SUV was perfectly warm. Clutching the coffee gave him something to do besides fidget. "What about those of us who want to open a local non-chain business?"

Kelsey shot him one of those sardonic half smiles. "Are you trying to pick a fight, or do you want me to absolve you of your sins?"

"Not sure. Let me think about it."

"It's a long drive and not usually exciting. You have time."

What might be not-exciting in Kelsey's world was still

scenic in Ian's. Once the outlying bits of Helen faded into the distance, he felt like he was being transported into another world—a wild one of rugged mountains and lush trees and endless sky. This was the backdrop that had driven him to beg his grandparents to take him to visit Alaska in the first place. He could imagine he was in the middle of nowhere, tossed into a fantasy world where yetis and talking wolves might show up any moment.

At least, as long as he could ignore the highway, the road signs, and the other vehicles zipping by.

Finished with his coffee, Ian set the empty thermos down and glanced behind Kelsey at the back seat. She'd tossed her jacket on it, and the SHS button was missing. Now, that was even more interesting than the scenery. It had been there two days ago when he'd run into her by the library. Had their conversation had an impact—*had* she been wearing it to goad him? Or maybe it had simply fallen off?

The silence in the car wasn't precisely comfortable, but it was peaceful, and just as importantly, it kept him from glancing at Kelsey as she drove. Ian broke it reluctantly. "I see your SHS pin is missing."

"Thirty minutes!" Kelsey slapped the steering wheel.

"What?"

"It took you thirty minutes to notice. Damn it." She smacked the wheel again. "I had you pegged for under ten. How dare you do this to me?"

Unsure whether to laugh or get pissed off, Ian stared at her, jaw open, for a second while he processed her unexpected reaction. "Who were you taking bets with?"

"No one, thank God. You'd have let me down for real."

He rested his head against the back of the seat and closed his eyes. "I don't believe you. Actually, I do. Not sure what's worse."

Kelsey snorted. "Please. It's funny."

"To you."

"Yeah." She paused. "Admit it—you think it's funny too."

The smile he'd been fighting made Ian's lips twitch. "Mildly, maybe."

"Whatever." She waved him off. "Yeah, I got rid of the pin when I found out it's the Lipins who are behind the SHS. Don't get me wrong—I agree with the sentiment. But I can't support them."

"Ah, right. Because of the feud. It's the Montagues and Capulets in this town." This time he did fully smile, thanks to the absurdity of it.

Kelsey, however, did not smile. "I hate *Romeo and Juliet*."

"Then why did you name your dogs after them?" He'd overheard her introducing the dogs to Micah, and that was probably why the play had popped into his head when thinking about the town. Shakespeare had been torture for him, but random bits and pieces remained lodged in his brain. Somewhere his old high school English teacher was cackling with glee.

"I didn't name them," Kelsey said, reaching for her water bottle. "They're rescues, so we're all stuck with the names someone else provided. But Helen's not as bad as fair Verona; no one's being murdered in the streets."

She grimaced in a way that made the unspoken *yet* practically audible.

"It's still something." *Seriously messed up* was the phrase that sprang to Ian's mind, but seeing as he was trapped in a car with Kelsey, insulting her family—especially as they were helping him—didn't seem wise. "Helen should come with a warning sign. You might keep people from moving there if it did. No one told me it was a war zone."

"Ha." Kelsey swallowed her water poorly and coughed.

"That wouldn't suit my father, who is all about development and profits. No way he'd have warned you about how screwed up we all are."

Ian was surprised to hear her describe the situation as screwed up, but on further reflection, perhaps he shouldn't be. For all her scowliness, Kelsey didn't seem like the sort of person to let her biases cloud her vision. Or maybe that was why she was so scowly—she realized how messed up the world was.

"Maybe not your father," Ian said. "But the real estate agent could have. It might have lessened the shock the first time Tasha tossed a permit request back at my face."

He'd added Tasha as an afterthought, mostly to himself, but the name caught Kelsey's attention. "Tasha who?"

"McCleod. She works for the town clerk's office. Do you know her?"

Kelsey was silent for a moment as she passed a slow-moving RV, but her lips—why was he staring at them again?—were upturned. Not exactly smiling, but knowing. "It's Helen. If someone's around my age, I probably know of them from school. And yeah, I know who Tasha is. She was a couple grades above me."

"At first I thought she was just a stickler about her forms, but I've lately discovered she's very involved in the Save Helen Society."

Kelsey snapped her fingers. "Aha! If I'd known that, I would have figured out what the SHS is about ages ago. Of course she's involved in it. Tasha is a Lipin on her mother's side, and she married into a Lipin-supporting family."

Ian burst out laughing. He couldn't help it. The town was so ridiculous. "Naturally you are fully informed about her heritage and her husband's family. And I thought my family had issues."

"Everybody's family has issues. Anyone who says otherwise is lying or naive. But you're not wrong. Ours are somewhat unusual." Kelsey shot him a quick glance. "Want to talk about yours?"

That killed Ian's laughter real quick. He might not be actively fighting with Kelsey at the moment, but she most definitely struck him as the sort of person who would use anything and everything you told her against you at some later point if you pissed her off.

Not that he ever wanted to discuss his family's issues regardless. "No."

"Good. How about some music instead?"

9

⚬————⚬

KELSEY HAD NEVER been so glad for the end of a long drive as she was this one, and it wasn't because her butt was falling asleep. Her plan to nurture her resentment against Ian was not going well. Probably because the resentment, in this case, wasn't his fault; it was her father's for pushing her toward him. Nonetheless, she thought she could have used it to keep her rebellious hormones in check. But no, her life wasn't allowed to be that simple. Ian had ruined everything by being agreeable when he should have been insufferable and hot when he should have left her cold.

Hell, even the word *insufferable* no longer packed the punch it used to. She'd need a new one, but Kelsey worried what word her brain might generate. When she'd taken her eyes off the road to glance at Ian, she'd had to admit his damn dimple was cute when he smiled, and the way his fleece collar rubbed against his chin was all kinds of cozy. Part of her wanted to pet him like he was some puppy.

"Here we are." Kelsey pulled into her grandparents'

driveway at last. She'd been to their new house only once before, and it was still strange to consider it their home.

"You said they'd downsized?" Ian peered through the window, sounding a touch incredulous, and she couldn't blame him.

Compared to their last home, the one-story white house was small. But the grounds held two outbuildings, and even from the driveway, it was clear the place boasted an amazing view of the lake from its back-facing windows.

Kelsey shut off the engine. "My grandfather was a geologist for an oil company. Trust me—this is downsizing. It's also why I'm getting their old furniture. They have too much now."

"Okay then." Shaking his head, Ian got out of the SUV. "Is there a plan for how we're moving and packing everything?"

Kelsey flinched on the other side of the vehicle, glad Ian couldn't see the oh-shit expression her face. "Yeah, of course. The plan is we fit as much as we can between here and the trailer."

She popped the hatch on the back of the SUV, and Ian stood aside as she opened her supply case and started yanking out bungee cords. "What are you carrying in there?" he asked. "A roll of tin foil?"

It took her a second to realize he was seeing only a part of her Mylar blanket. "It's just the usual supplies, you know." She turned to hand him some of the bungees and realized from Ian's expression that he didn't know. "For emergencies? Especially in the winter?"

Ian absently took the cords. "Emergency supplies are jumper cables and a spare tire, aren't they? That's a huge box."

Oh no. He was being a puppy again, and this time, not because he was cute but because he was clueless. Kelsey sucked on her lower lip. It shouldn't be her job to explain this stuff to him. If he wanted to live up here, Ian could damn well do his own research. And yet . . . Yet she couldn't withhold information from him if he might need it. She was neither that irresponsible nor that mean.

There was only one way to handle this situation. Put the puppy in his place. Remind him that he was an outsider and, in doing so, remind herself why she disliked him.

"Obviously a spare tire and jumper cables are good. But also . . ." Kelsey flung the crate fully open and started holding up its contents. "Collapsible shovel. Snow brush. Ice scraper. Mylar blanket. Wool blanket. Road flares. Hand warmers. Flashlight and spare batteries. Water bottles. Energy bars. First aid kit. Extra hats and mittens. Snow goggles. Reflective fabric. And that"—she pointed to the bag in the corner by the back seat—"is the sand you should be carrying. If I were doing a lot of driving outside of Helen in the winter, I'd bring other gear as well, but that's the basics for winter travel. Didn't you say you used to live in Massachusetts?"

Ian swallowed, his pallor a little paler than it had been a minute ago. "I did, but we left before I was old enough to drive. Besides, we lived in Boston. We were surrounded by civilization."

"Well, welcome to Alaska." Kelsey snapped the lid on her crate closed and pushed it as far back as it would go against the rear seat. Truthfully, she should have taken the bungees out at home and left the rest behind today, since the weather hadn't turned bad yet, but she'd forgotten. "You want to retract your statement about how I won't find you frozen like a Popsicle one day?"

It was absolutely the wrong thing to say. She'd been trying to sound bitchy, and judging from the pink that was replacing the white on Ian's cheeks, she'd probably succeeded. But bringing up the Popsicle remark reminded her of her previous fantasies of licking him—and all his frozen parts. Now she was annoyed and turned on, and clearly, asking for Ian's help had been such a bad idea.

Kelsey's confused and conflicted brain was half ready to offer an apology for her tone, but then the house's front door opened, and her grandmom called out her name. She let out a breath, thankful to put the awkward moment aside. But the tension in her shoulders remained, even as she hugged her grandparents. It was going to be a long day.

KELSEY HAD NO idea just how long. They'd only been moving furniture for an hour, but she might have aged a decade. Her grandparents weren't in much position to help other than to carry a few light chairs, so after she'd introduced Ian and they'd surprised her by not being nosy, they'd opened their garage, showed Kelsey where the furniture was, and let her get to work.

The thing about loading inconveniently shaped wooden pieces into square-shaped vehicles was that it required coordination between the people doing the loading. As a result, Kelsey found herself in some tight corners with Ian.

Like now. She was standing in the trailer because he was too tall to do so himself, even hunched over, and he'd just handed her the last chair to tie down. His head was mere inches below hers, and she could smell the soap or aftershave on him, and damned if it didn't smell good. Distracting, even.

That was the current word stuck in her head for him— *distracting.* She'd caught herself watching him lift things a couple of times. They'd both worked up a sweat, and Ian had taken off his jacket and pushed up the sleeves of his shirt. It was clingy, much like the T-shirt he'd worn in the website photo, and she could too easily imagine his muscles moving about underneath it. Maybe they were sweaty too.

Kelsey supposed watching him work was better than imagining licking him, but in the end, the activities weren't that different in what they implied about her state of mind.

"Watch your head," Ian called up after her, and Kelsey bit down a swear.

This was the problem with being distracted. All she really needed to improve the day was to give herself a concussion because she was picturing Ian naked.

God, she hated men. Cute, naive, puppylike men with arrogant cheekbones, potent-smelling soap, and tight shirts in particular.

"Um." Kelsey frowned at her feet. She'd gotten the last chair wedged in and tied down, but she'd managed to trap herself inside the trailer along with it. Freaking brilliant. Today was a day for a spectacular lack of planning.

Gingerly, she swung one leg over the upturned table blocking her path. There were about four inches between it and the edge of the trailer. Theoretically, that was enough for a foot to land on. In practicality, it sure didn't seem like it though.

Ian took a step forward and held up his arms. "Just go slowly."

Did she look like she was about to leap over this thing? Ian was probably enjoying her doing something stupid after she'd lectured him about his lack of car preparedness.

Grabbing a table leg with one hand, Kelsey concentrated on lifting her own leg over the bulk of the furniture. The table wobbled, and so did her balance. She managed to set her second foot down on the trailer, and for a moment all seemed fine. Then the precarious position of her feet caught up to her, her center of gravity shifted, and Kelsey screamed as it seemed like crashing into her grandparents' driveway was imminent.

Strong arms caught her, saving her face but not necessarily her sanity.

"Got you," Ian said, as though it weren't extremely obvious.

Heart pounding, Kelsey tightened her grip around Ian's neck. Her nose was buried in his hair, which smelled even better up close, and holy shit. He felt solid and warm. She hadn't missed having a guy's arms wrapped around her, but she was going to now.

It was just the adrenaline from thinking she was about to fall. That was all.

But while that explained her heartbeat, it didn't explain why the press of Ian's hands felt so nice or the way her nerves tingled beneath them. If a pair of male hands touching her through two layers of fabric was turning her on, maybe Kevin had been right and she did need sex again.

Ian lowered her, and Kelsey jumped back as soon as her feet hit the pavement. As it was, there was no way she would be able to ignore all those Popsicle fantasies tonight. "Thanks."

Ian adjusted his shirt and also took a step back. "Anytime."

Was it her imagination, or was there something flirtatious in the way she said that? Some heat in his voice? "I don't plan on making falling out of trucks a habit," she said, mostly to remind herself that falling into Ian's arms was a terrible idea.

"We can always skip that part next time." Ian was smiling. Smugly.

There was also no way to interpret that as *not* being flirtatious, although Kelsey decided to pretend he simply liked getting the better of her. Still, she was too tongue-tied with surprise to think of a witty comeback, so she opted to glare and lock the back of the trailer. As soon as she thanked her grandparents and said goodbye, they could hit the road. But getting back into a confined space with Ian held even less—or was it more?—appeal than it had this morning. She swore whatever scent he had on him had rubbed off on her.

After they separated inside the house to use the bath-rooms, Kelsey helped herself to a generous amount of hand soap, hoping to clear her nose of the remnants of eau d'Ian. It seemed to work, but the rose and hibiscus she replaced it with was cloying.

Her grandmom was emerging from the bedroom next door as Kelsey left the bathroom. It was probably inap-propriate to have favorite grandparents, but her maternal set absolutely held that title, for reasons other than giving her furniture. They were both a little short, and had gotten a little softer and squishier as they aged, but they were as sweet on the inside as they looked on the outside. That kind of sweetness was in short supply in her life.

"I've started heating up lunch for you and your friend," her grandmom said.

"He's not really my friend." She kept her voice low, although it seemed unlikely that Ian could hear her from the other side of the enormous house.

Her grandmom smiled knowingly. "I imagine not, but since you didn't tell us you were bringing a boyfriend, I didn't want to make assumptions. He's very handsome."

Kelsey could feel the blood rush to her cheeks, and she didn't know why. It wasn't *her* making an incorrect guess, yet it unsettled her for some reason.

Most likely it was all the Ian Popsicle thoughts.

"He's not that either. I'm doing him a favor, so he's doing me one. That's all."

"Are you sure? He's very cute, and I saw how he was looking at you."

Ian was looking at her? No, wait, of course he was looking at her. They'd been loading the trailer together. Kelsey pushed up the sleeves of her flannel, overly warm. "He was probably contemplating my demise."

Her grandmom placed her hands on her hips. "I don't have cataracts, you know. My eyesight is fine."

"But how's your ability to interpret what you see?" Kelsey tapped the older woman's head. Grandmom Brown was the same height as she was, and unlike with Grandma Porter, Kelsey felt she could get away with that sort of joking.

Her grandmom tsked. "My mental faculties are fine, but I'm starting to wonder about yours. From what I understand, you reject every guy you come in contact with. Are you just not interested in romance or sex? I understand that can be a thing these days, and I want you to know I will support you every bit as much as I support Kevin."

Kelsey rested her forehead against the wall, half laughing, half cringing, wholly contemplating crawling back into the bathroom and locking herself inside. But if she did, her grandmom would probably have this conversation with her through the door, and at that point, Ian was likely to overhear it.

"I'm pretty sure that's always been a thing. It's just not something that was always an option for people to choose. And no, that's not me, exactly." She simply hadn't found a guy worth her time or the risk of getting emotionally involved. Fictional men werc all she could tolerate.

"Well, what exactly is wrong with the one who came

up here with you? He's cute, he's considerate. I'm sure he could do a fine job of keeping you warm at night."

Kelsey was quite sure he could. Ian was big enough to wrap himself completely around her—and great, now she'd started thinking about what that might feel like. Those long arms. Those hard muscles. That damn *scent*.

How was this conversation happening to her? On the upside, Kelsey was finally looking forward to getting back into the car with Ian.

"I have dogs. They're plenty warm in my bed, and they have the added benefit of not fighting me for the TV remote." She lifted her head, choosing to believe her grandmom was simply concerned about her, and thus the fastest way to end this nightmare was to reassure her that she was fine. "I'm not lacking in company or affection. I'm happy."

Grandmom Brown nodded somewhat fussily, although she didn't look entirely appeased. "Dogs are fine company, but are you taking care of your other needs? A friend of mine's niece has gotten into this business selling products that—"

"I'm good!" Kelsey held up a hand. "Really. And we need to get going."

The older woman sighed. "Not without lunch you're not. Come on, the calzones should be almost ready, and your friend looked awfully hungry earlier. If you're not going to feed him what he really wants, then I should at least make sure he has food."

"DO YOU WANT to stop for any errands while we're in this bastion of civilization?" Kelsey asked, climbing into the SUV.

By some miracle, her grandmom had kept mostly quiet during lunch while her grandpop had grilled Ian about the brewery. Kelsey had no interest in beer, but that topic was infinitely preferable to her grandmom discussing relationships and sex. Ian had clearly enjoyed her grandpop too. So although Kelsey had no idea what the difference was between a stout and an ale, it had been interesting to watch Ian talk about brewing.

That he was knowledgeable about the subject was no surprise, given what he was doing, but it sounded like there was a lot more to it than throwing a bunch of grains in a vat. In fact, Ian made it sound a lot like chemistry, which did nothing to help Kelsey's understanding or pique her interest, but her grandpop seemed to get it. She ought to let him interview Ian for the newspaper article she was supposed to write. Then she could concentrate on the topics she did understand, like Ian's dimple, and imagine him lugging around heavy sacks of grain.

"No, I'm good," Ian said as she pulled out of the driveway. "It's been nice to get away from Helen. I haven't taken a full day off from working on the brewery in weeks."

"You're a workaholic?" If Ian was always at the brewery, that would make sabotaging it more difficult.

As if she was actually ever going to do that. She wasn't even fooling herself.

Ian made a sheepish face. "A bit. The rain doesn't help those tendencies. There's not much to do in Helen when it rains, so I might as well work."

Plenty of people, like her brother, didn't change their outdoor plans when it rained, but since Kelsey disliked rain herself, she shrugged. "I'm a hermit, so I don't mind being trapped indoors. You should be aware that it doesn't get much better in the winter. Even if the weather's nice, a lot of the town shuts down. Winters are long and dark. I recommend getting some indoor hobbies if you don't already have any."

"I think you should know by now what I intend my winter hobby to be."

The traffic light changed, forcing Kelsey to tear her gaze away from Ian's face before she could discern what he meant by that. He was smiling, not smugly for once, but that was all she'd been able to tell. Something inside her lurched about as she tried to figure out if it was a flirtatious smile. Or if she wanted it to be.

She told herself she didn't want it to be, but the heat she'd felt when Ian caught her tumbling from the trailer was back, and it told a different story. That was unacceptable. She *wrote* the stories; she was in control of the narrative. Her body shouldn't be usurping her brain, and yet her imagination was off and running.

Kelsey knew she couldn't let that comment of his go unremarked upon like she had the last possibly flirtatious comment. Yet it took her a couple of seconds to seize control of her mouth so she didn't say something stupid. "I should?"

It was only two words, and not the most creative reply. But at least it gave away none of the uncalled-for emotions racing through her.

"Well, yeah. I did tell you I got my library card."

"Ah." She was grudgingly pleased that Ian was a reader, but she was less so about his current expression. Smug again. What did that mean? Had he been trying to mess with her head? Ugh, men. Kelsey decided the wisest course of action was to play the whole interaction straight. "That's a good start."

Ian stretched out in the passenger seat, inscrutable once again. "Honestly, I'm looking forward to a long, dark winter."

"Why?"

"I don't know—because it's different?" He rubbed at his chin contemplatively. "It's a new experience. An adventure. Those are the same reasons why I wanted to open the brewery in Helen."

Right. He'd given her that same basic response to the questions she'd emailed him, and it didn't make any more sense now than it had then. Kelsey had a hard time thinking of Helen as a particularly adventurous place. There were adventurous kinds of activities you could do in the area—hiking, kayaking, cross-country skiing. But the town itself was just a town. "You thought it would be a fun adventure? Going from warm and sunny to cold and dark was a lark for you?"

Ian paused. "Mainly."

Kelsey would guess *partially* was more like it. There were clearly other reasons—there had to be—but if Ian didn't want to discuss them with her, that was fine. She had plenty of topics she wouldn't want to discuss either.

"I like winter," Ian said after another moment. "I missed it while I was in Florida."

"Why did you move there?"

"My bubbe is from there, and most of my family lives down there. My grandparents' plan had always been to move back after my grandfather retired. I don't think they expected to take me and my sister with, but . . ." Ian glanced out the window as though annoyed he'd said too much.

Unsure what part of that bothered him or why, Kelsey latched on to the one piece she clearly didn't understand. "Your bubbe? Oh, shit!"

She slammed on the brake as a moose trotted out into the middle of the highway. Next to her, Ian gasped, but she didn't glance his way this time. Her fingers tightened around the wheel, heart pounding in her ears, as she watched the other cars come to abrupt halts as well. When it became clear the guy behind her wasn't about to rear-end her trailer, Kelsey let out a breath.

Predictably, the moose gave not one shit about the mayhem it had caused. It continued its merry way down the road.

"Um." Ian sounded like he wanted to ask something but didn't know what it should be.

Slowly, traffic began moving again, and Kelsey took her foot off the brake. "Like I said earlier, welcome to Alaska."

10

⟡————————⟡

ASIDE FROM THE moose nearly causing a multicar collision, the day had gone well. Too well. Ian could recall with excruciating detail what it had been like to catch Kelsey falling out of the trailer—how soft her flannel shirt had felt in his hands, the way her cheek had brushed his, the lightly fruity scent of her hair. She was so short that her body fit against his perfectly, and he'd been unable to stop fantasizing since about what it would have been like if he'd slid his hands lower and cupped her ass. If she'd wrapped her legs around his waist. If he'd tasted those pouty lips with Kelsey's body clinging to his.

Not only were these thoughts he didn't want, they'd distracted him most of the drive home. And so did the way he'd melted down after he caught her.

Well, perhaps *melted down* was an exaggeration, but aside from his brain short-circuiting, he had no excuse for flirting with Kelsey. It wasn't the first time unintended words had slipped out of his mouth around her either. Every time they seemed to be getting along, he forgot that he didn't want to like her.

As such, it wasn't until Kelsey pulled her SUV into a driveway that Ian realized he had a problem. He hadn't only offered his services to load the trailer but to unload it as well. But unloading it meant going into her house. And going into her house meant there would be dogs. This was the second time today he'd forgotten all about the dogs.

Oy, he was an idiot, lulled into complacency by a flannel shirt and a perfect backside.

By some miracle, though, Kelsey had already planned for this part. "Do you want to come in for a second? Kevin was supposed to stop by and let the dogs out earlier, but they'll be desperate to to be let out again. I'm going to have to leave them in the backyard while we unload."

Ian hoped his relief didn't show, but he felt a bit like he had right after Kelsey had avoided an accident with the moose. "Actually, I need to make a quick call to Micah while you do that."

Ian got out of the SUV and made a point of playing with his phone while Kelsey went inside. He had no true need to call Micah, but so as to not be a complete liar, he did it anyway. Micah didn't pick up, so Ian left a message that he was back in town.

Kelsey reappeared a couple of minutes later as Ian was wondering whether it was finally safe to go looking for her. "Ready?"

"If you are." He stepped aside from the trailer so she could unlock it.

It became clear immediately that they hadn't escaped the moose incident as unscathed as he'd thought. The furniture had shifted, and the upturned table that had sent Kelsey crashing into his arms earlier had been punished for its transgression. One of the bookshelves had fallen to the side and snapped a leg.

"Oh no." Kelsey climbed onto the trailer, her face fallen in dismay.

"I might be able to fix it." The words tumbled out before Ian could think them through.

Here he was, being rash again. He didn't owe Kelsey anything else, and it wasn't as if they were friends. But his animosity toward her had evaporated today. It could have been that she no longer wore the SHS pin, or it could have been how cute she looked in her oversize flannel. Honestly, it was best to blame it on something superficial like that. But the truth was, talking to her had been interesting and had left him with the sense that there was a lot more to her than met the eye. He wanted to talk to her again, to learn what else she hid behind her acerbic tongue.

"You think?" Kelsey sounded doubtful. The leg hadn't been snapped completely in half, but it was too badly cracked for the table to be of use as it was.

Ian made a closer inspection, acutely aware that she was crouched inches away. Close enough that he could feel the heat radiating off her. "Probably. My grandfather's a woodworker. It's his hobby, but he taught me a bit. A dowel to stabilize the leg and some good wood glue should do the trick."

"That would be amazing, but really, you've more than repaid me for anything I'm writing for your website."

He suspected that was true. He also suspected Kelsey did not easily accept help from other people. She might be tiny and angelic looking, but she clearly had adamantine bones and muscles to match. He'd been impressed watching her lift furniture today. Despite her size, she could hold her own, and she struck Ian as the sort of person who would be determined to do everything for herself.

For some reason, though, that attitude made him want

to help all the more, and Ian told himself it was to prove to her that he was just as capable as she was, since she clearly thought otherwise. If he had other motivations, it was better to ignore them.

"Like I said, I don't think it'll be hard. I have the tools."

Kelsey looked like she was going to protest a second time, but the moment passed. "That would be great. Thank you."

It sounded like saying the words had cost her something, so Ian just responded with "No problem" and suggested they get to work.

Unloading took far less time than loading had, since they didn't need to cram furniture into unyielding spaces and tie it down. They did have to carry a few items up the stairs, however, and that proved challenging. Kelsey's stairs were tall and narrow, and she grumbled about how she'd just painted the upstairs walls so they needed to be careful.

They maneuvered the second of two bookcases into the room to the right of her staircase, and Kelsey let go and stretched her muscles. Ian averted his gaze, because lugging furniture around had done nothing to subdue his body's reaction to hers. Quite the opposite. With his testosterone flowing from the exercise, watching Kelsey was sure to be a bad idea.

The room wasn't large, and there was barely enough space left along the walls for the bookcase. There was a desk against one of the other walls that looked like it had come from IKEA and had nothing but a laptop on it. A couple of boxes that appeared to contain books sat next to it. Presumably they were waiting for their shelves.

While he studiously ignored Kelsey rolling her neck, Ian tested the shelves' stability. "The floor's uneven. You might need to wedge something under the front of this."

Kelsey stuck her hands on her hips as he demonstrated the bookshelves' wobbling. "Paint stirrers should work. I have a few left downstairs. Give me a sec?"

"Sure." He wasn't in a rush to leave, and if he was going to help her move stuff, he might as well do it right.

Kelsey disappeared down the stairs, and Ian glanced out the window. It overlooked the backyard, and her three dogs were running around without leashes. Which, of course they were, since they were fenced in. But it was enough to trip his pulse, and Ian quickly looked away.

Wandering over to her boxes of books seemed like a safer bet, and Ian absently pulled back the flap on the top one for a better view, curious what sort of books Kelsey read and any insight that gave him into her head. Oddly, they were all identical. For some reason, she had a box filled with multiple copies of the same book.

Confused, Ian pulled one out—*A Dog in the Fight* by Summer Austen. The cover showed a rugged man, his shirt unnecessarily unbuttoned, and a large husky against a backdrop of snow-covered mountains. The description on the back talked about a pack of shifters, their mates, and mortal enemies. Ian had never read a romance novel before, but his sister and bubbe did, and he knew enough to know one when he spotted one. The only question was, why did Kelsey have an entire box of this particular book?

Searching for clues, he flipped through the pages, listening to Kelsey curse as she rummaged around downstairs. Apparently *A Dog in the Fight* was the sixth book in a series called Dog Days. Ian found a listing of all the books in the front. Turning one more page backward, he scanned the dedication and copyright information.

And did a double take. Although the author was listed as Summer Austen, the copyright was to Kelsey Porter.

Ian had just enough time for the implications of that to

sink in when Kelsey reappeared in the room. He'd been so absorbed in searching the book that he hadn't heard her climb the stairs.

"Found some," she announced, and her gaze landed on the book in his hand. Her entire body froze like someone had halted time around her. Then, just as quickly, she unfroze. Seemingly making up for that lost half second, she dropped the paint stirrers and snatched the book away.

"Did you write this?" Ian asked.

Kelsey didn't respond. Ian had heard the expression "like a deer in headlights" before that moment, but he'd never experienced it on someone's face in real life. It was alarming, to say the least. Kelsey's eyes were wide and her face pale and blank, as though she were staring down a barreling tractor trailer and unable to move.

And he was the tractor trailer.

Obviously, he'd asked a bad question, and Ian's immediate urge was to apologize and take it back. But that was silly. He couldn't say *Never mind* and pretend he hadn't asked the question, and he couldn't unsee what he'd seen.

"Never mind." Ian cringed. It appeared he was going to say the silly thing anyway. Oy. "I'm sorry I asked."

Kelsey wet her lips and tucked the book back into the box with its clones. "Summer Austen wrote it."

"You're Summer Austen."

Slowly she nodded as she closed the box flaps. "Look, just pretend you don't know that, okay? No one's supposed to know that. Shit."

Her reaction unnerved Ian. Tough-as-nails, take-no-shit Kelsey should be cursing him out for stumbling onto something he wasn't supposed to see. Instead she was acting petrified.

He was the one who should have been petrified. He'd have expected her to be planning to feed him to her dogs and bury his remains in the yard. Hell, a few minutes ago, he would have thought her not turning on the snark suggested an improvement in their relationship. Now he'd have welcomed snark and outright hostility. A Kelsey out of snappy comebacks made him feel like a complete schmuck, and he hadn't even been trying to piss her off.

Maybe understanding the situation better would give him some idea of how to make it right? It didn't seem like he could make it worse. "No one knows that? The cover says you're a best seller."

Kelsey swallowed and gripped the back of the chair behind her. "People know who Summer Austen is. They don't know I'm her. And yes, I realize my name is on the copyright page. In my experience, most people don't check the copyright page, unlike you."

Ian smiled sheepishly. "I was trying to figure out why you had so many copies of the same book. If you don't want people to know, I won't tell anyone. That's easy."

THAT'S EASY? GOD, he was naive. In Ian's head, this was simple, not a situation fraught with complications and the makings of a potential disaster.

The key word was *potential*. Kelsey had survived disasters before. She could certainly survive a *pre*-disaster. So even as her pulse raced and her stomach churned, she sought a way to survive the situation. She'd always been daring and fast on her feet. A warrior, to use her father's language. She wouldn't panic.

As far as she could tell, she had two possible plays. The first was to let Ian believe he was right. The situation *was* simple and not a big deal. She only had to agree with him and hope he thought so little of her secret that he never had any temptation to mention it again. It was possible that would work. Ian didn't really know her, and he had no reason to care. And who did he know who might be interested in this random tidbit about her, anyway? It wasn't like she was secretly Stephen King or something. The name Summer Austen would mean nothing to him, and he might even forget it by the time he left her house.

Or he might not. If he didn't know how badly she wanted this kept quiet, he might have no qualms about mentioning it casually to someone—like to her father when he asked about her work on the website or the newspaper article. *Thanks for suggesting Kelsey would help, but she's not really qualified to write this sort of thing since she's a romance author.*

She wanted to throw up just thinking about it.

So no, as much as she disliked option number two, it was a better choice than option number one. She was going to have to swallow her pride and throw herself on Ian's mercy, then pray to whatever god was listening that he wouldn't betray her, either on purpose or by accident. So far, nothing had suggested that Ian was a total dick, or at least that he was more dickish than anyone of the male variety. There was a chance this could work, but it did mean she had to stop purposely antagonizing him.

That was going to suck, since purposely antagonizing Ian might have been the only thing that saved her sanity when she was otherwise tempted to fantasize about him.

Kelsey took a deep breath. She hated appearing weak, but there was nothing to be done about it. In a way, this was her fault. She'd forgotten the box with her author copies of *A Dog in the Fight* was sitting out in the office. She'd have shoved it in the closet before allowing Ian into the room if she'd remembered.

"You don't understand." Kelsey's voice quivered, suggesting she was closer to panicking than she wanted to believe. "Even my family doesn't know. That's why my father told you I could write stuff for your website. He thinks that's what I do for a living. You can't talk about this to anyone, not even them."

Especially not them.

Ian frowned. He was so clearly not getting it, but he hadn't mocked her yet or dismissed her anxiety. Under the circumstances, she should be grateful. Yet it was so hard to be grateful for small miracles when she could have used a bigger miracle that would have prevented this situation in the first place.

"If that's what you want, sure." Ian stepped away from the box, as though subconsciously distancing himself from her secret. "Can I ask why not? You're obviously successful."

Despite her blood pressure driving up her body temperature, Kelsey wrapped her arms around herself. She wanted her dogs. She needed comfort, and they had the added advantage of not being able to spill her secrets to anyone.

"Not everyone appreciates such a 'frivolous' occupation as writing novels." She picked up the box and stuffed it into the closet like Pandora ruing her mistake. "Especially not romance novels. I'm sure you're aware of the stereotypes about women who read them or write them. Now imagine that kind of fuel in the hands of the Lipins— people who would love to cause me grief. I can't give them that kind of ammunition to use against me or my family."

Kelsey couldn't tell if Ian was looking at her with pity or if she'd just blown his mind by relating her need for secrecy to the feud. Since today had shown he was still trying to wrap his mind around the feud, she'd choose to believe the latter. Pity would make her want to kick him in the shins, and as she'd already realized, being nasty to Ian was now dangerous in new and exciting ways. She wanted to hate him for putting her in this position, but once again, Ian hadn't actually done anything to earn her ire.

He was extra aggravating for it. Kelsey preferred enemies whom she had a right to dislike. It made the morality—and absurdity—of having enemies easier to handle. But lately, nothing about her life had been easy.

Ian held up his hands. "That's sad. I think writing books is actually very cool, and something you should be able to brag about. But you know best. Since it's not, you have my word that I won't tell anyone."

His word. Kelsey didn't like that. Words were easy; she ought to know. Unfortunately, making Ian swear a blood oath was something only the characters in her books might get away with. "Promise?"

"I promise. I swear. However you want to me say it." Ian crossed his heart and offered her a small smile. "Everyone has secrets they deserve the right to keep."

If her emotions hadn't been a whirlwind of bees buzzing through her bloodstream, that statement would have been worth following up on. Between it and Ian's reaction to her comment about family issues in her car earlier, she suspected he was hiding some interesting secrets of his own.

"Kelsey?" Ian sounded concerned.

She must have spaced out. Those damn bees were potent. "Sorry. Yes, thanks. It's just, no offense, we haven't exactly gotten along to this point, and I'm trying to decide whether I should trust you."

Ian raised an eyebrow. "And if you decided you couldn't trust me, what would you do? Sic your dogs on me?"

It should have been impossible, but the comment managed to provoke a tiny laugh from her. The idea of her three babies killing Ian with anything other than love was hilarious. "It's not a bad idea."

Ian sat on the edge of her desk. For a second, the room fell silent. With blood oaths out, she had to suck it up and trust Ian, but she couldn't let it happen so easily. Her brain turned over every word in her vocabulary, every phrase, as though seeking something she could say to give herself some assurance.

Ian seemed to be turning over something in his head as well. In spite of her anxiety—or maybe because she was so focused on Ian at the moment—Kelsey noticed the moment he reached a decision.

He rubbed his chin and braced himself. "Would it make you feel better if I gave you something to hold over me so we're even?"

It would. She didn't want it to, but it would anyway.

Before she could figure out how to respond, Ian continued. "I have a phobia of dogs. It's the most ridiculous and embarrassing thing in the world, and I've been trying to hide it from you, but there it is. I try to hide it from everyone, actually, because it makes me feel like an ass, so . . ." He spread his hands. "I won't tell your shameful secret if you won't tell mine."

Kelsey gaped. Shock finally wiped out the low-key (almost) panic running through her. When Ian had implied that he had secrets, this was not what she'd been expecting. That said, it put his odd behavior into sudden focus. Ian snubbing Josh over the summer. The way he'd slammed the door on her. His refusal to come over to her that day outside the coffee shop. She'd assumed it was his way of showing that he disliked her, but it hadn't been her he disliked. It had been her dogs.

But no, not *dislike* of her dogs. Something irrational that he couldn't control. That was just sad. Logically, Kelsey understood that not everyone was a dog person, but everyone should have the opportunity to decide if they were, and a phobia prevented Ian from gathering all the facts. She could happily dislike and distrust someone for not liking dogs, but she couldn't do that to someone who had a phobia of them.

"Um, Kelsey?" Ian's voice sounded as taut as hers had. "Are we even?"

Even? Of course not. He'd learned something that could screw up her life and possibly her career, and he'd told her he was afraid of dogs. Embarrassing to him, obviously. Ruin-your-life embarrassing—obviously not.

But.

But.

Kelsey appreciated the gesture. It was evident from the expression on Ian's face that he'd expected something from her besides silence. Derision or outright laughter, maybe? She wasn't sure, but Ian considered his phobia shameful, and sharing it had cost him something. And he'd done it for her. To make her feel better. He hadn't needed to, since she'd already chosen to put her trust in him, but he'd done it anyway, and damned if it wasn't getting under her skin.

He was *such* a puppy.

"I'm sorry." Those words didn't answer Ian's question, but telling Ian they weren't even wasn't a good choice, and she was sorry. Sorry not just because he had to live with a phobia, but sorry that he was missing out on all the good things dogs brought into someone's life.

Ian shrugged. "It's fine. Well, not fine, but I've been living with it for most of my life, so it's normal. Just do me a favor and leave your dogs in the backyard until I leave, okay?"

"Of course. If I'd known, I wouldn't have brought them along when we met before."

"I might have appreciated that." He laughed a little

shakily. "I guess it would make your life easier if you could be honest about your career, and it would make my life easier if so many people in this town didn't have dogs."

"We do like our dogs around here." Her family in particular. Reputedly, the feud had started because of dogs, but Kelsey considered any feud tales set before her time suspect at best. History was only one good storyteller away from fiction. "Have you ever seen a therapist about it?"

"I've thought about it. It's never been a high enough priority, and I'm better than I used to be. Small dogs don't freak me out anymore. Getting bigger helped with that. Dogs the size of yours are another story."

Again, the thought of her dogs hurting Ian was laughable, but this time Kelsey knew to hold in her smile. "My dogs would never hurt you. Jump on you, possibly. Lick you, absolutely. But that's only because they'd want to be your friend. Not because they were trying to decide whether you'd taste better with ketchup or mustard."

Ian did laugh at that. "I believe you and yet . . ."

"That's what makes it a phobia."

"Exactly."

"What about exposure therapy?" Was that what it was called? She'd taken an intro psych course to fulfill an elective in college, but that was the extent of her background.

Ian frowned at her, and, right—he had said he hadn't tried therapy. She couldn't believe she was suggesting this, but she plowed on before her better sense could kill her inner marshmallow.

"I could help. My dogs are super sweet, and if we met again so I could interview you for the newspaper article, we could figure something out. You got over your small-dog fear on your own, so maybe we could do this together."

Part of her hoped he'd say no. She was best off not seeing

Ian again. If you didn't want to adopt the puppy, you didn't play with the puppy.

Bad choice of words. She would not be playing with Ian.

But the point remained. Kelsey had no idea what had gotten into her, except she did—it was the man's damn dimple, and the way he lifted furniture, and the fact that he'd confessed something embarrassing to make her feel better. That last one was the biggest problem.

"That . . ." Ian might have been struggling with the same internal war as she was.

Say no.

"Can I hate the idea but also appreciate it and want to do it anyway?"

Yes!

Shit!

"Under the circumstances, that's probably logical." Kelsey glanced at her closet, surprised how long she'd gone without feeling like panicking.

She was positive the not-quite-panic would return later, just as she was positive she was going to kick herself after he left for offering to help Ian. She was also positive she was going to spend far too much time thinking about the man and what all his muscles had felt like pressed against her body earlier.

Absolutely positive she was going to hate herself for it too.

But if Ian got over his phobia, that wasn't only good for him, but for dogs. There would be one more person on the planet to pet them and dote on them. Honestly, this was like a public service she was doing for the canine community. She was being utterly selfless.

She'd been too fast to choose *distracting* as her word

for Ian. *Confounding* was a better choice. *Maddening,* perhaps.

"Just so we're clear," Kelsey said, "I'm doing this for the dogs' sakes as much as yours."

"That's what I assumed." Ian delivered the line with no hint as to whether he meant it.

Uh-huh. *Confounding* it was.

11

IT HAD BEEN twenty-four hours since he'd confessed his dog phobia to Kelsey, and Ian had yet to get over it. The look of terror on her face when she'd grabbed her book from him must have short-circuited his better sense. Although he might not like dogs, he wasn't a heartless monster. He'd flailed about for anything to make her feel better and had latched on to the one thing that had popped into his mind, possibly because he'd assumed she'd laugh at him for it.

That she hadn't done so had told him more about Kelsey than anything he'd learned on the trip to her grandparents' house. Beneath her snark and her open contempt for those who pissed her off, she was actually kind. He didn't know what to make of her offer to help him get over his phobia, only he wouldn't put it past her to be doing it for the dogs, as she'd said.

What made him accept the offer—that was the mystery that deserved to be explored, and therefore paradoxically the one best ignored. Therapy had never risen to a high enough priority in his life, but if he was going to work on his phobia, he should do it with someone trained for the task. Not a woman who believed he was an interloper and one bottle short of a six-pack when it came to life skills.

Down the hall, Ian could hear Micah starting the shower. His friend had just gotten back from a run and had connected his phone to a speaker so he could shower to music.

He should get up and do something about dinner, but instead he found himself searching online for Summer Austen's books. Burning curiosity had him clicking on the first in the series before he could question what he was doing. It was only when the shower turned off that Ian realized he'd devoured almost the entire free sample. He had to stop this nonsense before Micah caught him.

It wasn't that Ian particularly cared if Micah teased him about reading romance, but questions would arise since it wasn't his usual genre, and he wouldn't have a smart answer. Good thing then that Kelsey's books were available in digital format as well as print. Ian bought the first book—*Dog with a Bone*—and told himself that it was in no way strange to be interested in Kelsey's series, and surely the fact that the books were described as *steamy* had nothing to do with his decision. Kelsey had warned him he needed winter hobbies, after all. He wasn't just doing this because Kelsey and sex went together in his mind like peanut butter and jelly.

"Oh good, you're being lazy." Thanks to the incessant music, Ian hadn't heard Micah sneak up on him, but his friend spoke from right behind the sofa.

There was no way Micah could have read what was on his phone screen, but Ian tossed the device aside quickly anyway. "You startled me," he said as an excuse.

"Sorry. Came in to see if you'd started dinner, and since you haven't, all is well. We're going out."

Ian blinked at him. "We are?"

"Yes, to someplace that serves food and alcohol."

Ian's stomach rumbled. Yes, he did need food, but he'd already finished a second chapter of Kelsey's book since buying it, and he had been settling in to keep reading. "How about takeout?"

"How about going out? Remember the whole spiel about how we should be openly supporting other town businesses so they'll want to support us? Still in effect."

"I'm feeling antisocial."

Micah snorted. "No, my friend, you're feeling stressed and like working because that's what you always do."

Micah might have been wrong this time, but Ian had to grudgingly admit that usually his friend would have been correct.

"Exactly," Micah said when Ian didn't reply. "We're going out, and you're going to tell me how your road trip with Kelsey went yesterday."

If Ian's stomach hadn't audibly rumbled, he might have gotten away with protesting, but it had, and more to the point, he couldn't put off that conversation forever. Micah had dicked him over yesterday, and in retrospect, Ian couldn't be too pissed off.

"All right." He shut down his laptop. "But if I'm talking, you're buying the first round."

THE LAST TIME Micah had dragged Ian away from his work to be sociable, they'd patronized a Porter-affiliated bar. So this time Ian insisted they go to a Lipin-affiliated place. It was frustrating and ridiculous, but yesterday's adventures with Kelsey had done more to convince him of the feud's seriousness than anything yet. If there was a way to keep his brewery out of the fray, he had to do whatever it took.

Micah, who was far pickier about his food than Ian, had determined the perfect place was a tiny watering hole whose claim to local fame was its fish tacos. That was fine. As long as they served food with their drinks, Ian could live with it.

Micah questioned him about Kelsey on the drive, and Ian did his best to recite bland facts in a dry manner. He mentioned Kelsey almost falling out of the trailer, but not that he caught her. He admitted he'd made a fool out of himself by asking about the crate she kept in her car. And he declined entirely to talk about discovering Kelsey's secret career or that he'd agreed to let her work with him on dog issues.

Micah was visibly disgruntled with this recounting of events. "That's it? Nothing exciting?"

Ian wasn't sure what precisely Micah was waiting for him to say. That he was attracted to Kelsey? His friend had figured that out already, and Ian was doing his best to pretend otherwise.

"Oh, exciting things." Ian smacked his forehead like it had never occurred to him. "Actually yeah, one more thing. We almost hit a moose on the drive back. Those Moose Crossing signs are no joke."

"I see." Micah put the car in park, looking extremely disappointed. "Then what's up with that broken table sitting in our living room? Did you think I wouldn't notice?"

"The moose crossing and slamming on the brakes happened."

"So you offered to fix it?" Micah's smirk was too knowing.

"It seemed like the friendly thing to do."

Micah's smirk increased in power. "How gallant, especially considering you already overwork yourself, and how convenient that it gives you a reason to see Kelsey again."

Yeah, well, it wasn't like that *hadn't* been his subconscious motivation.

Shaking his head, Ian got out of the car.

The interior of the bar was packed and noisy, and Ian hid his grimace. This was much more Micah's scene than his. He wasn't even sure they could find a table. On the bright side, however, it was noisy enough to make continuing the Kelsey conversation challenging.

"Hey!" As Ian searched for two seats together to grab, he became vaguely aware that someone was yelling in his direction, but it wasn't until he heard his name that he realized the person was calling out to him.

There weren't many people in this town whom he was on such friendly terms with, but luck was on his side this evening. Ian turned his attention from the bar and saw Josh whose-last-name-he-didn't-know wave him over.

The first time they'd run into each other, Ian had stumbled upon Josh making out with his girlfriend outside the brewery. The couple's embarrassment had given Ian the laugh he'd needed after a long day, although he'd done his best to contain it. Since then, he'd seen Josh around a few more times. Helen was big enough that the strangers you passed in the store seemed faceless only until you began talking to some of them. Then you realized you were seeing the same people over and over. Apparently he and Josh did their grocery shopping at similar times. That was how he'd eventually learned Josh was a doctor at the local hospital and excited about the brewery opening.

Ian waved back as Micah entered the bar behind him.

"You have a friend?" Micah feigned shock.

"More like a friendly." Josh was sitting with another guy, whom Ian didn't recognize, but there were two extra seats at their table.

After a quick stop at the bar so Micah could schmooze with the owner and introduce Ian, they made their way to Josh's table. Thanks to the need for introductions, Ian learned that Josh's last name was Krane and the guy with him was Adrian, another doctor. A server came by, and while they waited on the famous fish tacos, Ian coddled his stomach with the complimentary tortilla chips.

"So you're the other brewery owner," Josh said, sipping his beer. "My cousin told me she met the two of you recently. How come we don't see you around as much?"

Micah laughed. "I've spent a lot of time on the road. I'm the sales and numbers guy. Ian's the one with the important job."

"Sales guy?" Adrian tapped the bar's draft menu. "So when is this place getting to taste the wares?"

"Soon, hopefully. We have a contract with them." Micah nudged Ian. "He's the one to ask about when the next batch will be ready."

"Soon, hopefully," Ian said, mimicking Micah's tone. He had two batches almost ready for bottling, and a few more only a couple of weeks away. But off the top of his head, he didn't know what had been sold to where, and he had to resist the urge to look it up on his phone. There would be no defense to the workaholic comments if he couldn't manage that.

"Who's your cousin?" Ian asked Josh. There was only one person he could think of who had met him and Micah recently, but she was a Porter, and this was a Lipin bar.

Josh waited for the server who'd brought over Ian's and Micah's beers to leave before responding. "Kelsey."

"Porter?" Micah looked around shiftily. "Should I not have said that out loud?"

"Kelsey's your cousin?" Ian asked while Josh chuckled at his friend's antics. "How does this work logistically?"

"Josh is our current best source of entertainment." Adrian smirked.

"I'm dating a Lipin," Josh said, seeing the confusion on Ian's and Micah's faces. "The chaos it's causing is all very entertaining, so I'm told. Personally, I'm tired of finding dead mice on my front step, and the person who used shaving cream to write 'traitor' all over my Jeep annoyed me, but as long as other people are amused . . ." He rolled his eyes.

"Dead mice?" Micah cringed. "Nice."

"A gift from the Lipins' cats, I'm sure. The shaving cream was my family."

Ian took a sip of his beer, a pumpkin ale from a microbrewery in Juneau. Pretty good. He tried to enjoy it and not think of it as competition. Northern Charm's own pumpkin ale was one of the beers that was almost finished.

"Porters and Lipins dating?" Ian pushed aside the work thoughts. "We really are living in fair Verona."

"Fair Verona?" Josh repeated.

"Kelsey and I were discussing *Romeo and Juliet* yesterday. She's surprisingly not a fan, considering the names of her dogs."

Adrian grabbed a chip. "It's romance. Can't see Kelsey enjoying that."

Actually, Ian was positive *Romeo and Juliet* was more of a tragedy than anything else, but in light of his discovery about Kelsey's books, he figured the safest thing to do was drink more of his beer. Credit to Kelsey—she'd done a great job of convincing everyone in town that she couldn't possibly be a romance writer.

"I don't know," Josh said. "Feuding families fighting each other seems like the sort of story Kelsey might like. On the other hand, it might hit too close to home. She's a former English major; she has feelings about Shakespeare."

Ian grinned into his beer. "I suspect she has 'feelings' about a lot of things, if that's the code word we're using for 'opinions.'"

Micah pointed a finger at him. "Aha. Was this the discussion yesterday? Because you failed to provide it during your half-assed recap." He turned toward Josh and Adrian. "Ian drove up to Wasilla with Kelsey yesterday on a very exciting road trip."

He should have expected Micah to chime in the moment Kelsey's name came up. All he needed was for Micah to share his theory that he had the hots for her, and then have Josh repeat it to Kelsey. While his accidental flirting had probably already given him away, he wouldn't put it past Kelsey to rescind her offer to help him if his feelings were confirmed.

"She's doing us a favor, so I did her a favor," Ian said quickly, hoping that explanation would cut off any further discussion.

"Was that to pick up her grandparents' furniture?" Josh swore. "I told her I'd help, but the timing kept not working out."

"Well it wasn't a big deal, and it's done now." Ian glanced toward Micah. "And it wasn't very exciting."

Adrian's head had been swiveling between them, and he raised an eyebrow. "Really? In my experience, being around Kelsey can definitely be exciting, particularly in an 'Am I going to live to see tomorrow?' kind of way."

Ian was too stunned that Adrian would say something like that around Josh to respond, but Josh chuckled. "It's true that Kelsey merely tolerates most people. She must like you to have been willing to spend that much time in your company."

Micah said nothing, but the expression on his face was significant. Ian pretended he couldn't see it. "'Like' is probably overstating things. More likely she was desperate for the help."

"Don't listen to him," Micah said. "They get along well."

"Really?" Josh looked curious, and Adrian disbelieving.

"No." Ian shot Micah a cut-it-out look. "That was sarcasm. Kelsey can be, um . . ."

"Bitchy?" Adrian suggested.

"I was going to say 'prickly,' but I figured that was just her attitude toward me."

Josh shook his head. "Nope, that's Kelsey. Don't take it personally. If Kelsey really didn't like you specifically, you'd know. She definitely wouldn't have tolerated an entire drive to Wasilla with you. She'd be doing everything she could to avoid you."

Ian made a noise of understanding and went back to drinking his beer, saved from further discussion by the arrival of the server and their fish tacos. If what Josh said was true—and Josh ought to know—then he was back to the question he'd been pondering earlier: What did it mean that Kelsey had offered to help with the dog issue? Doing it to help all of dogkind was no longer sounding as plausible. And what did he want to think about her motivations?

Ian swished the pumpkin ale around on his tongue,

contemplating its sweet-to-bitter ratio. He was trying to steer his thoughts back toward work, but even the words *sweet* and *bitter* made him think of Kelsey. He didn't have time for this sort of distraction, but it looked like he didn't have a choice.

12

AFTER LOCKING THE fence, Kelsey let the dogs off their leashes and stuffed her hands into her jacket pockets. She'd taken them on a three-mile walk, but did they have the decency to be tired? No, they did not. She, on the other hand, was wiped.

Sitting on her back stoop, she pulled out her phone while Romeo, Juliet, and Puck charged around her small backyard, loving life and confused as to why she wasn't joining them. Puck darted over to her and nipped at her ankles, and she could practically hear him yelling at her to come play.

"Mama needs to rest," Kelsey said, rubbing his head. "I only have two legs and get a whole lot less sleep than you."

Puck cocked his head to the side, giving off the eerie impression that he'd understood her. Then he backed away and joined his siblings in stalking the squirrels high over their heads in the tree branches. The three huskies chased their shadows in the grass, waiting for an unlucky animal to fall.

Kelsey's phone had alerted her several times on the walk about incoming texts, but she'd ignored them all. Opening the app now, she wished she'd continued to do so. Emily, Lauren, and Amy had been chatting about the rescheduled girls' weekend and making plans without her. Well, that was partially on her for ignoring the conversation while she was walking, but her silence did not mean she consented to what they'd agreed upon. Particularly since what they'd agreed upon was making their girls' weekend no longer a *girls'* weekend.

She should have seen this coming. Emily had gotten married last year, and Lauren was in a long-term relationship. Amy's status was less locked down, but she was dating someone at the moment. That left her as the lone, well, loner in the group—and now, the only one who wanted to keep the testosterone out of their vacation.

Kelsey scowled as she typed. Sorry to be the voice of dissent, but how are we supposed to bitch about men if there are men present?

Truthfully, she wasn't sorry at all, and she was pissed off that the others cared so little about preserving their together time. It wasn't just that the weekend was meant to be female-only; it had been their precious time to hang out like in the old days.

Romeo came over and set his head on her knees while Kelsey waited for a response. Poor, sweet boy. *He* understood group dynamics. Romeo was carefree around her and his siblings, but bringing anyone else into the mix raised his anxiety levels. It was why she'd had to abandon the idea of adding to their pack a couple of years ago.

It was also why Romeo wouldn't be the best dog to help out with Ian's therapy, although he'd been Kelsey's original thought. Romeo would be just as timid around Ian as Ian would be around him, but that made Romeo more unpredictable. Puck was out too. His smaller size might help Ian feel more comfortable, but his unrelentingly puppy-like energy made him too wild. Luckily, Juliet was more than up for the task that was hers by process of elimination. She was sweet and obedient, unless of course you were a squirrel, in which case she became a fearsome hunter. Kelsey watched her jump at a tree branch hanging ten feet over the fence whenever one dared step across the line dividing the yards.

You should bring someone! Lauren wrote back, so not-helpfully. It'll be fun.

Right. She, the woman they knew didn't date if she could help it, should bring a date.

So now she had a problem. She wasn't about to drag some random guy with her, but if she went without anyone, it would be awkward. There was no win here. Continuing to press the issue would get her nowhere. It was clear they'd made up their minds, and she'd lose any vote on the matter.

Romeo whined questioningly up at her, and Kelsey scratched his soft ears. "If more men were like you, I wouldn't be in this mess."

For a brief moment of madness, Kelsey imagined bringing Ian along to the no-longer-just-girls weekend. It was impossible to pretend she wasn't attracted to him. Since Friday, when she should have been worrying about Ian spilling her secret, her thoughts had continuously drifted toward more pleasant subjects, most of which had involved Ian without clothes on. It had been six years since she'd last had sex, and Kelsey couldn't deny that she'd thought about it more in the ten days since meeting Ian than she had in all that time. The last couple of days, specifically. Friday's trip had done a number on her body, and Ian's attempt to make her feel better had done the same to her head.

For the first time since her disastrous relationship with Anthony, she was contemplating the end of her self-enforced celibacy. The idea of it made her queasy, but in Ian's case, her libido was more powerful than her anxiety. The thought of him naked, of acting out all the scenarios she'd been fantasizing about, had the ability to override her common sense. Anthony had messed up her head, but she was no longer the insecure, clueless girl she'd been in college. She might not have gained a whole lot of practical experience when it came to men since Anthony, but she'd most certainly learned a thing or two, as her readers would attest. Whether book learning could translate into successful doing, Kelsey had doubts, but in Ian, she might have found her perfect test subject. Just sitting in her backyard, in the cold wind, thinking about the possibilities was making her nipples hard and her underwear wet. It was already a foregone conclusion that she'd be breaking out Mr. Happy before bed.

Another friend group text arrived, snapping Kelsey out of these dangerous thoughts, but she didn't bother to read it. She didn't have the bandwidth to deal with her friends at the moment, but it was a good reminder that considering testing her sex skills with Ian was a dangerous fantasy. He held her most precious secret in his (strong, manly) hands, and she had no choice but to trust him with it. That was a precarious position to be in, and she didn't dare disturb the balance of their relationship, such as it was. After all, when even the friends she'd known for years had no second thoughts about screwing her over, what hope did she have that a virtual stranger might not be tempted to do the same?

* * *

"THE GUYS JOSH recommended to help with the bottling this week seem solid," Micah said as Ian checked on another of the brewery's tanks. "We need to start thinking about hiring some people on permanently though. Once these next batches go out, we're going to be operating beyond the scope where the two of us can handle everything."

Ian entered the fermentation reading into his spreadsheet and sighed. Micah wasn't wrong, but until this place was fully open—including the tasting room—there was only enough work for additional hands periodically. Those periods would just be coming faster and faster. The income they generated, however, was still far from reliable. Until it was, Ian hated the idea of taking on permanent help.

That said, he knew he should trust Micah on this. His friend was the one with the business background, and he was better suited to crunching those numbers. But so much was riding on the brewery's success that letting any part of it get away from him, and that included taking on the additional risk of real employees, made Ian feel like vomiting.

Considering the thought of seeing Kelsey later for the first of what she'd dubbed his "dog therapy" sessions also made him feel like vomiting, his stomach needed a rest. And that didn't even touch on the news they'd gotten from the town today.

"Yeah, I know." Ian saved the spreadsheet and set his tablet aside. "Let's see how these guys work out and whether they're interested in more permanent work before we make any decisions."

"Sounds good." Micah tapped his fingers along the tanks as he headed toward the brewery's main room.

Ian followed, contemplating the time and how much more work he could get done before dinner. Then how much he should drink at dinner to prepare himself for what came after. Namely, the dogs. Seeing Kelsey again came with its own excitement, but more of the pleasant kind. The conversation with Josh on Saturday had kept her in the front of his mind, and the longer she stayed there, the more he wanted her there.

Reading her book didn't help. The story was entertaining on its own, but the woman could write sex scenes that burned up the page (or rather his phone screen). He inevitably got distracted while reading and started remembering how her body had pressed against his and imagining the curve of her ass beneath his palms and what it would feel like to have those legs wrapped around him as he pumped inside of her. Then he'd have to stop reading and go take care of business.

The plan was to meet Kelsey at seven at her house tonight, and Ian still hadn't told Micah what he was up to.

"We need to address the town problem," Micah said, taking a seat in the tasting room.

The town problem—the third and final issue that was making him sick to his stomach. They'd gotten word today, from Kelsey's father, of all people, that the SHS was petitioning the town to change their alcohol laws. Under the proposed new law, the brewery wouldn't be allowed to serve beer unless they served full meals with it or served alcoholic drinks in addition to their own beer. Either would be a disaster. He and Micah weren't trying to open a restaurant or a bar. These changes would force them to do so.

Ian rubbed his eyes. "Can they actually do that?"

"After consulting with our lawyer—yes, they can. Every town is free to impose whatever restrictions they want on top of the state's laws."

"Shit." Ian grabbed the back of a chair, fighting the urge to throw it and let out some of the tension inside. His own cursory understanding of the state laws had told him the same thing, but he'd been hoping an actual lawyer would say he was wrong.

Micah's eyebrows shot into his hairline. Ian rarely swore. "Relax. It's unlikely this is going to go anywhere, and if it does, we'll manage. We can strike a deal with another brewery. We'll sell their stuff and they'll sell ours."

"We'll need additional licenses to do that. It'll cost more money that we didn't budget for." It would push them one step closer to failure. Ian swallowed.

"Probably. Or we can go with my idea and open this town's first decent bagel shop. I've even come up with more names. Don't say no yet; hear me out." Micah spread his arms. "We'll call ourselves Lox of Lagers. You got to admit—it's catchy, right?"

In spite of himself, Ian snorted. "I don't even make lagers."

"And I don't make bagels—yet. But there's no time like the present to start."

13

"SORRY, MY DEARS." Kelsey closed the gate at the top of her stairs, preventing the huskies from following her. "I promise, this won't last long."

It wouldn't for Juliet anyway, whom she planned to bring down once Ian was ready. Kelsey figured not springing a dog on him the moment he walked through her door was wisest. Still, she didn't think Romeo or Puck would be trapped upstairs for too long either. She'd done a bit of research into exposure therapy, and she figured she should limit the amount of time Ian spent near Juliet. Slow and steady was the way to go. If she kept Juliet in the kitchen, Ian might not even cross the threshold between it and the living room, and that was okay if it was as close as he felt comfortable with.

Then Ian would leave. In all, the entire session might take only ten minutes.

She would not be disappointed about that.

Kelsey sighed. It wasn't like she even knew for sure whether Ian was interested in her, or for that matter whether he was okay with casual sex. Because that was all there could be, and even that left her second-guessing this harebrained idea. She didn't know what would be worse—Ian rejecting her outright, or Ian expecting more from her. If she contemplated these scenarios for too long, she'd lose her nerve altogether.

"And would that be so terrible?" Kelsey straightened the throw cushions on her sofa. She'd already gone through a whole list of reasons why kissing Ian would be bad, starting with him knowing her secret and ending with the possibility that he might not enjoy the experience. And what would happen to her then? She'd spent years rebuilding her self-esteem. Best not to risk anything.

At least her house was looking better. She'd painted the downstairs on Sunday, which was probably something she should have done before picking up her grandparents' furniture, but better late than never. The walls needed another coat, but with the addition of the tables and chairs, she no longer looked like she was living in a abandoned building. There was no reason to be embarrassed in front of company.

A knock at the door interrupted her brief moment of satisfaction and brought her emotional disarray back with force. Since there was nothing to do about that, Kelsey lifted her chin and welcomed Ian inside as though all was perfectly normal. After all, she was used to faking her way through life. Surely she could fake being indifferent to this man.

"It's looking good," Ian said, checking out the walls, and Kelsey couldn't help but notice he'd looked around the floor first, presumably for her dogs.

She stifled a laugh. "It's looking better. Don't worry. I'm not going to sic a dog on you if you're not overly effusive about my paint choices."

Ian winced and stuffed his hands in his pockets. "I appreciate that, but I don't think I was being effusive. Never mind overly effusive."

No, he was right. He hadn't been, but her defense mechanisms were kicking in. Being attracted to him made life difficult, and snark was her comfort setting. Trading barbs with Ian was the safest thing she could do for herself, but it wasn't fair to him. Especially when he was putting himself in her hands regarding the dogs (but alas, not literally).

"Sorry," Kelsey said. "I seem to default to sarcasm around you still."

Ian seemed surprised by her apology, as he should be, even if he didn't know her well enough to know why. If Josh were around, her cousin would have feigned fainting. "That's probably my fault. I'm the one who went on the offensive first."

"That's a matter of perspective. I was already inclined to dislike you before we met because of the whole outsider thing."

"True—and if I'd known that, I might have slammed a door in your face intentionally."

Kelsey shook her head, snark dissolving with her smile. It might be her comfort setting, but it was no longer her default around him, no matter what she claimed. "No, you wouldn't have."

Ian laughed, and some of the tension went out of his shoulders. "You're right. I wouldn't have."

"You're too nice."

"I'm not entirely sure that's the reason."

There it was again—the change in intensity of his gaze, the knowing lilt of his lips, and something more. Kelsey could have sworn the air between them took on a charge, like a storm was gathering, and it was disrupting her brain.

Disruptive—that was the new word she should have chosen for Ian. He wasn't just distracting; he was disrupting.

It was time to move on before she continued smiling for no good reason.

"Before we do this . . ." And by *this* she meant bring the dog out, but since she didn't say that, all Kelsey could do was rush on and think about how her words might be misinterpreted. "Um, do you want something to drink? To help with anxiety, I mean? I have this bottle of whiskey someone gave me. I don't drink unless it's the sort of thing that comes with a paper umbrella, but my brothers think it's good, and I thought it might help you to self-medicate."

"Thanks, but I'm good." Ian's hands visibly twitched in his pockets, suggesting that wasn't entirely true. "I had a beer with dinner. It was a stressful day—no dogs required for that."

"Everything okay?" Why was she asking? Kelsey told her feet to march upstairs and get Juliet, but they remained in place.

Ian's face spoke the answer before he could get out the words. "It's the town, or the SHS, to be more specific. They're petitioning to have the local alcohol laws changed to make our lives more difficult."

They could do that? She'd take Ian's word for it. It was nasty and underhanded and entirely aboveboard—the kind of move she could appreciate if it wasn't aimed at someone she liked.

Liked. Kelsey cringed. It was one thing to admit to herself that she was attracted to Ian. Liking him was another story. At best, she was willing to acknowledge that she didn't dislike him. It was damn hard to dislike a puppy.

"I'm sorry," she said, hoping that explained the cringe.

Ian crossed his arms. "Really? The fact that the Lipins

are behind it aside, isn't this what you want? To drive us out of town?"

He wasn't entirely wrong, but Ian had turned her into a contradictory mess. Kelsey flailed about for a way to explain her complicated feelings. One that didn't involve admitting that she wanted to jump his bones *or* that she was simultaneously worried that if she pissed him off, he'd spill her darkest secret. "Yes, but not really. I mean, it's not personal, as I've said. And anyway, it's not like your business is a chain store, so you could be higher on my shit list."

"Ah, thanks. I was worried for a second when you weren't being snarky."

In spite of her determination to do anything but smile, Kelsey laughed. "That worried you?"

"Well, I was getting used to it." He leaned against the half wall that separated her kitchen and living room. "You're funny, so I guess I might even have started liking it."

Funny was so not what she was aiming for when she turned her snark on people, and normally, Kelsey would have been offended by the suggestion. This was just one more example of men not taking her seriously. Except with Ian, that wasn't the case. She didn't want to truly cut him down, so she hadn't been aiming for cruel. Perhaps, subconsciously, she had been aiming for funny, or its proximity.

Heat rose up Kelsey's neck. "I usually have the opposite effect on people."

Ian rubbed his chin. "Maybe your tricks don't work on us outsiders, and that's the real reason you don't like us."

"My tricks?"

"You know, pretending to be unlikable so people will leave you alone?"

Kelsey opened her mouth to protest, but her words

failed. Damn him. Somehow Ian had figured her out too well. It was terrifying and fascinating, and she wasn't only feeling flushed anymore. Her pulse was pounding in her ears, and her head was swimming. She wanted to kiss him more than ever, but her mouth had gone dry.

She glanced around for something to fiddle with and came up empty. "You don't think I'm unlikable?"

That had to have sounded weird. Worse, she was certain it sounded hopeful. As if she wanted Ian to like her.

But she didn't.

Although she wouldn't have minded him pressing her against the nearest wall and smashing his mouth against hers. He didn't have to like her for that.

These emotions must have been flashing over her face, because Ian took a step away from the wall, bringing him a hair's breadth closer to her. The puppiness had left him again. He was 100 percent man, but with the kind of hungry look on his face that was pure animal instinct. She doubted he had any idea of it, but her body had become very aware, and her mouth was no longer dry.

"I did think you were unlikable at first," Ian said with a small shrug. "But I've changed my mind since. I now think you're an acquired taste, like beer. Lots of people don't like beer at first, but if you keep sipping, you develop an appreciation for it."

Kelsey had no idea if that was true, but truth was irrelevant. She watched Ian's lips as he spoke, and they were the only thing she could concentrate on. "I'd like to point out that you've never actually tasted me."

Those mesmerizing lips twitched. "We could fix that."

Fix what? Oh wait, she'd said the tasting thing out loud. Her heart, which had already been pounding hard, increased its speed. This was clearly a sign that she should run upstairs and get a dog—any dog—because her brain and her body weren't coordinating their actions, and who knew what she'd do next if left to her own devices?

Kelsey swallowed. *Take a step back,* she told herself.

She took a step forward. "Do you think that's a good idea?"

Ian also took a step forward. "Why not?"

Why not? She had an answer to that question, but it was seeming less relevant with every breath.

Did she really want to do this? Would she ever have a more exhilarating opportunity? What if it was a disaster? What if it wasn't?

"Kelsey?" Ian's hand had touched her cheek without her having any idea how he had gotten that close, but now that she was aware, she was very aware. The heat of his body seeped into hers. The scent of him filled her head. She could see every hair, every bit of stubble on his chin, and she wanted to rub her cheek against it and feel that stubble scratching the skin on her face. The skin in other places too. Then she wanted to climb him like he was a freaking mountain. Suddenly, she appreciated tall men in a way she never had before.

And she loved the way he said her name. Her friends, her close family—everyone called her Kels. Hearing her full name from Ian's lips made it somehow more sensual.

Or maybe that was just his voice. She'd never thought about it before, but Ian had a nice voice. Deep but not too deep, and rich like honey.

"Yes." She closed her eyes, and fear shot through her, a cold spike of iron that should have shattered her ability to continue. Anxiety, embarrassment—all the old emotions she'd spent years working her way through returned in a dizzying second of panic.

But they vanished as quickly as they'd come, because Ian was kissing her, and oh my God. Anxiety had no room in her emotional repertoire. Anxiety required repetitive thoughts and dwelling on old memories, and she was no longer capable of thinking coherently enough for either. Explosive lust completely drowned out everything but sensation and need.

Ian must have felt the same way. His kiss was not gentle and questioning like his hand had been. She'd welcomed his touch, given him the okay, and he was taking it, stealing her breath like he was afraid she'd rescind the invitation.

His mouth was hot, devouring hers, coaxing noises out of her throat that she wasn't sure she'd ever made before. Unbidden, her arms reached up, and she wrapped them around his neck and dug her nails into the patch of skin above his collar as her fingers and toes curled with pleasure. Ian slid his arms around her, cupped her ass, and together they slammed backward until she hit the wall behind her. He tried to pause for a second, possibly to ask if she was okay, and Kelsey didn't let him. She stretched for him again and ran her tongue over his lips and the prickly stubble on his chin. Ian groaned until he reclaimed her mouth. That was good. She didn't want to stop. If she stopped, those pesky thoughts might have space to breathe and unwanted emotions might return. She wanted to do this—she would do this—and for that to happen, she needed to keep kissing Ian, keep touching him. She'd never found a way to shut her brain off like this before.

Then Ian abruptly stopped, leaving her panting against the wall. "What are you doing?" she demanded.

He didn't take his hands off her, but he closed his eyes as though pulling himself together. "I don't know."

He wasn't changing his mind on her now, was he? "Ian!" She didn't care that she sounded desperate. She *was* desperate.

He looked up at her sharply. "Is this what you want?"

"No, this is not what I want. What I want is for you to get back to kissing me. Then for you to push me against this wall and do unspeakable things until we both come to our senses."

He wet his lips and stared at her, giving Kelsey a terrible second to believe she was the only one who wanted those things, despite what the bulge in his pants suggested. But she must have only shocked him, because the second passed, and Ian's mouth crashed back into hers. His tongue tormented hers, slick and demanding. His hands squeezed her backside, pressing her into his body. Pressing his erection into her abdomen and turning the ache between her legs into an unbearable throbbing.

She wasn't used to this. With Anthony, she'd needed tons of foreplay to get this aroused, and even then, she'd never been able to quiet her brain. With Ian, the past ten days felt like all the foreplay she needed. She was ready, painfully so, for the main event.

So why not do something about that? She didn't wait for a man to take charge any other time.

Kelsey unclenched her hands from Ian's sweatshirt and undid the button on his jeans. For her brazenness, she was rewarded with a most delicious moan and a sharp intake of his breath. Ian stopped kissing her, which was unfortunate, but she could see it was because he was fighting for control.

She liked that. She liked it a lot. The strain on his face might even be more arousing than kissing him.

Deciding where to focus her eyes was impossible, and Kelsey's gaze switched back and forth between Ian's face and his jeans as she unzipped them. His abdominal muscles twitched next to her hands. She took a moment to focus just on them—strong and lean—like she knew they'd be from his photos. A line of sandy blond hair disappeared into the waist of his boxer briefs. She traced a finger down it—soft skin, hard muscles, a veritable silk road of goodness until she slipped her hand beneath the elastic and wrapped her fingers around the prize.

Ian closed his eyes, and fell forward, bracing himself on the wall behind her. "Fuck."

It occurred to Kelsey that she'd never heard him swear before, and she liked that a lot too. She had half a mind to point it out, but that could lead to more talking, and she didn't want to talk. Instead she wet her lips in anticipation of all those fantasies she had of licking Ian becoming reality.

"Don't do that." He practically growled out the words.

She had no time to ask *What?* because Ian cupped her face with his free hand and kissed her again, impossibly harder than the last time. She squirmed in his grasp, unwilling to let go of his cock, and the harder she involuntarily squeezed him, the rougher his mouth was. And shit, she liked that too.

Ian released her mouth all at once, leaving her gasping for breath and too distracted to do anything else. It was a moment of weakness. He'd kissed the control right out of her and she could barely stand. While Kelsey tried to recover, Ian's hands tugged on her shirt, and reluctantly she let go of him so he could pull it over her head.

Her skin was cool without the extra layer, but she flushed anyway. Ian's eyes were bright, assessing her, and she tried to meet his gaze, but he was no longer looking at her face. His fingers looped around her bra straps, draping them over her shoulders. Her breasts were nothing special. They were as tiny as the rest of her, but under Ian's attentiveness, they felt swollen as he peeled her bra's fabric lower. His fingertips brushed her skin, hardening her already tender nipples, and Kelsey gave in and closed her eyes as pleasure shot straight down to her groin. She was barely aware that Ian was sliding her bra off. All her effort was focused on her breathing.

"You are so beautiful." His voice was thick. "These are so beautiful."

Kelsey whimpered as Ian's thumbs flicked over her nipples. "Stop torturing me."

"Revenge." The thumbs stopped, replaced by his tongue, and the comment on her lips dissolved with the rest of her.

"Oh my God." Kelsey grabbed him about the shoulders and tangled one hand through his hair to stay upright as slick heat circled her right breast. He sucked and nipped at her, one side and the other, until her knees wobbled. "Ian, please."

He paused, and that wasn't what she wanted either. "Please what?"

"Fuck me." She was begging. What the hell had gotten into her? The day Kelsey Porter asked anything of a man, never mind begged one, should have been a shameful day. But this didn't feel shameful at all. Not when Ian knelt in front of her, lips wet, eyes darkened with lust, his pants hanging open and revealing an enormous bulge in his underwear. One that made her body ache with need. No, this was perfection.

"I thought that's what I was doing." He smiled slyly.

She pulled more tightly on his hair for his audacity. "Get inside me."

"Okay." There was mischief on his face that she didn't have time to contemplate except to acknowledge that it looked good on him. Then Ian yanked down the leggings she'd been wearing, taking her panties with them.

But rather than stand and remove the rest of his own clothing, he pressed his face against her stomach. The stubble, the scratchy hair she'd longed to have rubbed all over her, now did as he kissed his way from her belly button down. She wanted to protest. This wasn't what she'd meant, and he damn well knew it. But she had no words. The noises coming out of her mouth as his lips brushed the patch of hair between her legs were nothing short of animal-like. Ian's fingers pushed her thighs wider, and she spread her legs because resisting was impossible. His tongue split her folds in two, and oh my God.

Time had helped her forget how good this was. She'd been with Anthony for almost two years, and he'd only ever gone down on her twice, because he hadn't liked doing it. Yet here was Ian on his knees for her. Ian, who'd just decided he wanted to do this with no prompting. His hot breath tickling her sensitive flesh. His tongue, wet and persistent. And his lips, homing in on her clit, circling and sucking. She was going to collapse against the wall.

She did when he slipped his first finger inside her. Kelsey tried to hold out, to prolong the release as long as possible, but she couldn't take it anymore. A cry that probably startled her poor dogs tore from her throat, but she couldn't think about that either as her body shook and her breath gave way.

Ian nursed her down gently, slowing his tongue, releasing the pressure on her clit as the orgasm subsided. Once all that was left was his breath against her tender skin, a sensation as strangely erotic as his tongue had been, she managed to catch her own wind.

"Holy shit." It was the only thing she could say, so Kelsey repeated it as Ian more or less held her upright and stood himself.

"I'm glad you enjoyed it."

She narrowed her eyes, wanting to respond with something snarky, but Ian's face was as flushed as her own, and his eyes continued to rake over her body like she was his to consume. And oh, that bulge in his boxer briefs remained.

Snark could wait. She'd rather be consumed.

Kelsey reached for him again, temporarily sane enough to register how big he felt in her hand, and she silently said a word of thanks to Mr. Happy for keeping her company. Otherwise she suspected this might be initially less than pleasant.

"I did enjoy it." She licked her lips. "But you still haven't had your way with me against the wall."

14

◇————————◇

DID KELSEY HAVE any idea how those words affected him? It had taken all of Ian's willpower to not ram his cock into her the moment she had unzipped his jeans. And when she'd wrapped her fingers around him and licked her lips, he'd been half a breath from coming right there like some overeager teenager. From the first moment she'd showed up on his doorstep he'd struggled to stop thinking about what he'd like to do to her. No matter how gorgeous she was, he'd had to remember he disliked her. So once he realized she was extremely likable, his imagination had been a force he couldn't contain.

And now she was standing in front of him, completely naked, asking him for more while the taste of her lingered on his tongue. Her pert breasts were wet with his kisses, her pouty lips red and swollen. His hands had left impressions on her soft hips where he'd held on to her. None of his fantasies had gone like this, and he clearly needed to fire his imagination for being wholly inadequate.

It was too bad he couldn't look at her and bury himself

in her at the same time. He didn't want to stop drinking her in, but his balls wailed with the torture.

"Ian." Kelsey reached for him, and he grabbed her wrist, pinning her against the wall and kissing her again.

She was so demanding, which shouldn't have been a surprise. It was Kelsey, after all. But even more surprising was how much he liked it. How much it turned him on.

She whimpered into his mouth, and Ian knew he'd go to bed hearing that sound over and over.

"Whatever you wish."

Kelsey gasped as he released her and yanked off his shirt. "You'll regret saying that later," she said.

Ian grinned. "It only works when you're naked."

"If I'm naked when I ask you to clean my house, will you do it?"

Probably, yes. "You can try it later."

"God, you're pretty. Will you clean naked?"

Ian almost dropped his wallet as he retrieved the condom he hadn't been entirely sure he had on him. Now that would have been a tragedy that eclipsed *Romeo and Juliet*. "I'm pretty?"

He was aware that he was at least attractive enough that he'd never had a hard time finding a date or a hookup when he made the time for such things. But the word *pretty* was new.

Kelsey was watching him, the blue of her irises seeming especially bright as her gaze roamed his body up and down. "Yes. You don't feel emasculated by me using that word, do you?"

Her voice held a challenge, but considering she was naked and gazing at him with unrestrained need, he might never have felt more potently male before in his life.

Ian closed the distance between them until he was

close enough that the tips of those perfect nipples brushed against him and his erection pressed into her stomach. The feel of that alone left him trembling. It was true he hadn't had sex since moving to Alaska, but that in no way excused his body for forgetting that he was a fully grown adult who shouldn't be ready to burst all over a gorgeous woman just because they touched.

"Do I look like I feel emasculated?"

Kelsey smiled, and her fingers curled around his length, forcing Ian to close his eyes and fight for control. "Now that you mention it, no. This is not the cock of a man who has any reason to ever feel emasculated."

"You. Are. Killing me." If she moved a single damn finger, it might be all over for him.

"Then get inside me. Do you like hearing me beg?"

Ian wasn't sure in what universe that tone could be considered begging, but yes, he very much liked it. "Whatever you wish."

He kissed her mercilessly, enjoying the squeal of surprise and using the moment of distraction to remove her hand from his cock before she caused more trouble. Then, once she'd quieted, he rolled on the condom.

Ian gave himself a moment, a breath, to pause as he pushed his tip into her. She was slick and warm and absolutely perfect, and he had to wait just a bit to savor this. He didn't see how he was going to be able to take it slowly, but he had to try for her sake.

Kelsey's hands slid over his arms and trailed down his chest until they landed on his hips, and she pulled him closer. "Why are you torturing me?" Her voice was barely audible.

"I'm trying not to lose control."

"You are the most insufferable man I've ever met. Lose

it." She yanked harder on him this time, positioning herself so that he slipped in deeper.

She'd given him permission, or more like orders. Who was he not to give her what she wanted?

Ian pushed her back against the wall, his mouth crashing into hers. He chased her tongue, sucking and feasting, trying to envelope her in the same heat she had around him. Kelsey's moan initially made him worry he'd hurt her, but before he could ask if she was okay, she raised her leg, leveraging him deeper inside her.

Ian obliged, grabbing her thigh and nestling himself more tightly against her. He could feel her grinding herself against him, so he wrapped his other hand around her, angling his fingers to apply more pressure to her most sensitive skin. Kelsey rewarded him for the slightly awkward position with a most gorgeous noise.

"Oh, God. Harder." Her fingers dug into his ass.

Yes, absolutely harder. He slammed into her again and again, unsure how much longer he could keep this up. She smelled so good, not just of the fruity shampoo, but of sweat and musk, and her skin was the most delicious thing he'd tasted in ages.

Kelsey's lips pressed into his chest, her teeth grazing him, biting him lightly. She was going to be the end of him. Normally, he tried to take it slowly, make sure his partner was fully benefitting before he let himself go. But with Kelsey, he was already half gone. He couldn't restrain himself; he wanted her too much. And that would be a problem if she didn't come soon.

Ian increased the tempo with his fingers as they glided over her. "Come for me, please. I can't do this much longer."

Now who was begging?

Miraculously, she did a couple of thrusts later, her

scream muffled as she buried her face in his chest. He wished she hadn't done that. He wanted to hear how loud she was, but feeling her breath on him and her mouth closing down on his skin wasn't a bad consolation prize. Nor was her tongue, running upward, licking his nipple and heading toward his shoulder.

It was her tongue that did him in. He came hard just as her own spasms were slowing down around him. Ian shuddered, struggling to hold on to her as his world temporarily dissolved.

Reality came back bleakly as he caught his breath. His chin rested on Kelsey's head. Her arms had crept upward, and she held herself up around his waist. Gently, Ian released her leg, helping her lower it to the floor and back to what was surely a more comfortable position.

He was exhausted. Utterly spent and temporarily confused as to why he was in Kelsey's house to begin with. Then it came back all at once, like the room's cold air hitting him: dogs.

He much preferred the sex.

"DOGS?" IAN WAS pacing around Kelsey's kitchen after she came back downstairs from cleaning up. He'd heard them greet her at the top of the steps. So much barking and clunking of feet. Under normal circumstances, he'd be a live wire, knowing how close they were and wondering how easily they could get out of whatever cage Kelsey had trapped them in.

But the absolutely amazing sex had blown out his nerves. Ian's stomach twisted with concern, but he was way calmer than he'd otherwise have been. Kelsey couldn't have planned a better way to get him relaxed. It was devious or genius—possibly both.

"In a moment." Kelsey's hands were buried in her shirt sleeves, and she crossed the living room with a contemplative expression. "We should talk about what just happened first."

That was probably a good idea, and it didn't hurt that it put off the dogs for a bit longer. "Right. So that was . . ." He intended to say *a onetime thing*, but his brain kept wanting to substitute words like *amazing* or *fantastic*. That sent the wrong message, so Ian faltered and he gripped a countertop to stop himself from waving his hands around in agitation.

"A fluke?" Kelsey suggested. "An act that's not to be repeated?"

Ian nodded, grateful that she was the one to say it. "Exactly. Good way to put it."

Normally, he'd have made his intentions regarding relationships clear in advance. That was, he didn't have time for them. But Ian was starting to realize phrases like *normally* and *under normal circumstances* didn't much apply to Kelsey. She somehow could not only push all his buttons, for good and for ill, but could shove him outside his comfort zone as well. Such was his entire reason for being at her house.

Kelsey's shoulders sagged with such relief that Ian almost took offense, regardless of the fact that they shared the same end goal. She poured a glass of water, which she offered to him. "It was good though?"

Ian couldn't tell whether she was asking or stating a truth, and her back was to him as she filled her own glass, lending him no clues. That made it easier to answer her honestly. "If I say it was amazing, will you accuse me of unwarranted effusive praise again?"

Kelsey's smile as she turned around was simply delightful, and it warmed him all over. "No, but if you say 'fuck' again, I can't promise I won't take that as an order."

He laughed, feeling his cheeks redden, and simultaneously tried to not give in to the temptation. They'd both agreed that there would be no repeat performance. He had to stick to that. "That's cruel."

"I can't help it. I don't think I ever heard you swear before." She narrowed her eyes as though assessing him in a new light. "Is that something you only do during sex?"

Ian sipped his water, thankful it was cold and might be able to cool him off. He'd been doing fine with any postsex awkwardness until this. Kelsey's perceptiveness gave him the feeling that he'd exposed more of himself to her than he'd intended. How many women had ever commented on his language before? None that he could recall. "No, but I try not to swear much."

"Morals?" Kelsey raised an eyebrow. "Religion?"

"No and no. My father swears a lot, and I try not to be like my father." If there was one topic he'd like to avoid more than dogs, it was his father. No matter how bad an idea it was to flirt, he was changing the subject. "However, if you're going to take 'fuck' as a command, I can rethink my policy on swearing."

Heat swept over Kelsey's face, then she steeled herself, pushing her shoulders back. "I don't take commands, but nice try. How about a dog?"

Since he'd told himself that dogs were preferable to his father, it was time for *him* to steel himself. "Let's do it."

Kelsey bit her lip, looking as nervous about this as he felt, which was still not nearly as nervous as he should have felt. "Stay in the kitchen. I'm going to get Juliet. I'll have her on a leash at all times. Okay?"

Ian swallowed, doing his best to project confidence. It might be too late to hide his phobia from the gorgeous woman, but he could avoid making a fool of himself at least.

He hoped.

Kelsey jogged upstairs, resulting in another chorus of barking, and Ian took a couple of deep breaths. Closing his eyes, he cast his mind back to ten minutes ago. Kelsey's mouth on his. Her legs wrapped around him. The taste of her on his tongue and her scent in his nose. It was difficult to be anxious and turned on at the same time.

The sound of multiple feet on the steps brought him back to reality, and Ian turned around. He'd hoped Kelsey had been getting the smallest of her dogs, the all-white one, but she had not. This one was a mix of white and black with patches around her eyes and a stripe down her forehead. Her tail wagged enthusiastically as Kelsey led her on a purple leash into the middle of the living room.

"Sit." Kelsey might not take commands, but she gave them with authority. The husky sat, her head swiveling between her owner and Ian. Kelsey kept the leash looped around her hand. "Juliet is the most chill, so you're going to meet her first. See the way her tail is wagging? She's excited to meet you. She likes you already."

"That's one of us." Ian attempted a smile.

Kelsey knelt next to her dog and gave her a hug. For her efforts she was rewarded with a bark and a tongue to the face. "She's way more likable than I am. If you can learn to appreciate me, you can learn to like her."

"I don't know. I'd bet your bark is worse than your bite."

Kelsey scoffed. "Don't be so sure. If we're speaking metaphorically, I can bite pretty hard."

"And if we're speaking literally?" He was thinking of the way her teeth had grazed his chest earlier, and damn if that didn't almost distract him from the forty or so pounds of fur and teeth next to her.

Kelsey shot him a look that clearly said *Don't*. "You can come closer anytime. If you want to get really close, first hold your hand out so she can sniff you. But only come as close as you feel comfortable. I've got her; she's not going anywhere."

Ian breathed deeply. He could do this, and it wasn't only because Kelsey was watching him, although he had to admit that was part of it. But as long as he had this strange post-sex calm, he should take advantage of it. Juliet still looked wolfish to him, but Kelsey didn't only have her leash, she'd wrapped the husky in her arms, snuggling her. His stomach twisted harder, and his pulse sped up, but Ian kept walking forward.

She's not going to hurt you. This dog is not a threat. He repeated it over and over, but his brain and his body were having a serious disagreement about the matter.

Don't think about the dog. Think about Kelsey. She kept turning her attention and those big blue eyes between Juliet and him.

Before he knew it, Ian was a mere couple of steps away. Somehow he wasn't fully panicking. Was it the sex, or was it that he trusted Kelsey? He wasn't sure.

"Hold out your hand to her," Kelsey said. Juliet was straining to get closer to him, but Kelsey didn't let go of her grip

Wincing—internally only, he hoped—Ian held out his hand a couple of inches from the husky's face.

Juliet attempted to stand and lunge for him, but Kelsey held her down. "Calm. Sit. Good girl."

The dog sniffed Ian's hand, tail wagging again, then barked once.

"What did that mean?" Ian asked.

Kelsey smirked. "It means you're tormenting her like you tormented me earlier. You're a damn tease."

Unbelievably, he laughed. "Not quite the same."

"So you think. She wants to kiss you and play with you."

Over the next few minutes, Ian let Kelsey talk him into

kneeling a couple of feet away from Juliet, which said a lot about both his state of mind and her ability to persuade him to do anything. He even, after a couple more minutes, got close enough to pet Juliet on the head. That went surprisingly well on his end until the husky decided it wasn't good enough and she wanted to lick him. Ian yanked his hand away and jumped to his feet, feeling stupid but unable to stop his heart from pounding in his ears.

"Hey." Kelsey snapped her fingers at Juliet. "No. I'm the only one around here who licks Ian."

Juliet barked at her, and Kelsey glared back.

It would have been funnier if he hadn't broken out in a sweat wondering which one of them had won the argument.

"Dogs don't exactly get the concept of consent," Kelsey said, giving the husky another hug. Juliet licked her face, and the two tussled on the floor. Ian supposed that's what Kelsey meant by playing, but he couldn't wrap his head around the idea that it was fun. "How are you doing?" she asked him. "Had enough?"

"I think so. Honestly, that went better than I thought."

Kelsey grinned. "It went way better than I expected. I think a good next step might be for you to hang around her some more. She's super excited because you're new. Once she gets used to you, she'll be a lot calmer."

Ian suspected the same couldn't be said for him, but on the other hand, this plan would bring him back into Kelsey's presence. "All right. Let's try it."

Ian wasn't sure what was driving him more—the chance that he might actually overcome his fear or the fact that having had sex with Kelsey was making him crave more sex with Kelsey. Both were strong motivators, but only the first was good for him.

15

◊—————◊

KELSEY PICKED A collapsible shovel off the shelves at Lucky Hardware and considered how many times she might have to hit herself over the head with it before her brain would move on from two nights ago. Once? Twice? If she did it enough, she might knock herself out. Theoretically that ought to do the trick, only she'd dreamed about Ian the last couple of nights, so maybe not.

This was ridiculous. No doubt she'd messed up by going for so long without sex. Her body and brain had forgotten what they were missing, but now they were like a dog who'd discovered the taste of steak, and going back to dry food was never going to cut it.

On one level, she was thrilled. Sex with Ian had been amazing—his word, not hers, although she agreed. She'd passed the test she'd created for herself, and that meant she could put the last stubborn issue preventing her from completely moving on from Anthony behind her.

On another level, it created these *complications*. These cravings for more. Ian had already been a potent force invading her thoughts prior to taking his clothes off. Now he'd basically taken up residency in her brain.

Naked residency. She'd called him *pretty*, but the man was such perfection that even the tight T-shirts hadn't done him justice. From his broad shoulders to the sprinkling of hair over his chest to the hard stomach and the impressive organ hiding beneath his pants . . .

"Hi, Kels."

Rather than smacking herself in the head with the shovel, Kelsey almost dropped it at the sound of Maggie's voice. Sticking it in her basket, she turned around. "Hey."

"Resupplying your car?" Maggie's gaze turned questioning as she glanced at the basket, which, along with the shovel, contained an ice scraper, a thermal blanket, and a prepacked first aid kit.

"It's for Ian Roth. He's woefully unprepared for winter, so I thought I'd give him a starter set for his car."

"Ah." Maggie smiled in a way Kelsey did not at all care for. "I told you the guys were nice."

"It's more like I owe him. He offered to compensate me for my help, and in doing so went way above and beyond what he might reasonably owe me. So now I'm stuck owing him. It's annoying."

She'd told herself the same thing since she'd come to the decision to buy Ian some supplies. It was a better reason than *I'm scared Ian will blab my secret profession to the entire town, so I need to placate him.* And it was a much better reason than *The man gave me the two best orgasms of my life and repaired the lingering hole in my self-esteem, and I haven't been able to stop thinking about him since.*

Way, way better than that last one.

But regardless of the reason, the decision was stretching Kelsey's monthly budget and yet she was doing it anyway. So possibly the real reason was temporary insanity.

"You're going to get locked into a cycle of owing each other." Maggie laughed, heedless of the distress her comment caused. "So, since I'm assuming you've spent more time in the men's company since we last talked, have you found out the answer to my burning question?"

Maggie had asked a question? Shoot. Kelsey's brain had dumped all nonessential, non-Ian information over the past several days. "Um . . ."

Maggie lowered her voice. "Are they together? Are they single? Are they looking?"

Kelsey glanced down the aisle to either side. Lucky Hardware was large, but it wasn't empty today, and it was possible Ian or Micah was roaming somewhere unseen. "That's three questions, and, uh . . ."

How did she answer that? *I hope Ian is single otherwise he's a shitty boyfriend for banging me against a wall on Monday?*

No. Best to keep that to herself.

"I haven't gotten the impression they're together," Kelsey said. That was true enough. Anything else would be an assumption.

Maggie chewed on her lip. "That's a positive sign. I might need to step up my flirting game the next time they're in the store. Too bad these work aprons aren't exactly flattering." She tugged at the maroon canvas with *Lucky Hardware* printed across the front.

"It's a good color for you," Kelsey said, recalling that Ian hadn't exactly cared that she'd been wearing leggings and an old sweatshirt when he'd come over. "For what it's worth, I get the sense that Micah is more your type."

She needed to shut her mouth. It was nothing to her—

nothing—if Maggie flirted with Ian, or if Ian reciprocated. As the two of them had discussed, the sex was a one-and-done thing. It wouldn't happen again, and there was nothing more to come from it. So if Ian wanted to screw every other woman in Helen, it had nothing to do with her. She had no right or reason to feel unhappy about it.

So damn it, it was beyond annoying that she did.

Ian was totally back to being insufferable as of this moment.

"You think?" Maggie raised an eyebrow. "I'm not much into long hair, but he does have a sexy lumberjack thing going on."

"Who has a sexy lumberjack thing going on?" A new voice joined the conversation from the other side of the metal shelving that displayed bags of ice melt.

Kelsey didn't bother holding in her groan. At least it wasn't Ian or Micah butting in, but Parker Ivanson was almost as bad.

He wasn't only a jerk because he'd broken into the Lipins' hotel over the summer and tampered with the guests' wine. Kelsey had taken a dislike to Parker as far back as elementary school, when he'd put earthworms in the girls' lunches, and his grossly sexist behavior hadn't exactly improved as he aged. She couldn't figure out why Kevin remained friends with him.

Rather than respond, Kelsey turned her well-practiced displeased, disgusted, and definitely dismissive glare on him through a gap between the bags of ice melt, and Parker took a step back. Kelsey smiled inwardly. Nice to know that, despite Ian taking over her brain, she still had it in her to wither a man's balls with a glance.

Her mood significantly improved, she opted to buy Ian a snowbrush too.

＊　＊　＊

"THAT'S THE LAST of them." Ian leaned the hand truck they'd been using to transport the kegs of pumpkin ale and a brown sugar stout against the brewery's wall. The deliveries would go out tomorrow morning. Two more batches down. One step closer to the brewery being financially solvent.

He felt good mentally, but physically he was exhausted. Filling the kegs and prepping the orders had taken most of the day, even with the additional help he and Micah had hired. His muscles were sore, and his shirt was coated with sweat. How he was supposed to be sociable later was a mystery, but if he were lucky, he might be too tired to be concerned about Kelsey's dogs.

Or, more to the point, too tired to imagine all the things he wanted to do to Kelsey that didn't involve her dogs.

Tonight would be an experiment. Could he handle being in Kelsey's house without her holding Juliet at all times? Could he handle being so close to Kelsey without fixating on jumping her bones? Both situations required a lot of his self-control.

Ian waved goodbye to the guys helping out and shut the brewery's back door. It was time to go home and shower.

"Are you leaving?" Micah sounded surprised as Ian grabbed his jacket.

It was also time to explain to Micah that he was going out. Somehow, he'd managed to "forget" his plans with Kelsey whenever there had been an opportune moment to mention them.

"It's after five o'clock," Ian said. "Aren't you usually nagging me not to work late every night?"

"I am." Micah stroked his beard thoughtfully. "And you're usually ignoring me. I'm not upset, just surprised.

I'm also beat. How does pizza sound for dinner?" It was Micah's night to cook.

"Actually, I have dinner plans, so knock yourself out."

"Dinner plans?" Micah positioned himself between Ian and the back door. "Do they happen to involve a certain blond-haired woman with an incredible ass?"

Since the description of Kelsey was apt, Ian shouldn't have wanted to punch Micah for it, but part of him did. What the hell? He'd slept with her once—an accident. He had no business getting possessive.

"I have to return her table." He'd fixed it over the weekend, and the glue should be good and cured. He hadn't wanted to take it over to her until he was sure it wouldn't fall apart again.

"Returning her table necessitates dinner, does it?" Micah did not look convinced.

Ian sighed. "No, but it's more complicated than that."

"Naturally."

"It's not what you're thinking."

His friend scoffed. "Sure it isn't. I called it back at the coffee shop."

"It's not like that." So Ian told himself. "She's working with me on the dog problem."

If anything, Micah's eyes opened wider. "You told her?"

"It kind of came out when I was helping her unload her grandparents' furniture." That was vague, but true, and Micah could concoct plenty of scenarios for how it happened on his own. "Maybe if you'd been there to help . . ."

"What?" His friend smirked. "And deny you these additional chances to spend time with Kelsey? Never."

"It's just to help me with the dog issue. Don't look so pleased. You're not some sort of matchmaker."

Micah's smirk broadened. "Bullshit. Is that where you were Monday night too?"

"Yes." Although running away was going to make him look guilty, Ian started for the main entrance.

"You hooked up with her, didn't you?" Micah called out. "I knew it. You were in too good a mood on Tuesday while we were dealing with the town nonsense."

"You didn't know anything."

"I do now—you just admitted it."

Ian closed his eyes, laughing even as he lowered his head against the door. "It's nothing. A one-and-done mistake."

"It's hardly one-and-done if you're seeing her tonight."

"That's for the dog problem."

"Riiiiiiight."

Ian waved a finger in his friend's face. "Doubt me all you want, but you'll be wrong. There will be nothing else between me and Kelsey except her help with dogs."

He didn't need the kind of complication that *anything else* entailed, so he would make absolutely, positively sure of that.

He hoped.

16

⤜━━━━━━⤛

IAN HELPED KELSEY maneuver the table next to her sofa. "I won't say it's as good as new, but it should be fine for most uses."

"Uses like holding my lamp?" Kelsey picked up the small lamp that had been sitting on her floor and set it on the table.

"The lamp will be no problem."

"A drink while I'm watching TV?"

Ian nodded. "Absolutely."

"A stable surface for sex?"

He caught himself before answering affirmatively. Kelsey grinned, and the evening was off to a great start, because now that would be all he could think about.

To be fair, he hadn't thought about much else prior to coming over. His shower time had, in fact, included many thoughts about Kelsey and sex, which Ian had told himself was okay since it was wisest to get the urge out of his system before he saw her. Only now that he was face-to-face with her in all her fake-perky glory, he realized it had been a futile effort. Simply watching Kelsey turn around and pick up the lamp had stirred his body. Her bringing up sex, even jokingly, had done him in.

"I wouldn't recommend it. If you want a sturdy surface for that, I'd suggest a wall. Or maybe try the sofa if you're looking for something new." He, for one, was definitely having thoughts about how they could use the sofa.

Kelsey made a noise Ian couldn't quite fathom. "Interesting. I note you didn't suggest a bed, which seems like the first piece of furniture that would jump to most people's minds."

Ian assumed it wasn't smart to admit that if he had the chance to act on all the ideas running through his head, they'd never make it up her stairs. So he settled for the next, less risky excuse. "I assumed your dogs were up there."

Kelsey laughed and ducked into the kitchen. "Aha! So you assumed that you would be involved in this hypothetical sex. I see how it is."

She had him there, and Ian cringed. "I can be a little self-centered, but it would definitely not be me involved. Not again."

Never, no way.

Damn it. He shouldn't be here if he meant it.

"Right." Kelsey agreed too quickly. "It was a one-shot deal."

"Exactly."

Hands on her hips, she stood next to her counter, and Ian couldn't help thinking the counter would work fine too. Kelsey's jeans were tight, the sweater she wore long and loose. The dark brown material swallowed her upper body, and he wondered if that was deliberate. If she was trying to make herself look less tempting. If so, it didn't work. The sweater wasn't exactly sexy, but it was cozy, and it left him to imagine what she was wearing underneath it.

Of course, the most likely scenario was that Kelsey had chosen her clothes with no regard to him whatsoever. After all, there wasn't going to be anything else between them, so why should she? Although in that case, she had more willpower than he did, since he'd made a point to shave while showering.

Ian realized he was staring, but then, so was she. It was Kelsey who snapped out of it first though. "Before I forget—I bought you something."

Shaking off his daze, Ian watched her retrieve a couple of bags from a corner of the kitchen. "You bought me something?"

Kelsey cleared her throat self-consciously as she handed over the bags. "You fixed my table, so consider it a thank-you present. Besides, I'd feel guilty if you died in your truck this winter when I could have helped prevent it."

Peering into the bags, Ian discovered a snowbrush, one of those blankets like the one she had in her car, and several other familiar items. Since his trip with Kelsey, he had made a list of equipment to buy, and it looked like she'd gone and gotten about half of it for him. Unexpected warmth bloomed in Ian's chest. Kelsey hadn't needed to get him anything for fixing her table, but this was both kind and thoughtful. How had she convinced everyone in this town that she was mean?

Well, okay, he knew how. She was very good at being sarcastic and standoffish. But Ian was beginning to see how pretty much everything he'd initially thought about Kelsey was an act.

Realizing he was gaping again, Ian closed the bags and set them down. "Thank you. That wasn't necessary, but your concern for my well-being is appreciated."

Kelsey's cheeks had turned a charming shade of pink.

"Don't read too much into it. My brother likes your beer, so I'm trying to protect his interests. Anyway, dinner?"

At her request, Ian had picked up burgers and fries on the way over, and they were getting cold.

Kelsey carried the bag and a bunch of napkins to the kitchen table. "Are you ready? Trust me, Juliet will be way more interested in the food than she will be in you."

Ready? No, he probably was not, but the thing that had helped him cope last time was not going to be an option. Ian attempted to feign confidence. "Sure. Ready."

He took a few deep breaths while Kelsey ran upstairs to get Juliet. There was less barking tonight. Kelsey had told him that her brother had the other two dogs. Kevin was working on socializing his puppy, so Romeo and Puck were on loan to him for the evening. It had worked out well, and she'd promised Ian that Kevin didn't know why she was keeping Juliet at home.

"You aren't the only one with anxiety issues," Kelsey had said. "Romeo gets antsy around other dogs, but Kevin's puppy was so little when they first met that Romeo tolerated him. I figure it's good for both dogs to be in each other's company."

Ian tried to take some reassurance from the knowledge that dogs got anxiety, but it just left him to ponder whether apex predators like lions or bears occasionally suffered from nerves too.

"Look who's here!" Kelsey's voice barely carried over Juliet's excited barking.

Ian forced himself to hold still. Like last time, Kelsey had the husky on her leash, but she was giving the dog more lead than before.

"You remember Ian, right?" Kelsey patted the dog's head, then looked his way. "Hold out your hand again."

He let himself be sniffed, then surprised everyone by laughing when Juliet's nose tickled his hand.

"Good girl. You didn't jump." Kelsey gave Juliet more freedom and pointed to the food bowl in the kitchen corner. "Go get your dinner."

The husky's ears perked up and she charged over, sprinting right past Ian, who hastily stepped to the other side of the table.

"See?" Kelsey said. "She knows the difference between you and food."

"I suppose that elevates her above the mosquitoes."

"Never compare my dogs to mosquitoes." Kelsey looped the leash around her chair. "Now sit and eat before she comes over to beg for your burger."

"No fear—begging will not work on me. I'm immune to doggie charms."

"Uh-huh." Kelsey opened her wrapper. "But you do like making women beg, and I won't have you torturing my dog."

The memory of Kelsey telling him to *get inside me* shot through Ian like a lightning bolt. He maintained that she hadn't been begging, more like demanding, but it hardly mattered. His cock hardened, and he quickly grabbed a seat before it became noticeable.

"So what movie are we watching after dinner?" Kelsey asked. "Assuming you last that long, that is."

"Oh, I can last." He didn't mean to turn her comment into sexual innuendo—or did he? Ian wasn't sure, but watching Kelsey pop a fry into her mouth was not helping his state of mind.

Her lips twitched. "I meant with my dog around."

"So did I."

Kelsey narrowed her eyes. "I question this. Greatly."

Was that in reference to him lasting, or to his meaning? "You did not just doubt my stamina."

"The anxiety would do you in." Kelsey shook her head. "You'd be too nervous to keep yourself together."

"We are talking about watching a movie, right?"

She opened her eyes innocently, but that expression didn't fool Ian in the slightest. Someone help him, because the desire to kiss her was overriding every rational nerve in his body.

"What else would I be talking about?" Kelsey asked.

Ian swallowed the pickle slice that had fallen from his burger, hoping the salt would somehow ground him, but he barely tasted it. He was too busy concentrating on the fact that Kelsey was trying to pin the blame for this conversation on him. "I don't know, but you're the one who keeps bringing up sex. And I'm just saying, if you have any doubts about my abilities in that regard, you're welcome to investigate them yourself."

"I do not keep bringing up sex."

"Yes, you do. And each time you do, my cock notices. I assure you, if you question whether being around your dog would prevent me from getting hard, the proof is under your table."

"I am not interested in the state of your cock." The color flooding Kelsey's cheeks and the way she bit her lip suggested otherwise.

"Uh-huh." He mimicked her tone from a moment ago.

Kelsey scowled, only it was a lousy scowl, because while her lips twisted, her eyes conveyed something very different. Amusement. Desire. And she claimed *he* was a tease?

"Fine." Kelsey tossed her hair. "I'll make an exception for science. If what you're saying is true, your anxiety issues must be improving. It's a breakthrough."

In a way, that was true. Ian had gone probably thirty

seconds without once thinking about Juliet. Mostly because, in those thirty seconds, he'd been thinking solely about pushing Kelsey up against her sofa and sinking himself inside her.

"We should test that theory," Ian said. "For science."

"For your therapy."

"I think it would be extremely therapeutic." It was also getting to the point where it was feeling like a necessity. Jerking off in the shower earlier had not done one whit to ease the current rampage in his balls.

"That would be the only reason, though, right?" Kelsey asked. "We're not breaking some promise to never have sex again without a purpose."

"I don't think we ever promised anything," Ian said. "We were in agreement before, and now we're agreeing this would be a wise move instead—for science."

"Makes sense." Kelsey stood and tied Juliet's leash around the fridge handle. The husky looked at her questioningly, then lay back down next to her food bowl, seemingly content and full. "That should hold her. There are some activities even I don't want my dogs involved in. But be aware, she can probably make it as far as the living room if she decides to stop being lazy."

In that case . . . Abandoning dinner, Ian jumped up and darted into the living room. "I'll wait for you over here."

"Smooth." Kelsey followed him at a much more leisurely pace. "Watch out for the corner table. I hear it might not be up to the task."

"No worries. I've been thinking about the sofa myself."

Kelsey stopped a couple of inches from him, close enough that Ian could detect whatever light scent she was wearing and feel her breath against his body. Far enough that he still had to move to touch her, and he resolutely stuck his hands in his pockets.

"What did you have in mind?" she asked.

What *didn't* he have in mind was a better question. Considering how much thought he'd been putting into this scenario—a scenario he *wasn't* supposed to be acting on, damn it—Ian had too many plans.

"First, you're going to take that sweater off." He curled his hands into fists so he couldn't do it for her. "Then I'm going to get down on my knees, and I'm going to kiss you, and lick you, and suck every inch of you until your legs give out. Then I'm going to carry you over to the sofa, lay you across the arm, and bury myself inside you until you come again. How does that sound?"

Kelsey whimpered, which Ian took as an initial good sign. Wetting her lips, she yanked off the sweater and tossed it aside. The T-shirt she'd been wearing underneath followed, leaving her in a lacy black bra. It was such the antithesis of the bulky sweater that, even if she hadn't meant it to be, it felt like a surprise gift just for him. He wanted to peel back the fabric and taste her breasts, too, and he wasn't sure he was tall enough while kneeling. And a plan was a plan—he'd stick to what he'd said.

Kelsey smiled in a way that suggested her choice of underwear had been deliberate after all, and she closed the distance between them. "I will never get tired of hearing you say 'fuck.'"

"Thanks to you, I've been saying it a lot lately in my head."

"Then you'd better get on with it." She grabbed the waistband of his pants and stood on her toes to kiss him.

Her mouth was an explosion of sensation over his, lips crashing and tongues tangling. He cupped her breasts and squeezed lightly, recalling she'd liked that last time, and they both moaned in unison.

"God, Ian." Kelsey's hot hands pressed against his stomach.

He dropped to his knees, trailing kisses down her throat, the sweet spot between her breasts, and her stomach as he went. The button on her jeans was torture. The zipper was like thunder in his ears. Peeling them off revealed that her bottoms matched the bra, and Ian smiled. He couldn't even recall the color of her underwear from last time, but he could slow himself down long enough now to burn the image of her into memory.

Because damn it, there would not be a third time.

"You're beautiful." With his face just brushing her skin, her scent was intoxicating.

Kelsey wrapped her fingers around a fistful of his hair. "Say it again."

"You're beautiful."

She tightened her grip, knowing he'd said what he had to tease her. "Not that."

"No?" Ian ran his teeth along the smooth patch of her stomach between her lacy waistband and her belly button, and Kelsey's breath hitched. As much as he liked her being demanding, he might like even more his ability to render her speechless. To make her only noises into short, breathy gasps. She delighted him with several as Ian lowered himself farther into a better position, nipping at the silky, damp fabric on the way down.

One by one, he kissed her legs. Down the left thigh to the knee, then up the right. Kelsey wobbled, and he held her tighter, his hands slipping under her panties and grabbing her ass. He had to pause at last, breathing deeply himself to calm the cry of need in his groin.

"Oh my God." Kelsey relaxed her fingers as he took his breath. "I don't know how you do that."

To be honest, he wasn't sure how he was doing this either. This going slow was killing him, yet he was loving every moment of it. There might be nothing hotter than listening to Kelsey moan.

"Oh, we're just getting started," Ian said, forcing a bravado he wasn't feeling. "Better hold on again."

Sliding his hands around to the front of her, he hooked his thumbs around the lace and pulled the fabric down to her knees. Kelsey inhaled sharply and stiffened with anticipation. Not that he could make her wait long. Ian pressed a kiss between her legs and ran his tongue over the slick heat lower down. It didn't seem possible that she should taste so good, but her skin was like a drug. Kelsey shook and cried out, but she parted her legs wider, giving him better access. Not demanding this time, but perfectly receptive and uninhibited in the noises she made for him. Ian licked her again and again, light and teasing, until Kelsey's knees began to buckle and the "Please" she uttered actually sounded like begging. Then he finally suckled the spot she'd been waiting for, and damn if he didn't almost come alongside her.

17

IAN HAD SAID he'd make her legs give out, and Kelsey shouldn't have doubted him. The man wasn't making idle boasts. She swayed on her feet, clutching him around the neck to keep upright. What in the world was going on here? The things he did to her body, the noises he elicited from her throat—she hadn't thought people could actually do those things to one another. She'd certainly never thought her brain could shut down the way it did when Ian touched her. After the way Anthony had messed with her head, it seemed like it ought to be impossible for her relax so much. But she hadn't worried once about being with Ian like this, just as Ian didn't seem to be worrying about her dog in the next room.

Ian pressed a kiss against her stomach as her trembling slowed down. "Ready for the sofa?"

There ought to be nothing left of her, but looking down at him, Kelsey was surprised to discover she was more than ready. Ian's eyes twinkled and his lips turned upward in what should have been an utterly smug expression. Instead, Kelsey found it charming and sexy as hell.

"Always ready." She kicked her jeans off the rest of the way as Ian carried her over to the couch, also exactly as he'd promised. Setting her down on the arm, he kissed her again. His mouth was delicious but not enough, and she tugged on his shirt. "You're wearing too many clothes."

"My apologies." Ian tossed off his shirt, and there, that was better.

Kelsey was glad he hadn't taken offense at being called pretty, because he really was like a perfect statue brought to life. Perhaps there was a better word for him—and perhaps, as a writer, she should be able to think of it—but when she was looking at him, her words failed her.

Ian stepped out of his pants, and that was better still. Even his cock was perfect. Kelsey had never thought of male genitalia as being attractive, but his might be the exception. He was hard as a marble statue, too, as she wrapped her hand around him.

Ian closed his eyes and sucked in a breath. "You'd better be careful with that."

"Or what?" She lowered her head and took the tip of him in her mouth. She never had gotten the chance to do this last time, but she'd wasted enough hours thinking about it. His skin tasted good and salty, and she was enjoying herself too much to worry about whether she was doing this right. The noises coming from Ian's throat sure made it sound like she was doing well enough.

"Condom." Ian pulled away and began going through his jeans.

Too amused by this to protest, Kelsey leaned back against the couch arm. "If you don't have one, I'm going to be most upset."

"Oh, I have one. I shouldn't, because I shouldn't have a need for one, but I did bring one."

"How presumptuous." How adorably insufferable.

"More like hopeful. Or maybe terrible, since we aren't supposed to be doing this."

No, they shouldn't be doing this, but at the moment, Kelsey couldn't remember why. She could reproach herself later when her brain was functioning again. "It's for your therapy."

"This is probably the sort of behavior that makes therapists lose their licenses."

"Good thing I'm not actually a therapist."

Ian rolled on the condom and kissed her hard, backing her into the couch, and Kelsey dug her fingers into his sides, holding on to stay upright. "A very good thing," he agreed. "Turn around."

Kelsey raised an eyebrow and turned her back on him. Warm arms wrapped around her as Ian slid between her legs, and whoa. As much as she didn't like not being able to see him, being bundled in Ian's long, strong limbs was pretty nice too. And when he kissed her neck and buried his face against her from behind, it might even be as good as being able to watch him. He moved slowly at first, the pressure building up inside her until she was gasping for breath.

"Good?" Ian raised one hand so that his fingers could toy with her breast, and Kelsey closed her eyes with pleasure.

It didn't matter that she couldn't see him. She could feel him so much—inside, outside. She was drowning in him, high on the scent of his skin. "God, yes. More."

She could feel his other hand slip down, and Ian's fingers pressed between her legs, seeking out her most sensitive skin. Pleasure, so strong it ripped a scream from her throat, almost overtook her. It was too much more. It was perfection.

She came a few seconds later, Ian's fingers moving in

rhythm with the rest of him. She caught her breath, listening to him cry out, feeling his body convulse against hers soon after. She still wished she could have watched him, but the heft of him against her back, the way he squeezed her almost painfully tight, was bliss too.

Shit, shit. Shit. They weren't supposed to do this a third time—or a fourth or more—but now all she was going to be able to do was contemplate other positions for sex with Ian. Sometimes having a potent imagination was a curse.

PULLING OUT OF Kelsey sucked as much the second time as it had the first. And this time, Ian was aware that they had an audience. Juliet was in the kitchen, stretched out on the tile floor, eyes barely open. Ian wondered if they'd woken her from her post-dinner snooze.

He also wondered how he'd managed to completely forget that she was there, probably no more than twenty feet away the entire time. Her leash could have gotten loose.

If it had, he wasn't sure he'd have noticed. And if he *had* noticed, he wasn't sure he'd have stopped with Kelsey. Apparently, his lust was stronger than his fear. Was that good or bad?

Also, was it any kind of lust, or did Kelsey simply arouse him more than his anxiety could bring him down? Oy. He hoped it wasn't that, because if this was all Kelsey . . . Ian shook himself mentally. No, he didn't have time for that. Besides, they agreed this wouldn't happen again.

Of course, they'd agreed that last time, too, and as he tore his gaze away from the dog and focused it back on the far more appealing woman next to him, Ian doubted his willpower. A naked, flushed Kelsey with red, swollen lips and skin shiny with their combined sweat was one hell of an aphrodisiac. He already wanted her again.

Kelsey seemed to notice Juliet as she was pulling on her underwear, and she cast him a questioning glance.

Ian did his best to ignore these heavy thoughts by offering her a light smile. "Told you I could last."

"Impressive. There might be hope for you yet."

There might be. But dinner was cooling off on the kitchen table, and Ian was far less certain about getting through it without his cock seizing control of the situation a second time.

Ten minutes later, though, Kelsey had reheated their dinners and brought them into the living room. Since the original plan had been for Ian to eat and watch a movie with Juliet nearby, they were combining those two activities. Kelsey said it was because they'd spent too much time doing unapproved and unexpected things, but Ian wondered if it was because she thought they were less likely to use the couch for sex again if they had dinner on it. If so, he was fine with that. It was smart. Disappointing as well, but he had to stick to the no-more-sex-with-Kelsey plan as well as he'd stuck to the how-I-want-to-bang-Kelsey plan. For some reason, the former seemed like it was going to be way more difficult.

"Movie?" Kelsey turned on the TV.

Juliet had crept into the living room while Ian got dressed, but as long as she kept to Kelsey's side of the couch, he wasn't too antsy about it.

"Sure." Ian watched her pop a fry in her mouth and couldn't stop from remembering how she'd taken him into her mouth. He might get over his dog issue thanks to her, but he was going to need a Kelsey intervention next. "Something with explosions."

Kelsey groaned. "Of course you'd want that. How about something with a story?"

Ian actually didn't care too much about what they watched, but he did need something compelling enough to keep his eyes on the screen and not on the woman next to him.

Or her dog. Funny that the dog was an afterthought.

"String enough explosions together and you have a story," he said.

"Seriously?"

"Just because you write romance . . ." Ian wasn't sure where he was going with that, but it didn't matter, because Kelsey smacked him with a throw pillow. "All right, that's what we need—a compromise."

Kelsey turned to Juliet, who was gnawing on something that might have been a bone. "Men. You know what it's like, don't you, girl? We both have two brothers." She ruffled the dog's head, and Juliet barked once in solidarity.

"Here we go, the perfect compromise." Ian had been scrolling through the movies available on Kelsey's streaming service.

Kelsey glared at him. "*Terminator*? Isn't that an old Arnold movie?"

"It's a classic. Have you really never seen it?"

"Before my time, and I don't go seeking out old movies about killer robots, and before you ask—I haven't seen the more recent ones either. I like movies with plots, and they get bonus points if the people in them are dressed in uncomfortable-looking, historical costumes."

Terminator was before his time too. Ian wasn't sure exactly how old Kelsey was, but he couldn't be much older than her. He did, however, go seeking out classic movies about killer robots. And tended to avoid those with historical costumes.

"Yes, Arnold is in it, and so are killer robots." He held up a finger to cut her off. "But so is Linda Hamilton. You will like Linda Hamilton. Trust me. Especially when we watch *T2*."

Ian could totally see Kelsey becoming Linda Hamilton's badass character if the situation ever called for it. She was secretly kind and caring, but she also had the take-no-prisoners attitude down flat. Any woman who bought him—a guy she supposedly disliked—a snowbrush for no good reason would totally threaten to kill a man with a pen if he stood between her and someone she loved. In fact, if he had to place bets on the winner between Kelsey and a killer robot, he'd probably go with Kelsey.

"We'll see about that." Kelsey grumbled something, but selected the movie. "And I never agreed to a sequel."

"We'll consider it for my next dog therapy session."

"You're being so presumptuous again." She was smiling as she said it, and a strange little ache awakened in Ian's chest.

He liked seeing her smile that way far too much.

18

KELSEY SCOOPED SOME of the whipped cream off her caffè mocha and closed the to-go lid. Sweetness melted against her tongue, and she would not . . . would not . . . Too late. She thought of Ian. Licking him. Sucking on him. Coating him in whipped cream.

Damn it. She should never have let herself get carried away the other night. They'd started texting each other over the past several days. Texting—like they were friends!

They couldn't be friends, because then this situation would mean they were acting like friends with benefits, and there could be no more benefits. She'd messed up majorly, and she feared doing it again.

She also craved it. Her entire life was currently a disaster. Hence the need for chocolate and coffee.

At least for the next half hour or so, she wouldn't be able to think about Ian. Kelsey was meeting Josh for their afternoon walk, and she had a list of questions to ask him about his relationship with Taylor Lipin and what was going on with the feud. Usually Kelsey would be the one to have the inside scoop, but she'd been too preoccupied with other topics lately—*cough*, Ian—to pay much attention. She'd also been avoiding her parents, who were her primary source of information—also because of Ian, and more specifically, because of the memory of her father suggesting she date Ian, which still pissed her off.

More so now than before, because she'd done it against her will.

And there went her thoughts, circling back to Ian.

Kelsey took a sip of her drink and burned her tongue on the hot coffee. That was a relief. For a second while she cursed the temperature, she thought about something else.

Her respite, however, was short-lived. The Espresso Express's door opened, and in walked Tasha McCleod.

As she was part of the Lipin family, Kelsey wouldn't normally pay Tasha any heed, but Tasha was no longer just a Lipin. She was a prominent voice in the Save Helen Society and was making Ian's life miserable. Merely one of those two sins, Kelsey could have ignored. Put them both together, though, and an irrational anger simmered in her veins. It was one part normal dislike for her enemy and one part irritation on behalf of a friend.

Irritation that was, honestly, completely out of proportion to what she should have felt. She and Ian were barely friends, yet the way she felt protective of him was like the way she would feel protective of her family. Or her dogs. If someone messed with them, they messed with her.

It was absurd, and yet Kelsey couldn't stop herself from sending a nasty glance in Tasha's direction.

"What?" the other woman snapped.

Kelsey pointed to the SHS pin on Tasha's jacket. "That. The way you're pretending to have some high-minded ideals about preserving our town culture when it's really an excuse to attack Northern Charm Brewing over a personal grudge. You make those of us who care about the town look bad along with you."

Tasha crossed her arms. "I do care about preserving the town, and I don't know what you're talking about."

"Sure you do. You're pissed off that Ian and Micah bought the old warehouse property from my father. I know your husband wanted to buy it to expand his garage, and I know my father chose to sell it to the brewery instead. So you're taking it out on Ian and Micah." Kelsey was very conscious of including Micah's name. That meant it wasn't only Ian she was thinking about.

To her credit, Tasha didn't deny these facts. "Your father's an asshole. We put an offer in first, but that's beside the point. Expanding DJ's business would have kept things local. Wallace sold to outsiders."

Just a couple of weeks ago, Kelsey would have agreed. She'd been annoyed for years by the way her father was determined to sell off Helen. What had gotten into her?

Oh right, Ian. In pretty much every sense of the phrase.

"What is it to you anyway?" Tasha bounced on her feet as she glanced toward the dwindling line at the counter.

"It's nothing to me, but I'm writing a piece on the brewery for the paper, and the topic came up. I thought I'd give you a chance to defend yourself."

"Yeah, I'm sure that's what you thought." Tasha stormed over to the counter to order.

As much as she despised letting someone else get in the last word, it was best to drop the subject. Kelsey had nothing else worth saying anyway. All she had were thoughts, and she'd had an epiphany during the conversation that required serious contemplation.

Kelsey took a second sip of coffee, which was no longer as scalding, and tried concentrating on the sweet mocha flavor, but it didn't calm her nerves. Worse than discovering she was feeling protective of Ian (and Micah by extension) was the discovery that part of the problems they were having were indirectly attributable to the feud.

Would Tasha and others be focusing so much of the SHS's ire on the brewery if Kelsey's father hadn't refused to sell the property to a Lipin? Kelsey thought not.

There had always been a niggling sensation in the back of her mind about why the SHS had chosen to direct its resources toward harassing Northern Charm Brewing when there were more logical targets. The brewery might not be owned by people who grew up in Helen, but it was an independent business, owned by two guys who'd moved here. It wasn't a franchise or a chain store putting one of the local families out of business. And yet, it was taking the brunt of the SHS's punches. The only reason that made sense was that Wallace Porter had pissed off the Lipins, and the Lipins were venting their anger on the convenient target—the brewery. Possibly, they even thought that if they could drive Ian and Micah away, Tasha's husband would be able to buy the building from them.

Once again, the feud was catching innocent outsiders in the cross fire. And that made *her* partially responsible for any problems Ian and Micah had to deal with.

ONE WEEK LATER, Kelsey still didn't know what to do about her revelation regarding the brewery and the feud. Really, she wasn't sure there was anything she *could* do about it, and yet guilt weighed on her.

Just as problematic was the question of whether she'd have felt that guilt if she hadn't been spending so much time with Ian. Before Ian, she'd probably have said something flippant, like *Every war has its casualties.* Now those casualties had been made into flesh-and-blood people. Kelsey could tell herself all she wanted that she didn't care about Ian, but each time she saw him, that lie became harder and harder to hold on to.

She'd seen him twice since the evening he'd returned her table and they'd broken their no-more-sex vow over her sofa. Both times, Ian had grown more comfortable with Juliet. He continued to tense up when she entered the room, but he relaxed over time. And although he hadn't started spontaneously petting her, he would when she was being calm. Ian had even started speaking to Juliet like she was a friend. Kelsey had therefore decided Ian was ready for the next step in his dog therapy—spending time with all three of her babies.

What the next step for the two humans was—that was another dilemma. It was occurring to Kelsey that calling these get-togethers "dog therapy" was as much for her own mental health as they purportedly were for Ian's. They had dinner together. Watched movies together. And yes, got naked together. Each time. If it weren't for Juliet, the more proper label for what they were doing would be *dating*. Or *friends-with-benefitting*, if that was such a thing. Kelsey didn't know, because she didn't want to find out. Anything with Ian other than a cursory acquaintance had been against her rules since the beginning. She was just apparently terrible at following her own rules, though she liked to believe she was emotionally astute enough to know that if she didn't start soon, she was heading for trouble. But how was she supposed to start when they'd fallen into a comfortable—and enjoyable—routine?

On a positive note, this whatever-it-was with Ian had gotten her on track with the book she was writing and given her a great idea for the next one in the series. What if the fated mate of a husky shifter had a phobia of dogs?

Kelsey grinned to herself, hoping her readers would find that setup as hilarious as she did. Then she jumped in her chair as someone knocked on the door below her office. Immediately, all three dogs began barking. With a sigh, she saved her file and peeked out the upstairs window, hoping she could ignore whomever had come to bother her.

It was her father, and so the answer was no. He would know she was most likely home if the dogs were.

Swell. Wallace had been texting her for the past two days about something he claimed he needed to discuss, and Kelsey had claimed to be too busy to go to family dinners and have that conversation. She felt bad about ignoring her mother, but she was too pissed off at her father to want to pretend everything was normal. It appeared her father had gotten tired of waiting.

Wallace knocked again as Kelsey tromped down the stairs. Good God, this must be where she got her impatient streak from.

"Back, back. You, too—back!" She herded all the huskies aside with one arm while opening the door with the other.

"There are my pups." Her father scooted in and showered the dogs with affection. "What were you doing? You took forever."

Kelsey rolled her eyes. "Working. The thing that pays my bills? What I'm supposed to be doing this very minute?"

He grunted. "Since you haven't made time to come to us, I made time to come to you. I need you to do something."

Another something? Wasn't it enough that she'd done something for him already by donating time and energy to the brewery? Sure, that had worked out unexpectedly well, but her father didn't know that, and she had no intention of sharing it. She still wanted to punch someone when she remembered him hinting about her developing a relationship with Ian or Micah for the good of the family. There was no way in hell she was giving him the satisfaction of knowing how close she'd come to doing that.

Truly, she needed to dwell on this point more often and with greater intensity. The way it was raising her blood pressure might be the best defense she had against falling for Ian's insufferable cheekbones.

"I'm working on the last mission you assigned me," Kelsey said, crossing her arms.

Her father chuckled. "'Mission'—I like that."

He would. Her bitter tone of voice had gone right over his head, which was her fault for never complaining about being a soldier before. Aside from her refusal to shun Josh, her father had no reason to suspect how her feelings about the feud had changed.

"This doesn't require much else of you," he continued. "I heard a rumor that Ian and Micah entered into an exclusive promotional deal with the Bay Song Inn. I don't want to ask them directly, but I figured you could work it in as you're interviewing them. Find out if it's true and what it entails."

The Bay Song Inn was the Lipins' family hotel and the business Josh's girlfriend helped run. Kelsey could see why her father might be interested if the brewery and the town's most upscale hotel had some kind of business arrangement, but not why it was so urgent.

Kelsey grabbed the doggie rope by the TV stand because she could feel her irritation building and needed to let off some steam. The rope was actually three ropes braided together so each dog could grab a piece to play. Puck and Romeo charged over and grabbed two of the fraying ends. "What's the big deal if they have some promo thing?"

"What's the big deal if they have a promotional deal with the Lipins?" Wallace sounded incredulous, and Kelsey couldn't be sure if it was because he didn't understand where her confusion came from or whether he was not used to his soldier questioning orders.

"The brewery is neutral," she said, glad for the huskies giving her a good tug-of-war workout, because the exertion kept her voice from becoming too sarcastic. "They've signed deals and sold beer to both Porter and Lipin bars and restaurants."

She had done her homework with Ian and Micah for the puff story, and Kelsey rattled off a list of the establishments to prove her point.

"This isn't the same." Her father was trying to get Juliet's attention, but the husky was too busy watching her brothers. "If what I'm hearing is true, this is bigger than just selling their beer to restaurants, and they did it before giving one of our family's businesses a chance to make that deal instead. It's allegedly an exclusive promotion for the hotel's guests once the tasting room opens to the public."

Maybe that was because the Lipins asked first? Ian and Micah weren't part of the feud, so there was no reason for them to pass up a business opportunity.

Kelsey managed to hold her tongue, but the effort caused her to lose her concentration on the rope. Romeo and Puck tugged hard, and she went flying halfway across the living room. The wall prepared to meet her face, and she raised a hand just in time to prevent a disaster.

The living room fell silent. Taking a deep breath, Kelsey turned around to find all three dogs gaping at her. Juliet looked alarmed. Romeo and Puck looked shocked, then guilty, although they hadn't don't anything wrong. The two boys rushed over to her, making sure she was okay. She'd never let them win like that before.

Her father laughed. "Strong dogs."

Yes, they were, but the dogs knew their limits—and hers. She was the one who'd messed up, and he was the reason.

Once upon a time, Kelsey wouldn't have questioned her father's ire. This was partially her fault for letting herself get friendly with Ian and feeling protective, but her exhaustion with her father and the feud had started before she'd ever met Ian. Then, more recently, Josh's relationship with a Lipin had brought her feelings into sharper focus. But it wasn't her cousin's decisions that had sparked this rebellion in her either.

Kelsey wasn't sure what had. Possibly it wasn't a single incident at all, but the inevitable result of growing up, growing wiser, growing more jaded. Of learning to see the absurdities of life for what they were. Or of being absorbed in reading and writing books that celebrated love—in all its forms—over conflict.

Whatever the combination of events, her exhaustion with fighting a ridiculous war had grown stronger over the last several weeks, and the way her family stressed that she not trust anyone who wasn't a Porter seemed more and more unfortunate. Especially as Porters kept letting her down, and as she'd been forced to put some trust in Ian. Of course, there was no guarantee Ian wouldn't screw her over eventually, but so far he'd upheld his end of the deal. It was an uncomfortable limbo to live in, but maybe if she hadn't been warned away from making deeper friendships with outsiders when she was younger, someone knowing her secrets might not keep her up at night as much.

"You all right?" her father asked, and Kelsey wondered how long she'd been staring into space as these traitorous thoughts raced through her brain.

"I'm fine. I'll see what I can find out about the deal."

Let her father interpret that how he would; she wasn't about to pester Ian with questions. He wasn't a part of the feud. He didn't owe loyalty to either family. And damn it, Kelsey couldn't shake the urge to defend him from the bullshit the rest of them had to live with.

Josh liked to call her a mother hen, but Kelsey preferred to think of herself as a mama wolf. And somehow, despite her best intentions to maintain her distance, she'd adopted the sexy, funny Ian puppy after all.

19

IAN HAD SEEN Kelsey twice since the night he'd dropped off her table and done the one thing he'd promised himself he wouldn't do again each time, but today would be the first time he'd see her with all three of her dogs. His fingers tapped the steering wheel as he drove to the trailhead where they were meeting, and he strongly suspected it wasn't the dogs that made him excitable. It was her. At this point, he felt strangely little concern about the dogs. His thoughts were more focused on the woman.

It had been a busy week, and he'd been feeling morose the last couple of days because of Rosh Hashanah. Rather than drive to Anchorage, Micah had found an online service they could attend, which was fine. For him, holidays were about family (and to a lesser degree the foods he missed), and video-chatting with Isabel and his grandparents simply hadn't been the same. He felt unsettled in his new home and not always welcome, and not being a part of the family celebration this year exacerbated that feeling.

But the promise of seeing Kelsey today had helped him get through it, and Ian wasn't sure that was a good thing.

If he pondered it too long, in fact, he was certain it was a bad thing. Reaching a truce with Kelsey had alleviated some of his feelings about not belonging, but sex with Kelsey was a problem he should be trying to fix. Until he cemented the *just friends* aspect of their relationship, Ian was wary of becoming too emotionally dependent on her. He couldn't afford to develop stronger feelings. It wouldn't be fair to either of them when he couldn't devote sufficient energy to a romantic relationship.

For that reason alone, Kelsey's idea that they meet for a walk instead of dinner was brilliant. Ian didn't know if she'd suggested it specifically because it meant they were less likely to tear each other's clothes off, but he valued the idea for that purpose.

He also cursed it for the same reason, but whatever. If his self-control continued to fail, his lack of interest in exhibitionism could save them.

The sun was hidden as Ian pulled into the trailhead parking lot about thirty minutes outside of town, but the weather was practically balmy in the midfifties, and it amused Ian how much his internal thermometer had recalibrated. Two other vehicles were in the lot, one of which he recognized as Kelsey's. Although he wasn't too nervous about meeting her other dogs, he'd declined the offer of being in an enclosed space with them for the drive. Ian was thrilled with the strides he'd made, but he was a work in progress.

Kelsey had all three dogs out of the SUV and on leashes, and Ian took a minute to identify who was who. Puck's white fur made him easy to distinguish, but Juliet and Romeo looked very similar, and he didn't want to confuse them. He recalled Kelsey saying Romeo was wary of strangers, and after all his progress, Ian didn't want to cause a canine incident by mistaking the dog he knew for the dog he didn't. Luckily, Juliet helped him out. It became clear quickly who was who as he approached— one dog's tail waved frantically, and the other regarded him warily.

Juliet barked, which seemed to excite Puck, and they both strained on their leashes.

"Yes, we're all very happy to see Ian," Kelsey said to the dogs, and Ian couldn't help but grin at the way Kelsey had included herself in that.

A few minutes later, he'd followed her instructions and introduced himself to Puck and Romeo. He was twitchy when they licked him, but overall, he was proud of himself for staying calm. Two weeks ago, he certainly would never have had it in him to kneel in front of not just one but three large dogs. So although he might be sweating a bit despite the cold and his muscles were tense, he owed Kelsey a lot. Sweaty and tense were a far cry from panicking. He could even admit there was a certain joyfulness in the way Juliet and Puck wagged their tails.

Romeo, however, like his tail, appeared unmoved. Since he was shyer than his siblings, Ian made an extra effort to control his own nerves and spent more time petting him in the spot Kelsey suggested. He could totally relate to that kind of wariness around the other species, and it was especially gratifying to see the dog finally relax enough to close his eyes and bask in the attention. "You and me both, boy. We both have trust issues."

Romeo barked in what Ian hoped was agreement.

As he stood, Ian realized Kelsey had been smiling down at him, and he was glad he hadn't noticed before. There was such pure, beautiful delight on her face that it knocked something around inside him, making it hard to breathe. He told himself her happiness was only for the dogs' sake, and maybe it was, but that didn't negate the effect her expression had on him. He wanted to know how to bring about that happiness again.

He also wanted to press her against a convenient tree and kiss her until they shed their clothes, and to hell with being in public.

With that in mind, Ian gestured toward the trail. If they were walking, they weren't kissing. "Shall we?"

"Let's," Kelsey said in such a manner that he suspected she was having similar ideas. "Come on, babes. It's walk time."

The huskies were clearly familiar with the word, because three pairs of ears perked up, and they barked happily.

Happily. Ian was even starting to recognize different types of barking and not just assume it all meant *attack!*

The trail Kelsey had suggested was wide, cutting through an open field. The air was pungent with a woodsy scent that made for a pleasant change from the bay smell of Helen. They walked silently for about a minute, Kelsey watching her dogs and Ian both watching the dogs and checking out the scenery.

"So, my father came by the other day," Kelsey said. She trailed off and chewed on her bottom lip.

Ian waited for her to continue, concerned about this new mood that was darkening her face. He'd just seen happy Kelsey, and he'd seen plenty of annoyed Kelsey. Also dubious Kelsey, horrified Kelsey, and turned-on Kelsey (which ranked up there with happy Kelsey if he was ordering them from best to worst). But this was a new emotion, and if Ian had to guess, it ran darker and deeper.

Before he could think better of it, he reached over and touched her hand. Kelsey startled, and she smiled at him, but she didn't take his hand in her own.

His touch did seem to focus her though. She took a deep breath, and when she spoke again, it sounded like she'd gotten a grip on whatever had been bothering her. "I thought I should warn you. He's heard a rumor that you and Micah entered into some kind of exclusive promotional deal with the Bay Song, and he's not happy."

Oh. Oy. Ian could almost laugh at the situation. He and Micah had spent so much time trying not to piss off one family or the other, only to have something they'd done before they'd even been aware of the feud come back to haunt them. It figured.

But pissing off Wallace Porter was not a laughing matter. Over time, Ian had picked up the knowledge that Wallace was one of the main players in the Lipin-Porter feud. If this were war, he'd hold the rank of general. So while Wallace didn't have any power over him or Micah, he did wield a lot of power over the rest of the Porter family. If they also became unhappy, that could be a problem. A far bigger one than Ian's inability to keep his hands off Kelsey.

That hamsa Micah had hung on their wall didn't seem to be helping much.

Sighing, Ian ran his hands through his hair. "Yeah, we made a deal with Lydia Lipin months ago, before we were aware of the feud. It hasn't gone anywhere since the brewery isn't open to the public yet, but we'd planned to offer discounts to the Bay Song's guests in return for the hotel promoting us."

"Ah."

"I'd forgotten about it because it won't even start until the spring." Ian shook his head ruefully. "Once we were clued in that most businesses are forced to choose sides, we've been so careful to try to work with everyone. I don't want to be involved."

Kelsey kicked at a tall patch of grass. "You shouldn't have to be. It has nothing to do with you, and I told my father that."

"Will he listen?"

She laughed sarcastically. "Who knows. Sorry. I wish I could be more optimistic, but that's not me."

It was Ian's turn to laugh in spite of everything. "I hadn't noticed. You're so bubbly and cheerful."

"Yeah, well, it's not like you've been a ray of sunshine since I've known you either."

"My grumpiness has solely been in response to your surliness." Ian placed a hand over his heart.

"What you *perceived* as my surliness," Kelsey said.

"Right." He rolled his eyes. "Because you bounced up the steps to the brewery the day we met all sunshine and smiles, and I misinterpreted that."

"You slammed the door in my face!" She pointed a finger at him.

"You brought dogs."

"How was I supposed to know you wouldn't love my dogs?" Kelsey appeared to be fighting down a smile.

The urge to kiss her was back, stronger than ever. Ian allowed himself a few breaths to clear his head and will his body to behave. He'd temporarily forgotten all about the dogs again, and the dogs had forgotten all about him. They were too busy sniffing the ground and investigating every rock or fallen tree limb in their path.

"I don't know," Ian admitted after a moment of watching Puck try to pick up a stick that was too big for him to carry. "They don't seem so bad really."

He expected some sort of snarky comeback from Kelsey, or if nothing else, commentary about how her dogs were much better than *not so bad*. But she kept smiling in that adorable way of hers, like she was basking in his change of heart.

He would be in trouble if he focused on her for too long, so Ian changed the subject. "The feud, on the other hand, is so much worse than I expected. I thought *my* family had issues."

"Everyone's family has issues," Kelsey said, echoing a comment Ian remembered her making on the drive to Wasilla.

At the time, he'd declined to discuss his family, but recent events made him more prone to talking. There was something amazing about walking down a quiet path in the woods with Kelsey and three huskies and feeling relaxed while he did it. She was responsible for that, and part of him felt like she deserved an explanation for how he'd gotten to this point.

"True," Ian said, stuffing his hands in his pockets. "When you were asking me questions about the brewery, one of them was why I lived with my grandparents."

"It was a nosy question. I shouldn't have asked it."

"It was, but it also flowed from the other questions you were asking, so I get it. Anyway, the answer is because my mom died when I was eight. My parents had divorced a few years earlier, and my sister, Isabel, and I were sent to live with our dad. That did not go well."

"I'm sorry."

Ian shrugged. "You don't have to be. My dad was a lousy parent. All he ever loved was being successful at his job, and to him, Izzy and I were inconveniences, and he made sure to let us know it. He's probably a good part of the reason I have—had—a phobia of dogs. I mean, the dog that jumped on me when I was knee-high started it, but my father thought he could cure me by exposing to me more dogs without any thought about how to do it. Loud dogs, hyper dogs, dogs that were bigger than me. He didn't exactly have a lot of patience, and he expected me to snap out of it to make his life easier. Of course, it only made things worse."

More amazing than the fact that he was calmly walking down a trail with three dogs was the fact that he could relate all of this without wanting to scream. But while Ian had adjusted to Kelsey's dogs relatively quickly, getting over his father's bullshit had taken a lot longer. Years, really. And in many ways, he knew he wasn't over it completely. His father was the reason he worked so hard at the brewery and why he sometimes lay awake at night, stressing about whether he and Micah would be successful.

What he'd gotten over was the rage. He still dearly wished to strangle his father when he'd do something like forget Isabel's birthday, but most of the time, Ian didn't even think of him. Some days that felt like a miracle.

Kelsey swore, and Ian fumbled on. "When I was twelve, my dad decided he couldn't deal with me or Isabel anymore, and so my mom's parents took us in. But by then, my dad had done a good deal of messing with our heads."

"I'm so sorry," Kelsey said again. Her free hand had balled into a fist. "My dad can be an asshole, but in some ways, yours seems almost worse. I don't know how you can talk about him so calmly. I want to punch him on your behalf."

Ian chuckled. He'd totally pegged Kelsey right when they'd watched *Terminator* together. "I made a conscious decision years ago to move on. I just thought you deserved to know where my dog issues stem from."

"Thank you for sharing." Kelsey offered him a tentative smile. "But be aware that if I ever meet your dad, I can't promise I won't unleash my inner hellhound on him. I have a lifetime of feud-fueled dirty tricks up my sleeves."

"You have my permission to do whatever. I can see that letting go of grudges does not run in your blood."

"No, it doesn't, although . . ." Kelsey sighed. "It gets

exhausting. But I can't see moving on working here. Porters and Lipins will never forgive each other for the past hundred years of shit."

"Who said anything about forgiveness? I haven't forgiven my father. Forgiveness needs to be earned, and although I'll keep giving him chances to do that, he has to want to take them. Until then, I just chose to stop wasting mental energy on someone who wasn't worth it. I don't want his actions to define my life."

"Like the feud defines ours?"

"Does it?" Ian asked.

Kelsey bent down and took the oversized stick away from Puck. "The feud has consumed my entire life. And for most of it, I've been like this silly dog here, trying to carry around a stick that's slowing me down, because it's a stick and I'm a dog, so I must have the stick." She tossed the offending tree branch several feet into the woods, and the dogs watched it go with longing. "Will you be okay if . . ." She gestured to the leashes.

Ian wasn't entirely sure, but he nodded anyway. He'd been with Juliet plenty of times when she was off-leash, and the huskies seemed entirely unconcerned with him. "Yeah."

Kelsey paused a second, as though assessing whether she trusted his answer, then she let the dogs off their leashes so they could run after their prize. "With the feud, some of the time, I didn't have any choice but to go chasing sticks. Now, when I do have a choice, I'm trying not to chase the damn things, but it's hard."

"I imagine it would be when it's consumed the whole town."

The three huskies returned to Kelsey, dragging a newer, even bigger stick with them, and she turned to Ian with a see-what-I-mean gesture. "Did it help to leave Florida? With your father, I mean? Is that why you're really here?"

"I moved on years ago, but I can't deny that putting some distance between myself and him factored into the decision."

Kelsey shot him a knowing smile. "Aha. I knew you couldn't actually have been attracted to our climate."

"There's a lot I'm attracted to in this state." Ian picked up a fresh stick and tossed it for the dogs so he wouldn't be tempted to watch Kelsey's reaction to that.

AS USUAL, IAN had given her a lot to think about. The idea that she could just say *screw it* to the feud shouldn't have been radical, and yet it was. Kelsey hadn't been taught to let go. She hadn't even been taught to forgive, and she wasn't sure she had it in her to do that. Hell, she'd been taught to be suspicious of people's apologies, but also that she had no choice but to accept them. Or pretend to, to be accurate. So to do none of the above, to simply shrug off the past and boldly declare she was done caring, was an intriguing proposition.

It wouldn't work for the feud, not unless lots of other people decided to do the same, but the feud wasn't the only baggage she carried around. There was the anger she nurtured about what Anthony had done. Writing books had rebuilt her self-esteem, and sleeping with Ian had rebuilt her self-confidence. But rage remained. Could she one day decide she no longer cared?

After another ten minutes or so of walking, Kelsey and Ian turned around and headed back to their cars. Luckily, the dogs were exceedingly happy to be out walking among so many distracting sights and smells, so she couldn't focus solely on the man next to her. She and Ian talked about lighter topics—TV shows, food, and whether skiing or sledding was more fun—and Ian kept making occasional flirty comments that she kept pretending to not hear.

It was early afternoon when they reached the trailhead. After the dogs were fed some treats and tied to a tree so they couldn't run far, Ian shared the sandwiches he'd brought, and she poured them both coffee from her thermos. Ian had spread out a blanket in his truck bed, and they sat on that to eat.

Kelsey had no idea how disheveled she looked, but Ian's cheeks were lightly pink and his hair blowsy from the wind, much like it looked after she'd run her fingers through it during sex. Kelsey tried to not to make that comparison, but it was impossible. She'd wanted to kiss him a hundred different times on the walk, and it was only because she'd had to keep control of all three dogs that she hadn't.

"I maintain that it's chilly for a picnic," Ian said. He'd been skeptical of the idea when she'd suggested it, and Kelsey had teased him about his Florida attitude until he'd relented.

"Don't know what you're talking about." They were sitting on opposites sides of the bed, and Kelsey stretched out her legs so that one was now touching one of his. "Body heat. Does that help?"

"You have to ask?"

No, she didn't. It was enough to assume Ian's blood heated as much as her own did from the contact. And now she was the one flirting.

Bad. Kelsey scolded herself like she was one of her dogs.

"You seem to have adjusted to being around dogs," she said, trying to think of things other than Ian's long leg rubbing against hers. "You barely flinched when Puck licked you a moment ago."

"I have." He sounded surprised, but pleased. "It's weird, to be honest. I expected it to take a lot longer and be a lot more painful."

So had Kelsey, and considering what Ian's father had put him through, she was surprised he'd agreed to try it at all.

The thought of poor younger Ian being neglected by his only remaining parent and tortured by dogs—even if it wasn't on purpose—made Kelsey want to punch his father all over again. She took a deep breath and sipped her coffee.

"I think it was you," Ian said after a moment.

"Me?"

"I trust you. That made it easier."

"Oh." Her mouth went dry, and Kelsey forced herself to swallow.

Ian trusted her—why? She hadn't done anything to earn that trust. Or was it less about earning it and more because he had leverage over her?

That didn't seem right though; it wasn't Ian's way. He was many things: distracting, insufferable. And in the past couple of weeks she'd add: smart, funny, caring. But he wasn't cruel. He would never lord her secret over her, that much Kelsey had grown to be sure of. Whatever else he was, he was a good person.

What must that be like? To be able to just trust someone, especially someone you hadn't known for years? Who you hadn't run a hundred tiny tests on to see if they'd have your back? And if Ian trusted her, did that mean it was safe to trust him?

Kelsey wanted to, but it was hard to shake the fear. Trust made you vulnerable, and vulnerabilities could be exploited. It had taken her years to patch herself back together after the last person had betrayed her trust. She wasn't sure she could put herself through that again, and yet something inside her ached with the knowledge that Ian had put his faith in her. He'd told her something that made him vulnerable just to make her feel better, then he'd let her help him work through his fear. Although she'd previously dismissed his actions as not being on the same level as the discovery of her secret profession, she was realizing that what he'd done was just as traumatic for him. Especially now that she knew what he'd gone through with his father.

She should say something other than *Oh*, but Kelsey didn't know what, so she did the only thing that felt right. She pushed aside her food, crawled across the truck bed, and kissed Ian.

Warm hands cupped her cheeks as Ian pulled her closer. Kelsey shifted, settling on top of his lap and wrapping her arms around him. The sourdough bread, pickles, and coffee they'd been feasting on should have been alarming, but mostly she tasted him, and Ian's mouth always tasted like perfection. Comfortable yet arousing. Demanding yet yielding. She didn't know how he knew exactly how to kiss her or where to touch her, but she wanted to consume him. She didn't even care that they were in public.

Ian groaned, and he lowered one hand to her thigh. That was all it took for heat to pool between her legs. Kelsey reached down through the slim space between their bodies and cupped the erection straining through his jeans.

"Kelsey?" Ian sounded incredulous as she tugged on his zipper.

"I need you." She couldn't bring herself to say *I trust you*, or *I like you*, or *I care about you*, although she was terrified that all three were true. So *need* was close enough. Her body was aching for him to fill it, and she might combust if he didn't.

Ian closed his eyes and swore, and his fingers pressed against her lips. "It's not that I haven't been thinking about this our entire walk, but anyone could pull into this lot."

"They won't. It's Friday, not the weekend. And it's getting late." She was completely making stuff up, but her confidence in these facts was high enough that she was willing to risk it.

The one other vehicle that had been here earlier was gone. No one else would arrive. She willed it to be so.

She was also counting on Ian to talk sense into her, something she hadn't realized until he decided not to and unbuttoned her jeans. Shit. Ian's fingers rubbed her through the fabric of her underwear, and Kelsey squirmed.

"I can't believe I'm doing this," Ian said, but he rummaged through his wallet and produced a condom.

Kelsey couldn't believe it either. She'd hoped that by sticking to the outdoors today, they'd avoid this. All she'd needed was one meeting with Ian that didn't result in sex for her to believe that maybe, just maybe, they'd get the whatever-it-was between them under control. Instead, they were doing the opposite.

Clearly it didn't matter what obstacles she put between them. She was going to jump his bones regardless.

Ian shoved her jeans down low enough so she could position herself above him, and holy shit. The truck was hard and cold against her knees, even with the blanket. But Ian was hot and hard in the best ways, and Kelsey's awareness of everything that wasn't him faded away. The length of him inside her. His hands on her hips, guiding her. His mouth crashing into hers, his tongue seeking her out, and his warm breath on her face.

She came fast, clutching Ian's body like a shield against

the cool air, and he followed seconds later while she buried her face against the crook of his neck. Her other senses returned slowly. Nearby, she could hear the dogs running around and the leaves rustling in the trees. Her skin cooled, and her knees ached. But she didn't want to let go. She wanted a second more, a minute longer, to hold Ian and feel his arms wrapped around her and inhale the wonderful scent of his skin. He felt so good.

When the first raindrop landed on her forehead, forcing them to hurry and clean up, Kelsey realized it was way too late to believe she could turn back the clock on whatever they'd started. The word *trust* might shrivel on her tongue, but that didn't mean she didn't feel it. Or that she hadn't already screwed up and started to care more about Ian than was good for her.

20

⚬━━━━━━⚬

THE DAY AFTER the walk with Kelsey, Ian found himself awake early. He was settled at the dining room table, his coffee growing cold, when Micah stumbled into the kitchen.

"Why are you up? Are you working again? That looks like a list." His friend pulled his hair back into a ponytail.

"Yes, I'm working," Ian said, aware of how defensive he sounded. "I had an idea for a new beer."

That was what had awakened him—an intense need to create. But it wasn't just any new beer. He had a particular person in mind for this one.

He and Kelsey had parted after the walk, but Ian's brain lingered at the trailhead, still trying to understand what had gotten into him. Kelsey had this power to make him do things he'd never otherwise consider, like pet dogs or have sex in his truck in a public lot. He was acting like a different person as a result of her influence, but he was enjoying it.

So the question that had woken him up was, could he have the same effect on Kelsey? She claimed to hate beer.

Could he change that the way she'd changed his opinion on dogs?

Already he had ideas. Ian had observed enough of Kelsey's eating and drinking habits over the past couple of weeks to figure out that her favorite food group was sugar. She puts lots of it in her coffee, only drank alcohol if it was sweet, and never turned down dessert, especially if it involved chocolate. From a brewing perspective, those were all things he could work with.

"Wait, does that say—?" Too late, Ian realized Micah was reading his screen over his shoulder. He minimized the file, but Micah had seen enough. "You're making a beer for Kelsey?" his friend asked. "I thought she didn't like beer."

"She doesn't. Yet."

Micah laughed obnoxiously as he sliced off a piece of the leftover challah. "But *you* like Kelsey."

Ian stuck his cold coffee in the microwave, debating his response. "She's been helping me learn to like dogs, so I thought I'd help her learn to like beer."

"So she asked for this help?"

"No, but it seemed fair. Anyway, it's my job to create new offerings." That was how he was rationalizing his decision. Creating new recipes, as well as re-creating successful ones from his aunt and uncle's brewery, was what he got paid for. Brewing a beer that Kelsey might like, therefore, wasn't a distraction from work. It *was* work. If Ian could win over Kelsey, he could win over new customers.

Micah's face turned serious. "You could just admit that you like her."

"It has nothing to do with liking her," Ian lied, both to himself and to Micah. "It's a challenge. If I can create something even Kelsey likes, that's a victory."

"Undoubtedly." Micah poured himself some coffee. "You know what else would be a victory? You admitting that you like Kelsey, that your therapy sessions are dates, and that the world won't end and Northern Charm Brewing won't fail just because you have a relationship with her."

"It's not like that." Ian retrieved his coffee from the microwave and sat back in front of his computer. Even to his ears, the words didn't ring true. But as long as he didn't declare his thing with Kelsey to be a relationship, none of those expectations would come along with it. Or so he hoped.

Micah might be correct that the world wouldn't end if he dated Kelsey, but Ian wasn't so certain about the brewery, and he couldn't risk it. Dating and relationships took time and energy, and he wouldn't split his between work and Kelsey.

The toaster popped up Micah's bread, and his friend turned his back on him. "If you say so. Personally, I like these Helen women. Did I tell you Maggie from the hardware store asked if I wanted to get coffee yesterday?"

"No. Good for you." Maggie seemed like a nice person, and it wasn't like Micah had more of a social life than Ian did since moving here. If it weren't for Kelsey taking over his brain, Ian might have been jealous.

"Well, she did," Micah said, "and I said yes because she's cute, and I'm not obsessed with my job to the point of refusing to have a life."

Ian narrowed his eyes. "I'm not obsessed, but there's a lot hanging on our ability to be successful here. My aunt and uncle are partially on the hook for the loans we took out."

"They are, but we both know they aren't what's driving

you, right?" Micah grabbed his toast and coffee and high-tailed it out of the kitchen before Ian could argue with him.

"THIS SUCKS." ON the couch, Romeo whined at Kelsey in sympathy as she checked her temperature. Unsurprisingly, it hadn't changed in the last five minutes. That should be good, considering it wasn't elevated before, but it meant the dogs were the only ones who cared about her distress.

A new text from Josh arrived, and Kelsey glared at it.

No fever so it's probably just a cold. Drink lots of fluids, get some rest, and Taylor or I can come by to walk your dogs tomorrow if you don't feel up to it.

Do people actually pay you for that advice? she typed back.

Not the dog part, but the rest, yes. Now go drink some tea, and I hope you feel better soon.

Kelsey tossed the phone on the living room table. "What good is being related to a doctor if the best he can do for me is offer to walk my dogs?"

Romeo's ears perked up, and Puck and Juliet both turned her way. Not only had she made the mistake of saying the W word aloud, she'd suggested caring for her babies wasn't important. Well, the dogs probably hadn't made the second association, but Kelsey felt guilty about it anyway.

"No offense intended. I just feel like crap," she told them.

After having gone to bed with a mildly irritated throat last night, Kelsey had woken up feeling like someone had punched her in the head. The slightly expired decongestants she'd dug out of her medicine cabinet were helping, but going up and down the stairs remained onerous. She was half considering going back to bed already even though it was only five o'clock, but the dogs would need to be let out soon, and she wasn't making that climb to her bed more than she had to. Possibly she should also eat something while she waited—Josh had told her that too—but she wasn't especially hungry.

Another movie, then. Sitting in front of the TV was all she'd been capable of. Reading required too much concentration, but movies were mindless, particularly ones she'd watched a hundred times before.

Kelsey scrolled through her offerings, her thumb hesitating for a moment on *Terminator*. She'd had to postpone Ian's dog therapy for the day because of this stupid cold, and she couldn't decide whether to be thankful for it. Logic said it was smart to stay away, but in her current mood, she really wished to see him. It was unfortunate, but he had a way about him that made her happy.

But no *Terminator*. She needed something soothing, not endless action.

Someone knocked on her door as Kelsey stuck her most-watched DVD into the player, and on cue, all three dogs started barking. She sighed, wondering who'd made the terrible decision to visit her plague house. A look through the peephole informed her it was Ian.

Swell. She was in pajama pants and an old sweatshirt, and her hair had been neither combed nor properly pulled back. Kelsey debated pretending she could sleep through her dogs' racket, then she decided, screw it. She hadn't asked Ian to come over. He knew she was sick. And she kind of did want to see him, even if she looked as awful as she felt.

"We did postpone getting together, right?" she asked, opening the door. "I wasn't having some feverish hallucination?"

"No, we definitely postponed." Ian held up the bag in his hands. "I brought you some homemade chicken soup."

Kelsey blinked at him, wondering if she was hallucinating now. "You made me chicken soup?" *Take that, Dr. Josh. That's how you treat a sick person.*

Ian made a noncommittal noise. "I brought you homemade soup. Full disclosure, I made a huge batch a few months ago when Micah was sick, and I froze a lot. I didn't have time to make any new soup, so it's more like I thawed some homemade chicken soup to bring you."

"I appreciate the honesty, and it's still nicer than being told to drink tea. Thank you." Kelsey opened the door wider, knowing she was grinning ridiculously. "Do you want to come in? I'll try not to breathe on you."

Ian stepped inside, seemingly no longer concerned about the threat of three excited dogs. "Something tells me if I'm going to catch this, it's already too late."

That might be true. Weren't people supposed to be most contagious before they had symptoms?

"Are you okay?" Her dogs were circling Ian with delight.

"I'm fine. Hey. Hi." He clutched the soup closer to his chest and greeted each husky with a tentative hello.

Even though every muscle in her face hurt, Kelsey grinned wider. He was adorable, and he'd brought her his own soup. Who cared if it wasn't a new batch? He'd made something and wanted to share it with her. The thought was alarmingly warming, and suddenly, her stomach was indicating it might be willing to give sustenance a try after all.

"You know, my mother loves to bake, but even she only fed us canned chicken soup when we were sick," Kelsey said.

"Oh, I ate plenty of canned soup while I lived my father." Wisely, Ian kept his distance as he followed her into the kitchen. "But my mother and my bubbe always made it from scratch."

"Bubbe?" Ian had used that word before, and she'd never gotten to ask him about it.

"It's Yiddish for *grandmother*. Homemade chicken soup is the classic Jewish mother cure for the common cold, or so she claimed."

"You're Jewish?" Why hadn't she known that? Why *would* she have known that?

Ian's expression turned wary. "Yes. So's Micah."

Something itched at the back of Kelsey's mind, possibly because of the trepidation in the way Ian responded. It came to her a second later. "But the calzones we had at my grandmother's had ham in them. Shit! Why didn't you say something?"

Ian's face turned blank, and then he burst out laughing. "Because there was nothing to say? I was well aware of that."

"But is that okay?" She knew she should have refused her grandmother's insistence that they stay for lunch. For other reasons, of course, but in retrospect, she should have checked whether Ian had food allergies or needs. He might be laughing, but her face was red. At least the shot of adrenaline had temporarily cleared out her sinuses.

"I'm fine. I eat ham. Not often, because I don't like it much, although the calzones were good. And I love bacon." He was chuckling like her reaction was the funniest thing ever.

Kelsey lowered the hand covering her mouth. "I thought . . ." Maybe she wasn't so sure what she thought after all.

"Micah doesn't eat pork, or mix meat and dairy, but that's how he was raised. Also, I'm not particularly religious, so . . ." Ian shrugged. "We're all different, like everyone else."

"Oh, right. Of course you are. Let's pretend I didn't

freak out, then." She might no longer be panicking, but her face might be perma-red from embarrassment.

"I appreciate your concern. I laughed because I wasn't expecting that reaction."

Kelsey cleared her throat, which proceeded to make it hurt again. "I just didn't want to offend you or anything."

"How far we've come since we first met." Ian laughed again.

"I was trying to be offensive then. Big difference."

"Huge."

Happy to put that misunderstanding behind her, Kelsey got out a bowl and offered one to Ian. "I know we canceled for tonight, but since you're here, if you'd like to stay I can heat up some soup for you too."

Ian clearly did not need to stay, judging from his lack of concern about her dogs. He'd been smiling at them, cautiously, to be sure, but smiling nonetheless. As for the huskies, since Ian was no longer an exciting stranger, they'd gone back to entertaining themselves.

"Are you sure you want company?" he asked.

Kelsey glanced down at her flannel pajama pants, decorated with cute dogs and bones, and at the hole in the sleeve of her sweatshirt. "I absolutely do not want company. Except for you. You can stay."

"As long as you think you can keep your germs at a distance. No climbing on my lap or anything."

She scoffed, but under any other circumstances, he would have a valid point, and they both knew it. She'd had sex with him in the bed of his truck, for God's sake. What was wrong with her? "You really think you're that irresistible?"

Ian stuffed his hands in his pockets, looking smug. "Apparently."

Yup, he was, which was why he was insufferable.

"I'm pretty sure even you cannot persuade my germs to

want physical contact at the moment. Besides, if I kissed you, I wouldn't be able to breathe, because my nose is stuffed. I like you, but I like breathing more."

Ian set the giant container of soup on the counter. "I'd like to keep you breathing too."

Puck chose that moment to wander into the kitchen and drop his ball at Ian's feet. Ian hesitated for a moment, then he picked it up and lightly tossed it into the living room. The husky shot after it, and Kelsey turned away to hide her triumphant smile.

"Now you're screwed," she said as Puck returned for round two.

"Story of my life when I come over here."

"You wish."

"I know."

Kelsey rolled her eyes. "Speaking of, if you're staying, it's my choice of movie, and we're watching my favorite one. No complaints."

Ian made a noise like a whimper. "What am I being subjected to?"

"*Pride and Prejudice*, and it's actually not the movie version. In this house, we prefer the BBC miniseries version. Five hours of Jane Austen, although I'm not sure I can stay awake for all of it."

"That makes two of us." Ian held up his hands in mock defense as she flipped him off. "I'm sure it's great. I'm finally starting to see the romance author side of you, aren't I?"

"You're seeing the English lit major side of me, but yeah, I guess that too. It's my favorite book."

Ian tossed Puck's ball a second time, with far more confidence. "I'll have to read it, then. All the better to understand you, and as someone pointed out, I'm going to need cold-weather hobbies."

"I have three copies. You can borrow one of them. The annotated version would probably be best to help you get some of the text references."

"You got way too excited about that."

Kelsey's cheeks flushed again, and really—what was wrong with her? There was just something so sweet about Ian reading her favorite book, or even joking about reading it, to understand her.

She'd blame the cold this time. Not enough oxygen was getting to her head. "Sorry. I so rarely get to push books on people."

"No need to apologize. Push away." Ian grinned. "But know I'm going to start pushing beer on you."

Beer sounded significantly less fun than a book. "You are?"

"Oh, yeah. I'm determined to make a beer you like. It's going to contain all your favorite things—coffee, chocolate, maybe some maple syrup. We'll see."

In theory, she did like all those things, but Kelsey was fairly certain the beer part would ruin them. That said, the thought of Ian trying to make a beer just for her made her all giddy. She was definitely going to blame the lack of oxygen for this. The only other possibility was that she was growing even more attached to Ian than she wanted to admit.

21

◦———————◦

THE TASTING ROOM was almost complete. The shelves
were hung. The bar was polished. There were decorations
and glassware. Ian had been sitting in the middle of it,
enjoying the sense of accomplishment while he worked on
writing descriptions for the beers they would be rolling
out for sale eventually. Everything, right down to the de-
signs on the labels, had to meet the regulations set out by
the Alcohol and Tobacco Tax and Trade Bureau, so it all
had to be prepared ages in advance. Fortunately, he wasn't
starting from scratch—he had the resources, including the
marketing expertise, of his family's brewery to draw on.

In all, and especially after spending time with Kelsey
on Sunday, he should have been enjoying this moment of
satisfaction and productivity. But the town had other plans
for him.

"It's not that bad," Micah said, grabbing a stool.

Ian turned to stare at his friend. "We lost two restaurant orders."

"We can deal with it." Micah spoke optimistically, but
he tore into a bag of mustard-flavored pretzels, and he nor-

mally hated mustard. "Do you have any idea why they canceled their orders?"

"Yeah." Ian shoved his laptop aside. "Kelsey said her father was furious about the promotional deal we made with the Bay Song."

Micah muttered something in Yiddish that Ian couldn't translate, although he got the gist. "That was months ago. So the fact that we've been dealing with both Porter and Lipin businesses since doesn't matter?"

"Apparently not."

"And the fact that you're screwing Wallace's daughter doesn't matter either?"

Ian glared at Micah and snatched the pretzels away. "That might make it worse. Who knows? And don't talk about it like that."

"Well, you're not dating her. God forbid you might allow her enough headspace and attention for that. So what do I call your *thing* with Kelsey?"

"It's . . ." Ian waved a hand around and then gave up.

The irony was, since Sunday night when he'd camped out on Kelsey's sofa for a few hours, he'd been giving a lot more thought to his no-relationship policy. There was something so nice, so comfortable, about hanging out with her. He'd loved the way her eyes had lit up when he'd brought over the soup, and that she hadn't freaked out over him seeing her in pajamas. He'd made her tea, let her explain everything that was happening on the TV, and massaged her feet since he wasn't allowed to touch her anywhere else. It wasn't dating, because it was far more familiar and relaxing than dating, but it made him want more.

If he could make time for this whatever-it-was with her, then maybe he could make time for a relationship. Kelsey claimed she didn't do those either, but he couldn't be the only one who was sensing how their circumstances had changed over the past few weeks.

But now there was this. Two Porter-owned businesses were backing out of their contracts because Kelsey's father was angry. The peace and comfort Ian had been feeling were ripped away, replaced by anxiety over whether the brewery could be successful. If this was what the future entailed, he didn't have time to give Kelsey any more of himself. He had to focus his energy on work; too much was riding on him not screwing this up.

"It's complicated?" Micah suggested, finishing Ian's sentence. "Everything in this town is, so why not your relationship with Kelsey?"

Ian didn't bother correcting Micah about using the R word. He just dropped his head to the bar.

"We're fine," Micah said. "Really. Demand exceeds supply. The sign issue has been straightened out. We just need to get the new labels approved, and you need to get that order finished. You know how long stuff takes to get here, and it's Yom Kippur in two days. No work allowed."

Ian rubbed his temples. "I'm aware. You going to Kelsey's with me?"

"Am I really invited?"

"Yes." He'd made the point that he wasn't leaving Micah by himself for a break-the-fast dinner, and Kelsey had rolled with it, extending the invitation.

Invitation to what—Ian wasn't sure. Kelsey had wanted to get together once she was feeling better, allegedly for more dog therapy that they both knew he didn't need, but the timing clashed with his holiday. After explaining the day's significance, and that even though he wasn't religious, he tried to mark it in his own way, Kelsey had offered to cook him dinner the following evening in lieu of a more traditional break-the-fast meal.

Ian's mother had been more culturally Jewish than religious, and his father's only religion had been professional success. When he and Isabel had moved in with their grandparents and ended up in Florida with most of their maternal family, the holidays had taken on a new significance. They'd become the times everyone—his grandparents, plus all the aunts and uncles and cousins on that side—gathered together for boisterous meals and shenanigans. Ian had never been thrilled with being taken to services, but he'd always loved what came after. Marking Yom Kippur with only Micah would be a lot more subdued than Ian was used to, so Kelsey's invitation had seemed like an antidote. If nothing else, it would distract him from all he was missing out on back in Florida.

"This ought to be good, then," Micah said, snapping Ian back to the present. "I want to see you playing with a bunch of dogs."

Ian narrowed his eyes and pulled his laptop closer to get back to work. His world had truly been turned upside down when dogs were the least of his worries.

KELSEY CLOSED HER eyes, took a deep breath (grateful that had become an option once more), and knocked on her parents' door. She was feeling 90 percent better since the weekend, and yet given the way she was burning up inside, she might as well have a fever. That heat, though, was solely due to anger.

The door opened a moment later, and her father's eyebrows shot up with surprise at seeing her. "Did your mother forget to tell me you were coming over for dinner?"

Wallace stepped aside, and Kelsey darted in so the neighbors would not hear any juicy gossip. Sadly, what was about to go down *would* be juicy gossip. There were pros and cons to being a member of one of Helen's most notorious families, and the interest everyone took in your personal life was a very large negative.

"No, I'm not here for dinner," Kelsey said after her father shut the door. The house was filled with the aroma of roasting meat and vegetables—likely her mother's pot roast—which made the true reason she was here all the more irksome. Kelsey loved her mother's pot roast. "I'm here to talk to you."

"Oh, about?" He turned off the evening news, oblivious to her mood.

She didn't know why she'd expected him to have figured it out. When Wallace Porter issued a command, the world jumped to obey. There was no questioning, no pushback, no complaints, even when the orders were a contradictory mess.

Until now.

She would not be staying for dinner.

Kelsey crossed her arms. "You told businesses to cancel their contracts with the brewery." She'd gotten the sense that Ian had been reluctant to confess this to her, but he hadn't been able to hide his mood the last time they'd spoken, and she'd eventually dragged the truth out of him.

Her father blinked, as though he wasn't sure what she was saying. Or possibly why she was bringing it up. "I told you about the rumor. I don't know if you ever got confirmation of it, but I did. There needs to be repercussions."

"Repercussions?" Kelsey thought her head might split open from the pressure she was containing. "Ian and Micah aren't your kids to punish. They aren't even Porters. Just a few weeks ago, you were determined for the brewery to be a raging success. And now . . . ?" She waved her arms around, unable to articulate how absurd she thought he was acting.

Wallace sighed heavily, as if this whole ordeal were as tragic to him as it was to the people feeling the knuckles of his metaphorical fist. "That was then. I still want them to do well, ultimately, but like I said—exclusive deals with the Lipins are unacceptable. I have to look out for the family's interests."

"How the fuck do you expect them to do well when you're kneecapping them? Helen isn't that big. Two restaurants is not a blip that's easy to ignore."

Her father cast a glance toward the kitchen, where her mother had probably paused making dinner to listen to the train wreck in progress. "Watch your language."

"Are you kidding me? I'm a professional writer. I always choose my words carefully."

Wallace looked less than impressed, but then, he'd never been particularly impressed with her fake vocation. There was no question he'd be even less impressed with her real one. "Calm down."

"Calm down? A month ago, you were telling me how important it was that the brewery be successful. You were suggesting I should strike up a relationship with either Ian or Micah for the good of the family. I'm getting whiplash here."

She also couldn't believe the turn her life had taken since that day. She and her father had done a complete one-eighty. The only bit of satisfaction Kelsey could take from this otherwise infuriating situation (and *infuriating* was definitely the word she'd assigned it) was that at least her non-relationship with Ian would no longer be playing into her father's hands. She could kiss him without feeling like she'd let herself be used in some ridiculous scheme.

"And now I'm telling you that you don't have to do any of those things," her father said. "You seemed resistant before, so what's the problem?"

If he really wanted to go there, she'd come prepared.

Kelsey took a last long inhale, savoring the scent of a dinner she wasn't likely to be invited to partake in for some time. "The problem is that I never *had* to do any of those things. I might have chosen to do them for the family's sake, but I never had to. And you know what? I did become friends with Ian. I saw how hard he and Micah are working. And now I see that you aren't treating them like people but like chess pieces in a fight with the Lipins. They're outsiders. They shouldn't be forced to be involved in your petty feud."

He gaped at her, color rising to his cheeks. "It's my petty feud?" He practically spit at her description of it. "No. It's this family's obligation. Our duty to those who came before us. I can't believe the words coming out of your mouth tonight. What happened to you?"

"I grew up and grew out of believing that being at war was a fun game with no repercussions to innocent people. I'm tired of being treated like a pawn in someone else's hundred-year grudge."

Wallace stared at her, his mouth open. Kelsey strained her ears, but she couldn't hear anything from the kitchen. If she were her mother, she'd be setting out the bottle of bourbon and going for a walk until her husband calmed down. Her father wouldn't take out his anger on her mother—he had plenty of faults, but not that one—but he wasn't exactly fun to be around when he was upset.

"Is this because of Josh?" Wallace asked when he seemed to regain control of his voice. "I know you're upset because I'm angry at your cousin for dating that Lipin."

Dating was hardly the correct word, seeing as Taylor had basically moved in with Josh. But there was a strong possibility that neither her father nor anyone else in the family besides Kelsey and Kevin knew about that, and she wasn't going to enlighten them.

She swallowed, trying to get her voice under control. "You know I support Josh. I also support Ian and Micah. And I cannot support the feud anymore. I'm sick of living this way, and I suspect I'm not the only one, although I might be the only one brave enough to say it out loud."

Kelsey didn't really have a lot to back that up; it was more of a gut feeling. But both her brothers had also stood by Josh, and as far as she was concerned, they were the Porters who mattered the most.

Her father was a healthy shade of pink, and she seemed to have stunned him into silence. Eventually he'd get over that and she'd have to deal with the fallout, but that was for another day. "Enjoy your dinner. I'm going home to have the last of the homemade chicken soup Ian brought me."

Kelsey left in a hurry before her father could sneak a last word in, but while she got out the soup, she discovered her father had made other plans. Since she'd hightailed it home, he'd called her brother. The big older brother.

Now Nate was on her case, and he'd sent a video chat request.

"This ought to be fun," Kelsey said to three unimpressed dogs. She hit the accept button. "I can't imagine why you're calling."

Nate grinned on her phone screen. The connection wasn't the best, and his image was highly pixelated, but he looked the same as ever. Which was to say, almost nothing like her or Kevin. He took far more after their mother's side of the family.

"You want to tell me what you said to Dad that had him calling me and blustering about you losing your mind?" her brother asked.

Kelsey propped her phone up against the wall so she could continue to move around. "He didn't tell you?"

"I was having a hard time following. You know how he gets when he's upset. What did you do, Kels?"

"I told him I was sick of the feud."

A moment of silence passed on Nate's end of the connection while Kelsey got out the dogs' dinners. "Say that again?" he finally asked.

"You heard me."

"No wonder Dad was losing it. His favorite child has gone rogue."

Kelsey couldn't be sure, because Nate was moving around on the screen, but her brother appeared to be laughing. "You're his favorite, not me."

"Bullshit. You were always daddy's little girl."

"And now you're the heroic firefighter, and I'm just some writer whose job he doesn't think is important."

"I left town. Lost a lot of points for that."

Kelsey snorted. "Why are you arguing with me? It's irrelevant."

"It is," Nate agreed. "But it explains a lot."

If he said so. She didn't see the point in continuing to argue, and she scooped out the dog food instead. All three huskies charged into the kitchen like they hadn't been fed in weeks. They watched attentively until Kelsey gave them the okay to go eat. Another reason to prefer dogs to people—they knew what was important in life.

"So what made you confront Dad?" Nate asked. "He said something about the brewery?"

Although she didn't feel like rehashing it, if she didn't, Nate's only source of information would be their father's biased summary. So Kelsey gave her own synopsis of everything that had happened over the last few weeks.

Almost everything. She left out some key points about the nature of her time with Ian.

"So you like this Ian guy?" Nate said.

Kelsey blinked. Possibly she hadn't done as good a job at leaving out those bits as she'd thought. "I consider him a friend."

"A friend you *like*." This time when he emphasized the last word, it was clearly not a question.

Swell. Her brother was fixating on the one thing she did not want to talk about. "What is it to you?"

"Nothing. I'm just curious about this guy. He's the one who helped you move furniture, right? You don't like many people, never mind *like* many people."

Kelsey groaned as she set her soup on the stove for reheating. "You sound like you're in middle school. There's nothing to be curious about. Just because I'm not on a mission to sleep with every single guy who comes across my path doesn't mean my *friendship* with Ian is noteworthy."

"Hey, I'm not on a mission to sleep with every *guy*. You're confusing me with your other brother."

"You mean my other brother who's in a stable, loving relationship and getting married, while you can't commit to more than two nights in a row?"

"Harsh, Kels."

"Accurate."

Nate grunted.

Honestly, Kelsey had never considered it before, but the fact that neither of them did relationships, yet handled their determinedly single statuses so very differently, was odd. She had her reasons, and for the first time, she wondered what Nate's were. Not that he would tell her anything if she asked.

"So what did Ian, who you definitely don't like, do with the Lipins that's got Dad so worked up?" Nate's question returned Kelsey's thoughts to the present.

"He struck some sort of marketing deal with the Bay Song," she said, getting out a spoon.

"Is Lydia still running that?"

Kelsey shrugged before recalling that Nate couldn't see her while she was stirring the soup. "As far as I know. Why?"

"Just curious."

"You're curious about an awful lot tonight. What's gotten into you?"

"Me?" Nate scoffed. "You're the one freaking out Dad with your heresy. I'm only trying to gather all the facts."

The soup was still cool, so Kelsey turned up the heat. She was not exactly pleased by the so-called facts her brother was gathering, and she was a little confused about his angle. Nate had left about ten years ago and never returned, which was not something typically done by Porters or Lipins. They might leave temporarily for school, but they came back to help their families stake their claim on the town. Of course, Nate had always lived for adventure, so it hadn't been surprising that he'd felt stifled in their small town. What no one had expected, however, was that he'd apply to the Forest Service and take a permanent position as a firefighter in the lower forty-eight. Kelsey didn't begrudge him doing a very necessary and risky job that he loved, but as far as she was concerned, he'd lost his right to question her actions when it came to the tricky side of living in Helen.

"Are you going to lecture me or tell me to apologize?" she asked. "Because my dinner is almost ready, and if we're going to argue, I'd like to do it before eating."

"I'm not arguing with you, and I need to get my own dinner. I'm checking in because I told Dad I would; that's all. I've concluded that you are fine. In denial or lying to me about this Ian guy, but otherwise acting normal."

Kelsey let out a breath. That was a relief, and smart of

her brother. She'd have hated to have to yell at him about judging her when he'd skipped town. "Good. Want to see your dog nephews and niece before you go?"

"Of course."

Kelsey gave the soup another stir, then brought the phone over to the huskies. Hearing Nate but only seeing part of him on the small screen never failed to confuse the dogs, and their reaction never failed to amuse Kelsey. Naturally, her brother only hung up once the dogs were good and riled, leaving her to calm them down so she could eat.

Annoying as that was, it was something like normal when so much else was anything but.

22

◇————————————◇

TRADITIONALLY, YOM KIPPUR was considered a holiday of atonement. It was a festive, joyful time but also one spent in prayer. Ian didn't pray, but there was a lot he liked about the general concept of the holiday. No work, no eating or drinking—for him, it was a time to reflect on the past year. What he'd gotten right. What he'd done wrong. How to do better.

The evening before, he'd sat through an online service Micah had found, and today, while his friend participated in additional services the same way, Ian tried to focus on the prior year's decisions and whether the choices he'd made had been for the overall good.

It was proving difficult. The better part of the previous year had involved his move to Helen and opening the brewery. By its very nature, those thoughts led him to think about work, and contemplating work led to him actually doing work. In his head if not in his spreadsheets.

Mixed in with that were his thoughts about Kelsey and the choices he was making regarding her. He should never have let things progress between them the way they had.

It had become too much like a romantic relationship, and regardless of what they called it (or whether they refused to name it at all), such an entanglement came with expectations. The issue hadn't arisen yet, but it would. Worse, it wasn't as though he wouldn't feel those expectations himself or subconsciously demand she meet them. Right this very moment, if Kelsey decided to date someone else, he would seethe with jealousy. If she said she couldn't see him for weeks because she was too busy with other things, he'd be gutted that she didn't prioritize him.

Since Ian already had expectations about her time and attention, he had to assume she had similar ones of his—ones he had a history of not being able to meet because his work had to come first. Yet he didn't want to hurt her, and he didn't want to be hurt himself.

It was probably too late for either of those to be possible.

If Ian had made one major screwup this past year, it wasn't choosing Helen as the place to open the brewery or striking an exclusive deal with the Lipins. It was letting himself get too close to Kelsey.

But damn did he like her. The thought of calling a stop to what they had was beyond painful already, and Ian didn't know what to do about it. It was so tempting to tell himself that it was always better to try than to not, but that was a lot of nonsense. Some tries, like a small test batch of beer, were harmless. Other tries, like jumping out of an airplane without a parachute, were best left as assumed failures. Ruining things with Kelsey was unlikely to be as lethal as the latter, but it could hurt every bit as much as breaking an entire body's worth of bones.

Of course, it was entirely possible they were beyond that point already. They were sure getting close to it, which was why he had to reach some kind of decision.

His phone rang, and Ian grabbed it, glad for the excuse to put aside these troublesome musings for a while.

"Hey, Izzy. What are you up to?" Ian glanced at the clock, trying to do a quick time zone calculation in his head.

"Stuffing my face with knishes. Oh wait, you can't eat yet for how many more hours? I'm sorry." She sounded gleeful.

Ian shut his bedroom door so as not to disturb Micah and glared at the phone. He'd been doing fine with fasting until now. The very idea of one of the cheese knishes his bubbe bought from the Jewish deli near her house made him want to weep with jealousy. "Glad to see you're already working on the list of things you'll need to atone for next year."

"Let it never be said that I'm a slacker."

"Never." They'd both heard enough of that over the years from their father. "It sounds noisy."

"It is. The whole gang's here. I'll pass the phone around in a moment, but I wanted to check on you first. Everything okay?"

Ian propped his feet up on his bed, frowning. "Why wouldn't it be?"

"I don't know. I keep having these worries. You and Micah up there in the cold north, all by yourselves." The background noise quieted slightly. Isabel must have walked into another room.

"So the last time we talked and you said your spidey sense was tingling—that was just you worrying?"

"I was right to worry then. Am I right now?"

Ian picked at the thick wool of his socks, contemplating his response. So far the brewery had lost two contracts because of the feud, and there might be more. But as Micah had pointed out, they were getting more demand than they could meet, and they'd been in the process of scaling up operations. As yet, there was no need to think that was a mistake.

That said, the Lipins' Save Helen Society hadn't gone away, so there was the potential for more trouble ahead.

Ian's desire to tell Isabel the truth warred with his desire to prevent her from worrying.

"I don't think so," he said at last. "But things are still challenging here. I still worry about you wanting to make the move."

Isabel clucked her tongue. "And I keep telling you not to. I'm looking forward to it. I've started a whole list of places I want to visit and things I want to try when I get there."

Ian could only imagine. He was probably the most boring person in the world for spending most of his days buried in work rather than going off exploring. Maybe once Isabel was here, he could make the time.

"Like dog sledding," his sister was saying. "I know you won't want to go with me, but it looks like so much fun."

The words *I could go with you* danced on Ian's tongue, but he held them in with a smile. Possibly he could surprise his sister when she arrived after all.

If she arrived. Obviously, just like she couldn't stop worrying about him, he couldn't stop worrying about whether her moving to Helen was a good idea. He didn't want his sister dragged into the feud along with him and Micah if he could help it.

"Is that Ian?" The sound of his bubbe's voice carried, distant but clear. "Pass the phone around."

Isabel groaned. "Everyone's holding out their hands. Ready to be interrogated?"

"It wouldn't be a family dinner without it." He cringed in anticipation, but his heart ached for the familiarity of it, too, and for all the people he was missing. Sometimes it seemed impossible to understand why he'd traded all that familial Southern warmth for the cold, foreign shore of Helen. Even the promise of seeing Kelsey later couldn't dull the ache in his heart, as happy as she made him, or drown out the worry that he would never truly be a part of anything here like he had back home.

UNFORTUNATELY, WITH NOTHING to do until sundown but reflect on life and everything he was missing, Ian was in a morose sort of mood by the time he and Micah left for Kelsey's. His friend tried cheering him up via commiseration about missing his own family, but that turned out to be an awful plan that made them both feel worse. So then Micah tried to cheer him up by teasing him about Kelsey, but that brought up the anxiety Ian had regarding their situation. Ultimately, it was for the best that the drive to Kelsey's was short.

There were two unfamiliar cars parked in front of her house, and when she opened the door, Ian discovered four unexpected faces. Before Ian could ask who the two he didn't recognize were, three dogs charged over to him and Micah. They were so excited to see him, with their tails wagging and their happy barks, that some of his dour mood slipped away in the chaos.

Once he would have backed out the door. Now, Ian smiled at the energetic distraction. It was nice to be wanted, and he petted each of the huskies in turn. Romeo especially demanded his attention, and Ian bent down so the husky could place his paws on his shoulders, and he gave the dog an awkward hug as if to say, *Just look at the two of us anxious folks bonding at last.*

It wasn't the first time Ian had greeted the dogs this

way, but it was the first time he'd done so without any trepidation. He'd needed stress relief, and he finally understood why Kelsey insisted her "babies" could provide it. Neither Kelsey nor Micah said anything about his reaction, but he could feel their gazes on him—one proud and the other shocked.

"All right, you three." Kelsey herded her dogs away from Ian and Micah. "Calm down. I know—it's a party. I never have this many people over."

"You barely let a single person in your house, never mind multiple," said one of the unfamiliar men. He was on the shorter side, with blond hair and a striking resemblance to Kelsey. That must make him her twin, which meant the guy with him was Kevin's fiancé. Ian didn't have all the details about Kelsey's family, but he'd learned some over the past weeks.

Kelsey scowled, and Ian couldn't miss the knowing glance shared between Kevin and Josh. "I'm aware. But Ian said the best part about the day was the dinner afterward when his family got together, so I thought I'd get everyone together—the important people, I mean."

Heat crept up Ian's neck. Clearly he wasn't the only one being given hell about their relationship.

Kelsey introduced him and Micah to Kevin and Peter, and Ian exchanged hellos with Josh and Taylor Lipin.

"Just to clear," Micah said, "is this a rare sight—Porters and Lipins spending time together? Should I be in awe that I'm privy to this?"

Kelsey shot Micah a wry expression. "Yes."

"I do enjoy being gazed upon in awe," Taylor added, striking a pose.

Josh planted a kiss on her forehead. "Some of us always gaze upon you in awe."

Kelsey groaned, and Ian chuckled along with the happy

couple. Given everything the feud was forcing him to deal with, seeing the relaxed way these members of the two families were coping with the situation gave him hope that sometimes sanity could prevail in this town.

"Does this mean we can eat now?" Kevin asked after the bad jokes died down. "I'm starving."

Kelsey shooed him out of the kitchen. "Back off. You weren't fasting all day. Ian and Micah go first. And maybe Josh."

Kelsey had said Josh was sort of Jewish, whatever she meant by that. Given how Josh motioned for Ian and Micah to go ahead of him, Ian took it to mean Josh was even less religious than he was and probably hadn't fasted.

"I wasn't sure what to get," Kelsey said, "so I looked up stuff online. I hope that's okay. I bought bagels and smoked salmon, and I made rugelach and apple cake and a noodle kugel. Although I'm not sure how great that turned out."

"Anything is wonderful." Ian wanted to add more— like that she was sweet and thoughtful and amazing—but too many people were already watching every move he and Kelsey made.

"I like you," Micah said to Kelsey, grabbing a plate. "I like you a lot."

Kelsey laughed. "You might want to try my baking before you say that."

Ian grinned, but he had a feeling Micah's comment was meant as much for him as it was for Kelsey. His friend not only approved of her, he was telling Ian to stop worrying so much about their relationship.

To be fair, Micah wasn't wrong. As everyone dug into the feast and the three dogs dove for the scraps that fell to the floor, the sadness he'd been feeling since his call with his family lifted off Ian's shoulders. For the first time since moving to Helen, he did feel like he could belong here eventually. Like he could have friends. It wasn't the same dynamic as he had with his family, and obviously it could never replace them, but it was a hopeful substitute. If Ian had a tail of his own, it would be wagging, especially as he watched Kelsey. She grumped and scowled and traded barbs with everyone, but Ian saw the pink flush on her cheeks and how she turned away, as if trying to smile in secret, whenever someone's teasing amused her.

He also saw the way she looked at him when no one else seemed to be paying them attention. There was no question anymore about what he should do with regards to her. To pretend otherwise was pointless. He'd fallen for her, good and hard, and walking away was impossible. Ian didn't know how they could make it work, but the solution to his dilemma was obvious: he had to try.

23

SOMETHING HAD BEEN bothering Ian when he arrived. Kelsey had seen it in the tightness around his eyes. But she'd also seen how his mood had lifted when her dogs rushed him. If there was one positive she could take away from this whatever-it-was with Ian, it was that. She'd helped him, and by extension had helped dogs everywhere. But mostly, she thought about Ian. And when she did, she didn't want his overcoming his fear of dogs to be the sole defining triumph of their relationship.

That meant she didn't want him to walk away now that he was "cured." As much as it scared her, Kelsey didn't want her no-relationships policy anymore either.

It wasn't supposed to have happened this way. Ian was supposed to have been a test of her bedroom skills and nothing more, but she'd screwed that up spectacularly, and she wasn't even upset. Finally, she'd found someone who was worthy of keeping around beyond a first date. Ian the puppy and Ian the man had become one and the same, and he'd charmed his way into her heart.

Insufferable was no longer the word. *Adorable* was.

God, she was so screwed.

Kelsey shut the door as the last guest left, leaving her alone in the house with her three dogs and one man. She'd looked at Ian, and he'd looked at her, and by some silent conversation, they'd decided he was going to stay. Kelsey was equal parts pleased, excited, and terrified.

"So?" Ian had helped her put away what was left of the food, the dogs had been let out for the last time, and now he wrapped his arms around her waist from behind. "Does staying over mean I finally get to have you naked upstairs?"

Kelsey relaxed her body against his. Judging by the pressure in her lower back, Ian had been anticipating a positive response. Not smart on his part, because feeling him growing hard was going to make it challenging for her to let him get as far as the stairs before she tore off his clothes.

"You think we can make it up there?" she asked.

"You doubt my self-control?" His breath tickled her ear.

"No. I doubt mine."

She could feel him chuckle, and he kissed her ear. "As much as I like it when you get bossy, I think I'm going to refuse to obey any demands for downstairs sex. So you'd better come after me."

Ian let go of her waist, darted across the living room, and ran up the steps. Damn him. "You're going to pay for that," Kelsey yelled. She turned off the downstairs lights and charged after him.

Ian was waiting for her in the hallway, and he pulled off his shirt as she reached the top.

"Tease."

"I've never been in your bedroom," he said. "Seemed wrong to barge in without an invitation."

"Consider this your invite, then." She grabbed the waistband of his jeans and pulled him down the short hallway to the last room. Her bedroom was as small as the office, and Kelsey had to scoot across the bed so she could lower the blinds on both windows. That accomplished, she settled against her pillows and raised an eyebrow. "You may continue the strip show. Was that bossy enough for you?"

Ian seemed to consider. "The 'you may' was more polite than I'm used to, but I'll allow it." He dropped his jeans and crawled onto the bed to hover over her. "Your turn."

He didn't wait for her to do it herself. Ian dropped a kiss on her lips, then worked his way down her throat until he'd pushed her flat against the bed. She had zero resistance as he kissed her lower and lower, and layer by layer peeled off her clothes.

There was something different about the way he touched her tonight. Softer. Gentler. Slower. All their previous encounters had an air of desperation and franticness about them, but tonight Ian seemed to be savoring each moment and she did too. She concentrated more fully on the taste of his lips and the curve of his muscles under her hands. He was pretty—so pretty—but instead of just admiring his chest or the swell of his erection, Kelsey focused on the feel of his hair through her fingers, the mole on his neck. He was gorgeous not because of his stupidly perfect cheekbones but in spite of them. Because there was something delicious in the unique scent of his skin and the calluses on his hands.

Kelsey came with his name on her lips, her fingernails digging into his back, and she didn't want to let him go. There was no better, more comfortable place in the world than with her flannel sheets beneath her and Ian's warm body pressed against hers. Letting him go so she could clean up and he could dispose of the condom was a crime, but it had to be done.

Ian crawled back into bed with her a few minutes later, and she wasted no time getting as close to their prior position as she could. "You're too muscly to be a good pillow," Kelsey said, resting her head against his chest.

"My apologies, but your head isn't the softest body part in the world either." He kissed the top of it and lightly squeezed one of her breasts. "These, on the other hand, are perfectly soft."

Despite being completely satiated and sleepy, Ian's fingers aroused more glorious sensations in her body. "You can play with them all you want, but are you going to tell me what's bothering you?"

She could feel him shift with surprise. "Nothing is bothering me. Thank you for this, for everything you did tonight. It means a lot to me."

Kelsey propped herself up on one elbow so she could see his face. It was true that whatever had been bothering him earlier appeared to be long gone, and the way he was smiling at her did all kinds of funny things to her insides. She might as well have been melting. "I'm glad you liked it. I was afraid I'd screw it up."

"You couldn't if you tried. It was wonderful. You're wonderful."

"You're not so bad yourself." She kissed his nose. "But something was upsetting you when you arrived. Is everything okay?"

Ian groaned. "I was missing my family."

"Even the father who made your dog phobia worse?"

"No, not him. Good point." He closed his eyes. "The dogs were the least of our issues."

Kelsey nodded but chose not to prompt him. She'd definitely gotten the sense from their time together that there was more to Ian's relationship with his father than the dog stuff, but if he wasn't comfortable enough to share it with her, it wasn't her place to ask. Although it hurt to see him hurt, and it hurt to be walled off, they'd never admitted that there was anything more between them than this—dog therapy and sex. And it wasn't like she'd opened up to him, as tempting as doing so had sometimes been. So far Ian had given her every reason to trust him, but her own issues died hard.

"He's an asshole, my father." Kelsey had resigned herself to the silence when Ian's voice broke it. "About a lot of things. It's not only that he didn't want to raise me and Izzy, but he made it clear that he never saw any potential in either of us."

"Potential?"

Ian tucked some hair behind her ear. "My father has a limited idea of what it means to be successful. We were never ambitious enough for him, or driven enough. Isabel liked art and music, but he didn't consider those worthwhile. I wanted to be a scientist. I actually majored in chemistry in college, believe it or not, but that wasn't good enough for him either."

"Chemistry wasn't smart enough?"

"Chemistry wasn't likely to make me lots of money, and I was good enough to get a degree, but I had to work at it. I wasn't some genius saving the world by age twenty. That's what he believes makes someone successful—money or fame, preferably both."

"How many people become rich and famous?"

"If not rich, then well off," Ian said. "He's successful enough by those standards, but he's a workaholic. I got the brunt of his dissatisfaction, being the boy. If it wasn't about grades, it was about hobbies, and it wasn't just about what we liked, it was about how well we did those things.

To give you another example, I played baseball in school. He wanted me to play tennis or run track—any sport where there was more opportunity for personal glory. In his opinion, teams could only drag you down, no matter how good you were. You had to put yourself first."

"Wow." She hadn't guessed quite how bad it must have been for Ian. It was almost ironic in the way it was so vastly different from her own father issues. With her family, personal glory only mattered if it came at the expense of a Lipin. Otherwise, it was more important to put aside your personal desires and goals to support the greater cause. Still toxic, just in a different direction.

Ian laughed at what had to be the stunned expression on her face. "That about sums it up. I heard my whole life about what a failure I was and how I'd never make anything of myself."

Kelsey kissed him, because the only words that came immediately to mind were *Yup, your father is a major asshole*, and she wasn't sure that was helpful. Poor Ian. Her father—and possibly her mother—might not approve of what she did, but they weren't so openly disparaging. Her heart ached for the boy who'd had to grow up being told he'd amount to nothing.

How wrong his father had been.

That was what she ought to tell Ian, and so she did. "Screw him," she concluded. "Everyone I know who's had your beer likes it, and you're selling lots of it from what I heard tonight. You're very successful, but more importantly, you're a good person. You're smart and sweet, and my dogs love you, despite the rocky start there. Dogs are excellent judges of character. That's also success."

"Thank you." He kissed her back, making her toes curl. "I appreciate the pep talk, but I swear it's not needed. I know his warped ideas are just that—twisted. But people like him get inside your head. I'm not going around angry at him all the time anymore, but. . . ."

"Words stick." She ought to know. She believed in the power of words, and her ex's had certainly stuck with her.

Ian winced. "They do."

Kelsey swallowed. Now that Ian had opened up, part of her wished he hadn't. Ian talking about his past and his pain meant a lot to her. It meant she should trust him. *Could* trust him. She was finally having to face the way everything was changing between them.

Kelsey trailed her fingers down Ian's chest as she collected herself. "My ex still lives inside my head sometimes. I told you I don't do relationships—he's why."

Anger flashed in Ian's eyes. "Was he . . . ?"

"Abusive? Not in the way you're thinking." Recounting the tale was humiliating, but it wasn't like no one else knew it. That was the problem—lots of people knew it. "We were together for almost two years in college. It was my first serious relationship, and he was the first guy I ever slept with. Only eventually, I found out he was less than satisfied with that part of things. Not that I had a clue, because it sure wasn't like he had a hard time getting off with me. But apparently he'd been regaling his friends with tales about what a lousy lay I was the whole time."

Kelsey thought she did a good job of keeping her voice steady, but she could feel her cheeks erupt in flames. Damn Anthony.

Ian gaped at her. "You're serious."

"Yup. I've basically refused to get close to anyone like that again. Who needs the hassle? That's why I started reading so much romance and writing my own. I needed to know the truth and work through the massive hit my self-esteem took."

"I can tell you the truth." Ian pulled her closer, forcing

her to straddle him. "The truth is he sounds like a clueless dickhead. Trust me when I say no one has come close to blowing my mind the way you do, every time. You are the sweetest." He kissed her. "The sexiest." And again. "The most amazing woman I've ever been grateful to for giving me the time of day."

God, didn't he know when he said shit like that she turned into a pile of smoldering, smiling goo? Kelsey buried her face in the crook of Ian's neck while his hands roamed down her back and cupped her backside. The desire to hold him tighter warred with the urge to kiss the hardening length she could feel on her stomach. This perfect man was knocking down all her well-built walls.

"What I'm saying," Ian continued when he'd reached the limits of where he could kiss her without them rolling over, "is that I'm one hundred percent confident that any bedroom problems you experienced with your ex were his fault."

Kelsey raised her head. "Oh, so am I. Now. At the time, I did wonder if I just sucked."

"I happen to like it a lot when you suck."

Groaning, she poked him in the side before applying a playful nip to his shoulder. "I kicked myself for giving you that opening as soon as the words left my mouth."

Ian grinned—smug and adorable at once. "You can't tempt me and expect me not to take the bait. You should have figured that out. But are you really feeling better?" His expression turned serious. "No more believing a word from your evil, inadequate ex?"

Anthony the Inadequate Ex. Kelsey approved of this unintentional rhythm, and she mentally filed the nickname away. "Believe him? No. But like you said about your father, pieces of him live on in my brain."

Ian cupped her cheek before deciding he was tired of

her on top, and he flipped her onto her side. "Then I'm formally requesting permission to kick him out of your brain. I want to take up that space instead. I want to re-place every awful thing he said to you with lavish praise, not just about your bedroom skills—or not-bedroom, as is our usual—but also about how wonderful you are. And I want to override any memories you might have of un-satisfying naked encounters with lots and lots of mind-blowing orgasms."

Kelsey's brain was suddenly racing, along with her pulse. "What exactly are the details of this request?" Was Ian saying what she thought he was saying, or was he be-ing cute? He'd said he didn't do relationships either.

"Details?" His lips brushed hers, light and toying, and infinitely arousing. "I'd say I think we should agree to stop seeing other people and make us exclusive. But since that's not something we need to worry about, how about we stop pretending that we only get together for my dog therapy? How about we admit that we're willing to make an exception to our no-relationships rules for each other?"

Ian's eyes were hopeful, but his voice told Kelsey that he wasn't as sure of her response as he'd like to be.

So she reached up and kissed him, a solid, affirming kiss to let him know that his proposition was more than agreeable. That she was happy, and the quickness of her heartbeat when she was with him wasn't as scary as it had been a day ago. It was more than finally feeling the ground between them settle. It was knowing he wanted her as much as she wanted him.

Ian tucked her closer against his body. "So that's a yes?"

"Obviously. Now shut up and kiss me again."

He did, and a lot else too.

24

KELSEY SUPPOSED *DATING* was her new official word. She was *dating* Ian, even though when they'd had dinner together or hung out and watched movies over the past week, it hadn't felt like dates. Dates were awkward and dull, and they required effort. Spending time with Ian was fun and mostly effortless.

Mostly because she was trying to make him watch all her Jane Austen adaptions and he was trying to spark a love of mindless action movies in her.

But since they were officially together for more reasons than her dogs, Kelsey had convinced Ian to take the weekend off and go with her on her former girls-only trip. The timing was perfect, and until recently, Kelsey hadn't thought much about her once-beloved vacation. In the end, she figured she probably would have asked Ian to go with her regardless of their status so she didn't have to be the odd woman out. With them being an official couple, though, plenty of awkward explanations about the state of their relationship had been avoided.

As a bonus, she got to unabashedly dote on him. Official couple-hood had freed her up to spread some of the attention she normally reserved for her dogs onto a human for the first time in years, and she was a little out of practice. Kelsey used every opportunity to kiss Ian, but she frequently also found herself rubbing him or ruffling his hair.

"You're petting me like I'm one of your dogs," Ian had pointed out once, and he wasn't wrong. Luckily, he seemed to enjoy the affection, and had taken to doing it back to her in what had started as revenge and often turned into foreplay.

Or he had when they weren't in public. Emily's parents' cabin had only two rooms, and with four couples squeezed inside, the only moment of privacy available was in the bathroom. And there had almost always been a line for that. By Sunday morning, Kelsey had been eager to hit the road and return to Helen, and not just because she missed her private time with Ian.

"It's pretty, and the air smells great," Ian said as they loaded their bags into the back of Kelsey's SUV. "But it's still serial killer territory out here."

"And yet you didn't get murdered."

"No. True." He rubbed the two days' worth of scruff on his chin. "But Paul almost did. I thought Emily was going to beat him up with her crutches for stinking us out of the cabin."

Kelsey smirked. "Nah. Dying of embarrassment was more her style. I told you it would be fun."

They were neither the first nor the last to leave, and Kelsey waved goodbye to her remaining friends before putting her SUV in reverse. Already she was imagining a nice, hot shower, preferably shared, when they returned to civilization.

Ian, on the other hand, seemed to be thinking about his

messages. He had his phone out as the SUV headed away from the cabin, but it would be a bit yet before cellular service returned.

The unpaved road was narrow and in need of fresh dirt to fill the many potholes created by the fall rain. Trees branches hung low over the nonexistent shoulders, and shrubs reached out with leafy fingers to caress the car. It had been an uphill drive to get to the cabin, and on the right, the dirt sloped off at a steep angle as they drove lower, winding their way back down.

"You've got several more miles to go before your phone's going to work," Kelsey said. "It's supposed to be peaceful, you know. A break from the daily grind."

Ian's expression was unimpressed. "Peaceful with the possibility of serial killers or being eaten by bears? It was fine when there were people around. Emily had a busted foot. I could have outrun her."

Kelsey snorted and smacked his arm. "That's what you get for watching too many action movies and reading too many thrillers. Try picking up a romance once in a while. You might start associating 'secluded' with 'romantic.'"

"I've been reading *your* series."

She almost drove off the road. "You have?"

"I'm on book three."

"Do you like them or are you just reading them because they're mine?" Immediately Kelsey wished she hadn't asked. She didn't want to pressure Ian into saying yes, and she didn't want him to feel bad if he said no, since logically, she understood that taste was subjective.

"I started reading the first one because it was yours. I *kept* reading because they're entertaining." He grinned. "Also, you have a filthy mind."

"I haven't heard any complaints about that in real life."

"Because I have none, although your books give me ideas."

Kelsey winced. "Just remember, things in books don't always translate well to real life. Sex outdoors around here will result in mosquito bites where you really don't want them."

Ian sighed. "I got two on my legs during truck sex. I was hoping it had gotten too cold for them."

"Never underestimate their staying power. But what are your thoughts on shower sex?"

Not surprisingly, Ian had positive thoughts.

The next leg of the drive passed in happy comfort. Sometimes they talked. Sometimes they fell into comfortable silence. Kelsey watched Ian from the corner of her eye as she drove. The lack of privacy notwithstanding, she'd enjoyed every moment of cuddling with him to stay warm the last couple of nights. She could get used to waking up to the sound his breathing and his scent clinging to her skin.

She'd anticipated the weekend would irritate her to no end, and that her annoyance with her friends for changing the rules would spoil her mood the entire time. But Ian's presence had been like a soothing balm, smoothing out her edges and cooling her temper.

There was no question she was getting soft. Ian just had an effect on her, something even her friends had noticed when she'd let him carry the heavy box of food they'd brought to share into the cabin. Normally, Kelsey hated allowing anyone to help her, fearing it made her look weak. But she'd never resented Ian's help. Whether it was fixing her broken table or bringing her chicken soup, she'd been touched instead. It was a sure sign she'd always viewed him as different from everyone else, and that she'd

been developing feelings for him far earlier than she'd
been willing to admit to herself.

No doubt it was also a sign that she'd fallen hard. She
trusted him. She preferred his company to anyone else's.
It was highly possible that she loved him.

Kelsey didn't have a lot to base that suspicion on. She'd
once thought that she loved Anthony, but since then, she
hadn't let herself get close enough to anyone else to gather
much experience with the emotion. Just the fact that Ian
had sneaked passed all her barriers was probably proof
enough of what she felt.

Screwed. The new word she associated with Ian now
was *screwed*, because he'd utterly screwed up her life, and
she was grateful.

ALTHOUGH HE LIKED teasing Kelsey about the possibility
of serial killers, Ian could see the appeal of a secluded
cabin. As long as it was only the two of them. In fact, this
weekend had made him look forward to winter. He imagined long nights curled up naked with Kelsey by a fire,
pretending the cold world outside their doors didn't exist.

By the time cell service reappeared, these plans had
put Ian in a very relaxed state of mind, but it wasn't meant
to last. The constant chiming from his phone, as all the
messages he'd missed since Friday evening arrived, killed
it pretty quickly.

"You're obviously more popular than I am," Kelsey
said. Her phone had barked only twice.

"You know, you were right. There was something nice
about not being able to be reached." Ian held in a groan as
he counted the texts.

By sheer determination to maximize his time with
Kelsey, he refrained from reading any of them for another

half hour until she stopped to refuel—with gas for the SUV and coffee for herself. He had a couple of texts from Isabel, but Micah's messages were what ensnared his full attention.

Call me when you get this, Micah's first text read.

Not even a minute later: I mean that literally. Whenever you get cell service back. We have a situation.

And finally: Don't panic.

Ian panicked.

Micah picked up immediately. "You're panicking, aren't you? I specifically said not to panic."

"People only say to not panic when something is worth panicking about. Talk to me."

"Several Lipin-affiliated businesses are canceling their orders . . . Ian?"

With a start, Ian realized he'd spaced out for a moment after Micah's information. He'd glitched as his brain tried to process this, and his stomach threatened to return his breakfast. "Which ones?"

Micah rattled off a few names. "So far."

Ian thought he might hyperventilate. Those were most of the Lipin-affiliated businesses they'd signed contracts with. Even if several of them would be shutting down for the winter soon, those contracts had been instrumental in his planning for the spring. "So far?"

"I have a feeling there might be more coming."

"Why?" He was leaning against the SUV, and he grabbed the door to keep himself upright. First Wallace turning Porter-affiliated businesses against them, and now this? The brewery wouldn't be able to survive it. He was going to fail. Just like his father had told him all his life that he would.

"Word has gotten around that you're dating Kelsey," Micah said.

The implication didn't need to be stated. Clearly, the Lipins were taking that as a sign that he and Micah were declaring their support for the Porters in the damn feud. And so the Lipins were withdrawing their support.

Shit. *Shit.*

"Don't panic?" Ian cast a glance over his shoulder. After offering to buy him a coffee, too, Kelsey had disappeared inside the shop attached to the gas station. He'd been so happy just a couple of minutes ago, but that bliss had been snatched away. "This is exactly the sort of situation that requires panicking."

"It's not great," Micah admitted. "We'll have to rethink some plans. Reconsider some options we'd ruled out."

Micah was right. There were options—deals they'd considered making with other breweries, contracts they'd worked on with businesses outside of Helen but discarded for a variety of reasons. None of them had been ideal, but before, none of them had been necessary. Now they almost certainly would be. With every reason to believe they needed to scale up production, he and Micah had spent more money to buy additional equipment and hire people. Money for all of that would be due, and it wasn't only *his* name, reputation, and credit on the line, but his family's as well.

He had to pull himself together, and Ian stood straighter, physically adjusting to his changing priorities. "I'm on my way home. Should be there by late afternoon."

He hung up as Kelsey stepped outside. Her brow immediately furrowed when she saw him, a sure sign that his mood was showing.

Ian's heart sank down in his torso until it met the mess that his stomach had become. This wasn't Kelsey's fault, but he'd made a grave mistake where she was concerned. For a short time, she'd made him feel so good that he'd been delusional enough to think he could finally have everything. Love *and* success.

There was no point lying to himself about whether he loved her. Nothing short of it could have distracted him so thoroughly and disastrously from everything he'd worked toward. But that delusion had been shattered.

No, this was his fault for taking his head out of the game. For always taking two steps forward with her when he should have been taking one step back. He'd compromised both their hearts, and the only fair thing to do was to admit his mistake, apologize, and set her loose. Kelsey deserved someone who could give her everything, and he was no longer deluded into thinking it was him. Not now, anyway. One day in the future when the brewery's situation was more secure, things could be different between them. But until that day, the brewery had to come first, and that meant he had to prove to the town that they were a neutral business. That they could—and would—work with everyone. And there was no way the Lipin half of the town would believe that while he was dating a Porter.

Ian had to choose, and his obligations, familial and financial, to Micah and his aunt and uncle had to win out.

25

IAN EXPLAINED TO her what had happened with the Lipins, and Kelsey spent the remainder of the drive wondering what she could do to help. In a way, this was her fault. Not directly, but the feud was the reason, and she was part of the feud. She'd told her father that she was done, but that was after more than two decades of gleeful participation. She might not have started it, but she'd thrown plenty of fuel on that fire, heedless of how many innocent people prior to Ian might have gotten burned.

Her guilt, of course, was no longer the only reason she wanted to help him. She cared too much about him to stand aside and merely say sorry. Unfortunately, positive intentions didn't necessarily translate into useful actions, and Kelsey couldn't come up with many ideas. She might have some influence among her family and family friends, but it was unlikely any of the Porter businesses that were balking at their contracts would listen to her over her father.

That was frustrating in its own right, but her feelings paled in comparison to the frustration and worry plastered over Ian's face. After he'd told her about his call with Micah, he'd fallen into silence, staring morosely out the window or scrolling through his phone. Kelsey let him be with his thoughts. She had no doubt he'd open up and share in time.

That time turned out to be when she dropped him off at his house, but what Ian shared was nothing like she'd been expecting.

"What are you saying?" She'd parked in his driveway behind the truck. Her SUV's air was thick with tension, but Kelsey had assumed that was from everything weighing on Ian. And in a way it was. But it sounded like more had been weighing on him than she'd realized, and she felt like someone had knocked the wind out of her. She did not like being blindsided, and she was hoping against hope that she had misunderstood Ian.

Because it sounded like just a week after they'd decided to make their relationship official, he was breaking up with her.

Ian winced. "I can't do this, do us, now. I'm sorry, Kelsey. I need to focus on the brewery, and that means I don't have time for distractions. I probably never did, but I wanted to be with you so badly that I lied to myself and said this could work."

A distraction. He was really calling her a distraction. And he was breaking up with her.

Kelsey thought she might vomit. "A distraction?"

She tried to summon some rage over that, and there was a little. Over time she might be able to build that spark into a fire. But at the moment, it couldn't overpower the deadness and hurt that Ian's words had caused.

Ian rubbed his eyes. "Maybe that's not the right word, but you do distract me, in a good way, and that's a problem. We're losing Lipin businesses because I'm with you. And because I've been so distracted by you, I didn't even realize what a problem dating you would be. The brewery has to remain neutral in the feud. It's the only way we can survive. I shouldn't have chosen Helen without understanding the town, and that was my mistake. I screwed up. But if the brewery fails, a lot of people are going to get hurt. This is my aunt and uncle's investment—I have a responsibility to them, to take that seriously."

Her jaw was aching, and Kelsey realized she'd been clenching it. Better that than to let out the pressure building inside her. She didn't cry, especially not in public. A good Porter soldier didn't show weakness. She got angry, not hurt. Then she got vengeful.

She hadn't been a good Porter soldier in a while, though, and if she didn't get the hell out of here soon, she wouldn't be able to hold back the tears.

She'd been right to choose *screwed* as her new word for Ian. Because that's what he'd absolutely done to her—he'd screwed her up, screwed her over, and apparently now was screwing right the hell off.

Well, fuck him. Her sense of guilt for whatever role her past actions played in bringing about this moment had depended on him not blaming her for it.

"Fine." Kelsey restarted the engine. "I was feeling bad, like I'd dragged you into this mess, but if you're going to choose your job over letting me work through it with you, then whatever. I don't want to be with someone whose priorities are that messed up. Get your things and good luck."

Ian reached toward her, and she snatched her arm away. "Kelsey, please. Listen to me. When things settle down maybe, when we're better established, we can—"

"No. Don't you dare expect me to wait around until you have your shit together. Life never gets easier around here, and I'm not waiting for you to figure that out. The only *when* you should be thinking about is when are you going to kick your father out of your head? That's what this is about. You won't listen to me or let me help, because all you can hear is him telling you that you're going to fail. My voice counts for nothing, so why should I believe that's going to change?"

Ian flinched, which was all she needed to know that her punch had landed. "That's not fair. I have people relying on me—family, friends, employees. I can't just tell them 'Sorry, I have other priorities.' I'm not like you."

"Excuse me?"

Ian clamped his lips shut, then broke a second later under her glare. "I mean you have no right to lecture me about choosing to prioritize work. You lie to everyone, even your friends and family, about what you do. To protect your job. I'm at least trying to protect my friends and family by putting my job first."

Oh, how dare he. She'd explained to him why she had to lie about what she did. Their situations were not even close. Kelsey's knuckles whitened around the steering wheel. "I said—get your things and get out, before I drive away with them."

A wall crashed down over Ian's face, and he got out of the passenger seat. As soon as he'd unloaded his bag, Kelsey backed out of the driveway. It was time to pick up her dogs. She'd been right all along—they were far superior to any humans.

KELSEY FOUND IT hard to be creative when her life was in turmoil, but writing romance specifically, even romance as far-fetched as one involving husky shifters, was like trying to outrun a pack of sled dogs. She couldn't make it past the starting line.

For that matter, she'd barely made it past her couch for the last two days, but who was counting? Not even her beloved collection of Jane Austen adaptations was helping. Silly Jane had given her characters happy endings.

Kelsey had officially declared a war on happy endings. A feud, if one would.

It was particularly troublesome given that she needed to write them to earn her living. She'd briefly considered switching genres to something more fitting to her state of mind, say, revenge thrillers, but that would not help in the short term when she was under contract for romances. Besides, any type of creativity, even preparing meals, was out of reach.

It didn't help that Ian's accusation was stuck in her head. She told herself she did not put her job ahead of her family. That, if anything, she was putting her family ahead of her job. She was protecting them by keeping her secret. Yet at the same time, Kelsey wasn't so sure she'd be keeping secrets if she did write revenge thrillers. And that made no logical sense. While revenge thriller writers projected an air of don't-mess-with-me that could be useful in her situation, the fodder any semipublic career provided the Lipins wouldn't have changed. So what was the difference—why was one lie okay and the other unnecessary? Her only conclusion was that she just didn't want to deal with the extra baggage that came with the title of *romance writer*, and in that case, she wasn't lying to protect her family nearly as much as she was lying to protect herself.

For the first time, she felt a little guilty about all the lying, and that made her angrier at Ian.

Kelsey circled her spoon around the empty container of rocky road ice cream, feeling more forlorn. She was out of ice cream, which meant she needed to put on real pants and get to the grocery store. Her stock of comfort foods was running low.

Maybe she could beg Josh to do the shopping for her.

Then again, that would require responding to the half dozen messages her cousin had left her. Ugh. Human interaction was so overrated.

Kelsey flopped back on the couch, and Romeo let out a tiny yelp of surprise. "Sorry."

The husky didn't seem to mind her accidentally smacking him, and he licked her hand. Her entire pack was distressed. The dogs might not know why, but they'd picked up on her mood and had been especially snuggly and affectionate with her since she'd returned on Sunday.

"You're so much better than people." Kelsey scratched Romeo's head, and he nuzzled her shoulder. "Yes, you are. No wonder you don't trust them. You see where trust gets you?"

As if anticipating a lecture, Juliet and Puck lifted their heads and wandered over. Puck jumped up on the sofa, too, burying her under an additional forty pounds of fur.

"I trusted Ian," Kelsey said, not about to deny herself a willing audience. "Not only with my secrets, but with my heart. He made me believe that maybe love wasn't just fiction. That maybe some men could be as deserving of my heart as the three of you are. But it was bullshit. When things got tough, he picked up and ran. He chose his work over me. He didn't even give me a chance to help, so it must have been an easy decision for him. Obviously, I was an idiot to think I meant as much to him as he did to me."

Juliet barked her disgust with Ian. Female understanding about these sorts of problems evidently crossed species.

"Exactly. What an asshole to have led me on like he did."

Although had he ever led her on, or had it all been in her

head? Through her misery, it was hard to tell, and Kelsey no longer trusted her judgment. Ian had opened up to her, and he'd made her soup and done her favors, but what if he'd never done more than what he considered to be reciprocating? What if he'd told her about the dogs and his father only because he knew about her career? What if he'd only brought her soup and fixed her table because he thought he owed her for the website work and the car supplies she'd given him? In her head, the exchanges that had started off as an attempt to be even with him had morphed into things she was doing because she cared. But perhaps Ian had always seen these moments as a way to maintain the balance? If she made a move, he had to counter so he didn't owe her.

Of course, that wouldn't explain why Ian had indicated he wanted to try again with her in the future. She must have meant something to him if he didn't want to write off a relationship completely. But Kelsey wouldn't let herself put too much emphasis on that. The future was nebulous, and Ian might have just been tossing that idea out to make her feel better. Besides, she didn't even know exactly what he would have said. She'd cut him off because she hadn't wanted to hear it, and she didn't regret it.

Kelsey's stomach rumbled with unhappiness, ungrateful for the steady diet of junk food she'd been feeding it. New question—what if she pulled her head out of her ass and started acting like the warrior she'd been raised to be? Or, barring anything so ridiculously dramatic, just a functional adult again?

She'd allowed herself only two days to mope when she discovered what Anthony had done to her. Then she'd picked herself up and gotten her life back. Or started to. Given how much more pain Ian's betrayal was causing her, she deserved more time to mourn her crushed heart. But she'd take no more than one additional day—two max—to manage her emotions. She would absolutely not allow Ian more than that.

"It's a plan," she told the dogs. Since they didn't argue with her, Kelsey assumed they thought it was a good one.

Her phone barked with a text, and given the time, Kelsey had a feeling she knew who it was. The same guy had texted her at this time yesterday.

Still, it was best to confirm that it wasn't Ian admitting he'd screwed up and begging for her forgiveness. Which she wouldn't give, naturally. He was the one who'd told her it was okay to make people earn it, and that would be an impossible task.

My good opinion once lost is lost forever, so Mr. Darcy proclaims in *Pride and Prejudice*, and that seemed like an ideal to live up to. Dearest Jane hadn't intended it to be (probably), and Darcy had been called out on it in the book. But Kelsey was certain Darcy had been onto something. Giving people second chances gave them second chances to hurt you. Only a fool made the same mistake twice.

She'd been fool enough, trusting a new man after the first had hurt her. She would absolutely not let the same man take another swing.

So it would be ridiculous for her to feel disappointment when she checked her text and saw it was from Josh, as she'd expected.

She was not disappointed.

Totally not.

Come walk the dogs with me, Josh wrote. I have Tay's double chocolate brownies to share.

Kelsey groaned. Her cousin knew her weaknesses well.

Josh also knew what had happened with Ian. She'd have avoided telling him if she could have, but Josh had been dog-sitting, and when she'd shown up at his door with tears on her cheeks, he'd demanded answers. Since Kelsey had felt guilty for interrupting his dinner, she'd given him a quick rundown.

She'd also denied any emotions other than a serious case of being pissed off, but surely Josh had seen through her ruse. Ignoring his texts for the last few days hadn't been the wisest move if she'd been attempting to hide it.

Too bad for Josh, though; she was in no mood to talk. Her dogs, on the other hand, could use a good walk, and they loved spending time with Josh and his huskies. It was a beautiful day out too. Possibly her first step in recovering from Ian ripping her heart out should be to take advantage of the weather. For the dogs if not for herself.

Fine, Kelsey wrote back. But I'm not talking about you-know-who.

Josh's response was prompt. I have no idea who you're talking about. I just have chocolate to share.

Slick. Kelsey almost smiled.

"The things I do for you guys," she said, peeling herself off the couch and out from under Puck. But who else was she going to do anything for? Her dogs might be the only creatures worth her effort.

26

◇━━━━━━━◇

THE TAVERN DOESN'T offer a huge beer selection," Lydia Lipin said, referring to the restaurant associated with the hotel she managed, "but I think we can add one more of yours to our taps this winter. That'll make my sister happy."

Ian sank back into the chair in Lydia's tiny office at the Bay Song Inn, hoping the relief he felt wasn't entirely visible on his face. Nor the desperation.

A couple more Lipin-affiliated businesses had canceled their orders since Saturday, adding to the already impressive list of restaurants, bars, and stores in town that had decided they couldn't do business with Northern Charm Brewing for one reason or another. Micah had been busy over the past several days searching for new opportunities outside of Helen, while Ian had been working on a plan to adjust their production. The stress of it had left him lying awake in bed at night.

Although not all of that stress was brewery-related. Hell, not even half of it was. Every time he closed his eyes, it wasn't his spreadsheets or the bank statements that he saw. It was Kelsey, her big blue eyes gaping at him as he'd told her he needed to end things between them. It was the red-tinted anger on her face when he'd told her she put her job above her relationships too. And it was her voice he heard, the pain, honed to a razor's edge in the way she'd said *Fine* before kicking him out of the car. That *Fine* had left him bleeding internally.

Ian didn't believe he'd been wrong about her prioritizing her job the same way he did, but he regretted his words—how he'd snapped. He hadn't wanted to end things between them at all, and he'd done so in the worst possible way.

Not entirely your fault, a desperate voice in his head reminded him. And it was true—he had tried to leave open a possibility for the future. One day, he hoped, the brewery would be successful enough that Helen and its feud wouldn't matter as much to the bottom line, and then being with Kelsey wouldn't be as big of a deal.

But Kelsey had shot down that option before he'd finished getting the words out, and given how upset she'd been, Ian couldn't blame her. But it still stung. He'd wanted to close the door just for a moment, but Kelsey had slammed it shut, locked it, and boarded it over.

They'd only owned up to the emotions between them for just over a week, but he missed her with all the longing of the entire time he'd known her. More, really. She'd fit into his arms and his life so perfectly it was like they'd kindled their weird non-relationship for years. Breaking up with her was supposed to allow him to focus on work, but so far he was focused at least as much on missing her as he was on the brewery.

Since that part of the plan hadn't worked out, Ian reminded himself that this was what was best for her. If they were together, Kelsey would be expecting to spend time with him. She'd put demands on his attention that he couldn't meet, and she'd be hurt because of it. Yet here he was, wishing he had her around to hold at night so he might be able to sleep, dreaming of her kissing him to distraction, and craving her wicked sense of humor, which might have helped him laugh at the things that otherwise made him want to howl with frustration.

Damn it, he even missed her dogs. They were part of the Kelsey experience, and there was nothing about that he'd change. Romeo, in particular, worried him. At some point, the husky had decided Ian's lap was a good place to rest his head, and Ian recalled Kelsey saying Romeo got anxious if separated from his people. Ian had assumed he'd become one of them.

Still, Ian was not ready to consider the possibility that he'd made a mistake. No, the mistake had been letting himself take his eyes off the prize in the first place. He would succeed. The brewery would not go under before it had truly begun. He would not fail.

In the end, that was what mattered.

So he'd always believed.

So he'd continue to ignore the pain and doubt that crept into his heart.

"Ian?" Lydia was twirling a pen around in her hand, a cool trick that was mildly hypnotic, and Ian realized he'd spaced out.

He'd been doing that a lot since Sunday.

"Sorry. That would be fantastic." Despite his best efforts, there was no way Lydia could have missed the relief in his voice. The Tavern buying more beer wouldn't solve all their problems, not even close, but every bit helped.

Perhaps even more helpful than the purchase itself was the meaningfulness of the sale. Lydia wasn't simply one of the many Lipins in Helen. She was the mayor's daughter and the granddaughter of the woman behind the Save

Helen Society. A series of framed photographs on the wall behind her showed the hotel and her family over the last five decades. The Bay Song and this branch of the Lipin family tree were formidable. Ian hoped Lydia's continued willingness to do business with him would send a message to the other Lipin businesses that had backed out.

"Not a problem," Lydia said, setting the pen aside. "Honestly, I felt kind of bad when I heard some Porters were throwing a fit because of the marketing deal we signed. I should have anticipated something like that would happen, and I didn't, so I didn't warn you. I was too excited by the idea. Tay has that effect on me. She's great with ideas, but not always with the gritty details for implementing them."

The *Tay* being referred to was obviously Lydia's sister, Taylor, who was dating Josh. Ian wondered if her sister's willingness to cross feud lines had influenced Lydia's willingness to overlook his (former) relationship with Kelsey. He was also afraid to ask.

"The feud is a weird thing to have to take into consideration when doing business," Ian said, choosing his words carefully.

Lydia laughed as though she'd read his real thoughts. "That's a kind way to put it. I try to keep my head down and stay out of the fray, but it has its way of finding you. As you've discovered."

"I'd guess staying out of it would be hard when your sister is dating a Porter."

"Taylor's relationship with Josh quite literally brought it to my doorstep." She frowned. "If you don't mind me asking, how are you holding up?"

Not wanting to take any more of Lydia's time, Ian had been starting to get up, but her words made him pause. "Holding up?"

"I heard you and Kelsey broke up." Lydia's face was sympathetic. "I wouldn't usually intrude, but I'm afraid to ask—was it because of my family?"

"I . . ." Ian didn't really want to discuss his breakup with Kelsey with anyone, and he certainly didn't know Lydia well enough to feel comfortable talking about it with her in particular. But seeing as he had broken up with Kelsey because he needed to get Lipin businesses back on board with the brewery, knowing the news had spread should have been a positive sign.

While he faltered for a way to exit the conversation without being rude, Lydia plowed ahead. "It *was* my family, wasn't it? Damn it. I'm sorry, Ian."

"It was my fault." By some miracle he didn't fall back into the chair, but the hollowness he'd felt since Kelsey had driven off on Saturday was more intense than ever, a growing pit in his gut that could swallow him. "I should have known dating a Porter would be problematic."

"You shouldn't have had to worry about it." Lydia's pen went accidentally flying across the desk in her agitation.

Her reaction surprised Ian. Yes, Lydia had been the easiest Lipin to work with, and the fact that he was here in her office said a lot. But there was a bitterness in her voice that suggested her anger was personal. Maybe it was simply concern for her sister, but Ian wondered, and curiosity gave him the will to speak more.

"I shouldn't have; you're right. But I don't have a choice. I have to put the brewery first. There are too many people depending on me, and I can't let down my aunt and uncle, who have invested so much." Bitterness or not, Lydia ran the Bay Song. As one business owner to another, she should understand his decision.

Ian needed someone to understand his decision. It would go a long way toward validating his choice.

"I get it," Lydia said, and strangely, the words did not have the effect on Ian that he'd hoped. "I probably would have made the same choice. I admire Taylor and Josh for what they're willing to do, but I don't think I could handle that kind of pressure."

Ian nodded. *That kind of pressure*, right. But wasn't Lydia saying that while she'd have made the same decision he did for the business's sake, she admired the ability to make the other choice? That was absolutely not what he'd wanted to hear.

"Taylor and Josh aren't in the same situation as either of us would be," Ian said. He was willing Lydia to agree with him.

She acknowledged the point with a shrug, but her gaze went unfocused for a second, again leaving Ian to wonder what she was thinking about.

"You weren't put in an easy or a fair situation," Lydia said at last. "I thought things might calm down around here. Like Tay and Josh being together might bring people to their senses. But the way you guys have been dragged through the feud by both sides doesn't give me hope. I have a bad feeling shit's picking up again. It's going to be a long winter."

Aren't they always? Ian wanted to ask, but he couldn't dredge up the humor. Kelsey had said something to that effect once—winters were long and dark, and he needed to find indoor hobbies to entertain himself. But lately, he'd been counting on her for that, and he'd lost her.

None of this boded well for the future.

KELSEY WASN'T SURE she was ever going to be able to walk her dogs again. She didn't know who had spread the news about her Ian and dating, and she didn't know how the news that they'd broken up had spread, either, but it hardly mattered. Small towns would be small towns. Anyone who didn't know yet would tomorrow or the day after—especially considering she was Porter royalty, Ian was the interesting new guy, and their relationship was what had gotten the Lipins all riled up in the first place. Their star-crossed romance and subsequent implosion was the stuff of Helen tabloid dreams.

She felt the town's eyes on her as she walked, and for that she was grateful that she'd put in some effort before leaving the cozy confines of her house. It wasn't easy being dumped, and it was even harder going out in public not looking like you'd been dumped. But while Kelsey might have spent the last several days bingeing on sugar and wearing pajama pants, she wasn't about to let anyone know it. She had a reputation as the take-no-prisoners, suffer-no-fools Porter alpha bitch to uphold. And damn it, her pride required it of her.

Her pride was especially stinging this evening after her visit to her parents' house. Her mother, predictably, had wanted to coddle her and stuff her full of dessert. Her father, on the other hand, had mostly ranted through dinner. Somehow she'd endured it. At the time, Kelsey had thought that made her strong, but in retrospect, as she made the half-mile trek back to her house, keeping her mouth shut no longer felt strong. Hence, the wounded pride.

Her father was furious at Ian for the breakup, and even more furious at the Lipins for being the cause of it. Kelsey hadn't been able to help but notice that her own feelings posed little concern for him. When she'd gently reminded him that he'd instigated a campaign against the brewery himself because of the Bay Song deal, he'd repeated his earlier insistence that it was different. She'd been able to ignore that, mentally rolling her eyes.

But when her father had asked her if she'd written the article about the brewery for the town paper yet (she had) and subsequently suggested she pull and revise it, that was when she'd almost lost her temper. No one was getting any more free work from her. Even if *she* didn't want to see her own words in print, Ian wasn't worth the effort.

She'd brought this on herself, though, by never telling her family the truth about her career. Kelsey hated to admit it, but it was true, and Ian's accusation had been haunting her the way Anthony's commentary on her bedroom skills used to. Every time she got upset, she tried channeling her pain into anger. And every time she tried doing that, she had to contend with Ian's voice telling her she acted no differently than he did.

It was slowly dawning on Kelsey that there was only one way she was going to be able to shake Ian's ghost. By healing herself—the same way she'd shaken Anthony's ghost.

Sex with Ian had helped with that, but before Ian, she'd done the hardest work on her own. Years ago, she'd channeled the pain and humiliation Anthony had caused her into reading and writing, and she'd turned the writing into a successful career. Anthony had never written that "great American novel" he'd talked about in college. But her? She was making money doing something she loved, and she owed that to him. Success really was the best revenge.

But success was also one of her biggest sticking points in dealing with Ian's accusation. The more Kelsey had thought about what he'd said, the more she'd come to realize that if she kept quiet about her writing—if she wasn't openly proud of it—then the lies she told were about more than just her career. She was lying about who she was and the person she'd worked for years to become. And at the same time, she was making assumptions about how her friends and family would react to that person. Not to mention that there were readers out there who were devoted to her genre—some who were huge fans of *her* books—in spite of society telling them they should be ashamed of what they loved. By needlessly hiding her truth, she contributed to that message. In essence, she was lying to everyone and assuming the worst to protect a career she ought to be proud of.

So that was that. If Step 1 of healing from Ian had been to put on pants, Step 2 would be to stop the lies. It wasn't only the right thing to do. It would also let her reclaim the moral high ground, and it would be a lot easier to maintain her anger at Ian if she had that. Maybe she'd even get a good night's sleep again.

Kelsey had failed the chance to reclaim that position by opening up to her parents tonight, which was why she was kicking herself, but her parents had never been the right people to go to first. Possibly Josh was for the family side of things, and Maggie for her friends.

Raucous barking snapped Kelsey from these thoughts, alerting her to the fact that she was almost home, since the barking wasn't from her dogs but from Mr. Silvester's terrier. The huskies regarded the tiny ball of brown fluff with something like pity as it bravely defended the Silvester property from behind its fence.

Two properties later, the barking died down as Kelsey opened her door and let her dogs inside. "I'm so glad you guys are usually quiet."

Romeo's expression was one of pure disdain, as if to say dogs only had to resort to barking if they couldn't look intimidating.

Or maybe she was projecting, given she snarked a lot precisely because she knew she couldn't look intimidating herself.

Kelsey wasn't sure it was Ian's fault that she was now comparing herself to a terrier, but she'd find a way to blame him eventually.

More barking erupted, this time coming from the phone in her pocket. Kelsey grabbed it, seized by an irrepressible and irrational hope that it might be Ian. Then she cursed herself. She didn't care about Ian anymore, and more to the point, she'd blocked his number for the sole purpose of trying to kill that bit of hope. So much for that plan.

Nate's name showed on the caller ID. My, wasn't her older brother being chatty these days? Two calls in one month. Usually they texted a couple of times a week and that was it.

"Did Dad put you up to this?" Kelsey asked by way of greeting. It was the only reason she could think of for her brother calling.

"Hello to you too," Nate said, entirely unfazed. "I haven't spoken to Mom and Dad for days."

"Oh. Then what's up?"

"I wanted to check in on you. Kevin told me what happened."

Kelsey flopped on the couch. Of course her twin brother hadn't been able to help spilling everything to their older brother. And people claimed women were the gossipy ones. "I'll be fine."

So she kept telling herself on multiple fronts. In truth, she wasn't sure she'd ever be fine again.

"You sure you don't need me to kick this guy's ass?" Nate sounded doubtful. Possibly she hadn't put much force into her answer.

"I'm quite capable of kicking ass myself, you know."

Nate was silent for a second, and Kelsey was getting ready to be offended, but then he finally spoke up. "I know. It's just that there are times when it's appropriate to stand back and let other people do the ass-kicking. I'm good at being the mean older brother, and you can have the satisfaction of knowing that an ass was kicked while claiming you were so over it and it was totally unnecessary and Ian-who, you barely remember him anyway. It's a double win."

Kelsey laughed in spite of everything. "I appreciate the offer, but that would mean you need to come home for a visit."

Nate sighed. "Yeah. It might have to wait until Christmas, then, assuming I can make it."

With Nate's schedule, there was no guarantee. When he wasn't fighting fires, he volunteered for rescue missions with the Humane Society, and he could end up being sent out on short notice. Her older brother did not do well with inactivity. While Kelsey admired his dedication toward helping people and pets, the idea of living that way was beyond her understanding, and she hated how little she got to see of him.

On the other hand, his not visiting often gave her an idea. Why not let Nate be the first to know about her secret? Josh had been her first thought, since they were close, but Nate's physical distance was a point in his favor. That, and Nate wasn't a big talker. His speech about kicking ass was the most words she'd heard him string together in a long time. Combine those two things, and Nate wasn't likely to spread the gossip. Plus, Nate was far more chill than most members of her family. If anyone was going to take the news in stride, it was him. She could tell Nate, see how it went, and move on (or not) from there. Her brother's protective streak was a mile wide. He'd beat *himself* up if he told anyone after she'd asked him not to.

"You'd better make it." Kelsey ran her fingers through

Puck's fur. The husky had settled on her feet, and she appreciated the comfort. Her mind was made up, but her stomach twisted with what she was about to do. "Change of topic. There's something I need to tell you."

"You already killed the brewery guy, and you need help disposing of the body?" Her brother didn't pause a second before coming up with that.

Kelsey had put her phone on speaker, but she wished they were video chatting so Nate could see the what-the-hell face she made. "That's what your mind jumps to?"

"You sounded serious."

"I am, but no murder and no help required. I have entire files filled with ideas for how to make murders look like accidents and how to dispose of bodies."

Nate snorted. "That doesn't surprise me."

"It's research. I'm a writer." She braced herself. "That's what I wanted to tell you, by the way. I write books."

A brief silence followed. "I thought you wrote magazine articles."

"I've been lying."

"To me?"

"To everyone. You're the first person I'm telling the truth to."

"Okay." Nate sounded confused. "Why are you telling me now? I mean, thanks for no longer lying, but I'm confused."

Yeah, she'd figured that out. Kelsey swallowed, vowing to keep her voice steady, and gave her brother a quick overview of what had transpired between her and Ian and how she'd reached her decision to tell the truth. She also filled him in on her books, leaving out the part about Anthony and why she'd started writing romance. She wouldn't put it past Nate to track down Anthony and give him a belated ass-walloping.

"I haven't been fair to anyone," Kelsey said, "and besides, now I can prove Ian wrong."

Nate chuckled. "I figured spite had to play a part in there somehow, but I appreciate you telling me. And telling me first. I knew I was your favorite. But romance? Really? I'm actually not surprised you write books, since you always had your nose glued to one growing up. But I'd picture you writing something with blood and maybe swords. Something violent."

Kelsey looked down at the dog snoozing on her feet, wondering if she'd done too good a job of convincing everyone that she was heartless.

"They're paranormal romances," she explained. "They have swords and knives, and sometimes guns. There's lots of blood and probably as much fighting in them as there is kissing. You should try one someday. You might be surprised how violent a romance can be."

"I'm trying one now. I just downloaded your first book."

She almost jumped off the sofa, to Puck's displeasure. "I didn't mean mine! You can't read mine. There's sex in them."

"So? You mentioned sex and violence. Honestly, Kels, you were pushing these pretty hard for someone claiming you don't want me to read them."

Kelsey flopped back on the couch. "Why do I feel like I just made a horrible mistake?"

"I have no idea."

She could hear him grinning, and her cheeks flushed, but overall, she supposed the conversation had gone well. Embarrassment aside, it was nice to know her brother wanted to support her.

"I'm still wary of how this might affect the feud," Kelsey said after enduring a couple more minutes of Nate teasing her. "But I'm also sick of letting the feud dictate my life."

And she was super sick of Ian letting it dictate his, but she pushed that thought aside. She'd managed to go more than five minutes without thinking about him.

"Yeah." Nate's tone changed, drained of all the good-natured humor. "So it's still going strong despite what Josh is doing, huh?"

"Yup. You okay?" she asked when Nate had fallen silent again.

"I'm okay. I was just hopeful when I heard about him."

Nate had been hopeful that the feud was waning? That was interesting. As kids, he'd never been as into it as she'd been, but Kelsey had always written that off to Nate's live-and-let-live attitude toward life. Before she'd been forced into the role, Nate had been the peacekeeper.

"I didn't realize you cared that much about the feud," Kelsey said. "Especially since you don't live here anymore."

"I care."

She waited for him to elaborate, but it seemed like her brother had used up all his words for the day. "And?"

"And what?"

"That's all you're going to say about it?"

"I think so," Nate said. "Maybe I'll tell you more one day, since we're sharing secrets now."

"You have a secret?"

"Got to go. There's a fire somewhere. Bye." Nate hung up on her.

Kelsey glared at the phone, 100 percent positive the only fire had been in Nate's head. She hadn't even had the chance to threaten her brother with bodily harm if he told anyone about her books.

"One down," Kelsey said, ruffling Puck's fur. The gesture made her think of how she used to do that to Ian's hair, and her throat tightened.

Kelsey gritted her teeth. Nope. Her body had to stop with that nonsense. She was healing, damn it. One more day down. One person given the truth. Her heart didn't hurt any less, but when she thought about it, her shoulders did feel lighter.

The heart, she hoped, would eventually follow.

27

IAN SWISHED A sample from the test batch of porter around in his mouth, trying to be objective. It was heavy, far heavier than a typical porter, but it would make a good winter beer. It was also extremely sweet, with hints of maple and coffee. Some people would hate that; others would love it. Ironically, the one person he'd made it for would likely never even taste it.

Misery overpowered the flavors on his tongue, and Ian swallowed the sample before he choked on it. Another week had passed without Kelsey in his life. Another week that felt wasted.

"Well?" Ian asked his friend and business partner. He'd lost all hope of objectivity. Any time he started thinking about how much he missed Kelsey, all things in his mouth turned to ash.

Micah held up his dark amber sample to the brewery lights. "I'm not sure whether I'm supposed to drink this or pour it over a stack of pancakes."

"It's strong on the maple intentionally."

"It's also as thick as syrup." Micah preferred lighter, crisper beers, so his opinion was no surprise.

Ian would drink almost anything except lagers, which was why he didn't brew those, although he liked heavy beers himself. This one might be a touch too heavy even for him, but would Kelsey have liked it? He'd abandoned all pretense of brewing this beer as a test of his skills weeks ago. The question—could he brew a beer even a non-beer-drinker liked?—had always been a poor excuse. He'd made it for Kelsey, and her alone. And now . . .

"I'm kidding!" Micah said, misinterpreting the cause of Ian's distress. "It's good for what it is, but it's definitely a sipping beer."

"It's fine." Ian set their glasses in the sink. "I don't think I'll bother scaling this one up, so never mind."

"Why not? I thought we could use more winter beers?"

They could, and he had to make smart business decisions no matter what his heart was telling him, but his heart couldn't get on board with anything that made him think of Kelsey. That wasn't an acceptable answer, though, either to himself or to Micah, so Ian turned on the water and started the dishes.

"Oh wait." Micah snapped his fingers. "This is about her, isn't it? This is the beer you made for Kelsey."

Apparently he didn't have to say anything after all.

"Let me get this straight," his friend continued. "You dumped her because dating her was interfering with your focus on the brewery, but because you dumped her, you're incapable of focusing on the brewery."

"I'm focusing fine."

"By abandoning a promising recipe because it reminds you of your ex-girlfriend?"

Ian shut off the water, in danger of breaking a glass. "What was I supposed to do? I couldn't have both."

"You know that how?" Micah crossed his arms. "The brewery is going to survive. I'm less sure about you. Or me, for that matter, since living with you has been a real joy lately, what with you acting miserable all the time."

"I'm not acting miserable all the time."

"Oy, no." Micah snapped his fingers. "It's worse than that. You know what you're acting like? Your father."

Ian stared at him. "Excuse me?"

"Isn't that what you said your father did—he put his job over the people in his life?"

Yes, that was exactly what his father had done. It was why he'd dumped Ian and Isabel on their grandparents. He'd chosen work over his children.

"It's not the same thing," Ian grumbled.

"How is it different?"

"I told you." He collapsed on one of the barstools. "The brewery needs to stay neutral in the feud, and I couldn't do that for us and be with Kelsey at the same time. I should have figured that out before I got involved with her, but I was too focused on her to see it. It was my mistake, and so it's my responsibility to get us out of this mess."

Micah shrugged. "Seems to me the mess is manageable. It isn't Kelsey's fault that people in this town have issues, and there is nothing we accomplished in the last couple of weeks that we couldn't have accomplished with her around. In fact, I'd argue that you would have been far more productive if you hadn't had your head up your mopey ass the whole time."

Ian wanted to argue, especially that last point, but Micah wasn't wrong. He'd been so lost without Kelsey (and her dogs, strangely enough) that half the time he was supposed to be focusing on work, he was thinking about her. Or sometimes he just stared into space, absorbed by the emptiness in his chest. He was supposed to have been overcome with fear and desperation for the business, but once his initial panic had subsided, it wasn't the brewery's possible fate that had dismayed him. It was missing Kelsey.

"I take it from your silence that you don't disagree," Micah said.

Ian lowered his head to the bar, wishing he hadn't tossed the rest of his beer sample. He was feeling sick, but also like he needed to get terribly drunk so he could forget how badly he'd screwed up. "I love her."

"Yeah, I figured that out." Micah thwacked him on the side of the head. "So, since you're finally removing your head from your ass, might I suggest you try telling her that?"

His friend made it sound so simple. Ian knew her better. He hadn't tried contacting Kelsey since she'd told him to leave her alone, and he wouldn't be surprised if she'd blocked his number since.

"I don't think an 'I'm sorry' is going to cut it," Ian said.

"Probably not, but I've always found it a good start." Micah grabbed his jacket. "Now, since it's Saturday and I'm supposed to be resting, I need to go home."

He kindly didn't add it, but Ian knew it was also because Micah was making plans for his latest date with Maggie.

After Micah left through the back, Ian stared at his phone. As tempting as it was to believe he could call Kelsey and make things better, he doubted it. But maybe Josh would have some insight. Kelsey's cousin had sent him a couple of messages over the last few days, and Ian had ignored them. He'd assumed Josh was telling him off for treating Kelsey like crap in that weird mafia family–

like way that seemed to be the norm in this town, but that didn't mean Josh wouldn't hear him out. It was an idea, anyway.

Before he could settle on whether this was a smart plan or a terrible one, someone knocked at the brewery's main door. Surprised out of his misery, Ian slid off the stool as he yelled, "Come in!"

A flashback to the day he'd met Kelsey popped into Ian's mind, and his heart skipped with hope for a half second that it might be her outside. Instead it was her cousin, the man he'd been considering texting, and the coincidence was unsettling.

"Sorry to bother you," Josh said, stepping inside. "I sent you a couple texts and hadn't heard back, so when I saw your truck outside, I thought I'd pop in."

"No problem. Sorry, I've been busy, but I was about done here today. What's up?" He wanted it to be news about Kelsey and also feared it would be more like a lecture about her.

Josh was looking around the almost finished tasting room and nodding. "Are you done? It looks nice."

"Mostly. Thanks." It did look nice, if he thought so himself. He'd had electricians do the wiring and plumbers take care of the sinks, but he and Micah had installed the bar and stools, built and hung the shelves, and decorated the walls. The result was a little rustic but with lots of modern touches. It fit in with the town but maintained its own style.

"So what can I help you with?" Ian asked again.

"Oh, right." Josh rubbed his neck sheepishly. "This is going to sound weird, but would you mind if I trespassed on your property later?"

"You're right. That does sound weird."

"This is where Taylor and I went on our first date, and

I was thinking it would be fun to propose to her here. In your parking lot." Josh cringed. "When I say it out loud, it doesn't actually sound that romantic, does it?"

Josh's request was so not what Ian was expecting that he had to laugh. "Not in the usual sense, no, but in your case, yes. Sure. That might be the best thing that ever happens to the parking lot."

"Great. Thanks. Now I just need the girl to say yes."

Some of Ian's laughter died away as Kelsey returned to the front of his mind. Josh wasn't worried about the feud. Nor was Taylor. They were plowing ahead despite it. "Is that really in question?"

Josh smiled. "No, but you've lived here long enough to know what a *thing* this is going to be. Porters and Lipins getting engaged? Taylor and I have discussed it, and prepared for it, but it's still going to be a bit like jumping in the bay in the middle of January. On the positive side, all the chaos we're going to cause might take some attention away from Kels. I'm not sure how aware you are, but Kelsey's as close to a celebrity as we get in Helen thanks to our family, and your brief romance and subsequent breakup have lots of people talking. She did me and Taylor a huge favor a few months ago. We might never have reached this point without her, so the timing is all the sweeter if it benefits her. "

Although Ian knew the news about their breakup had spread, he hadn't been aware that people were still talking. Another part of being an outsider—no one had clued him in to the extent of it.

"How is Kelsey?" When Josh didn't answer right away, Ian rubbed his eyes. "Do you want a drink? I need a drink."

Being talked about all over town required it, despite having wanted the news to spread.

More of the beer sample he'd drawn off was sitting in a measuring cup in the fridge, and Ian poured it into two small glasses, passing one to Josh.

Josh sipped it. "This is heavy but good."

"I was hoping to tempt Kelsey with it. See if I could make a beer drinker out of her."

Josh was silent a moment, leaving Ian to wonder whether he wanted to discuss his cousin or avoid the topic. "Kelsey's hanging in. She's tough. It's hard to know exactly what's going through her head."

"I noticed. She doesn't like to show weakness, or emotions other than anger."

"Which isn't the same as not feeling them."

Very much not. Ian had learned Kelsey felt deeply. It was one of the things he loved about her. "She has a big heart underneath her icy exterior."

"You noticed that?" Josh chuckled. "I guess you would have. You're the first person I've seen Kelsey willing to get close to in a long time. She's kind of a marshmallow beneath that skin of hers."

"Her devotion to her dogs should have been a clue."

Josh nodded. "She's good at hiding it until you realize all of her tells. I think she was annoyed that I wasn't more surprised about her writing romance."

Ian swore, aware that this was another way he'd begun imitating his father, but at least the swearing didn't hurt anyone. "She told you that?"

Josh took another sip of his beer. "I had the honor of being the second person. Well, really the third person, I guess, since technically you were the first to find out."

Ian swallowed. There was no way it was a coincidence that Kelsey had started telling her family about her writing. She had to be doing it because of what he'd said to her, and what did that mean? Had she taken his words to heart?

Was she doing it to prove to herself that she wasn't like him? The questions were going to torment him. He could ask Josh, but although Josh might be sympathetic, there was no question he was also Team Kelsey.

Ian lowered his head. "I screwed up with her, and I don't know how to fix that. I panicked and pushed her away."

Josh drained the last of his beer. "Been there, done that."

"Any advice?"

"Grovel a lot?" Josh shook his head. "Kelsey's a marshmallow, but she's a murdery marshmallow. She holds grudges amazingly well."

"Seems to be a family trait."

"It is. You're going to have to convince her that you won't make the same mistake again, and since I don't know the details about how things went down between you, I don't know how to tell you to do that. But that would be my advice."

There was no question—he would not make the same mistake twice. Once what he'd done had hit him, the brewery had become almost an afterthought. But knowing that in his heart and making Kelsey believe it were two different things.

Ian finished his beer, mulling this over. "Thanks for the pep talk, and the parking lot is yours. I hope Taylor says yes."

Grinning, Josh got up. "I'm less worried about that than I am about the fallout. But it won't be the first time we've managed to piss off everyone in town."

Ian silently wished Josh and Taylor luck with that. He, too, now had firsthand experience with pissing off the entire town.

"You know . . ." The beginnings of an idea took shape

in Ian's head. If he had to convince Kelsey he wouldn't put his work before her again, here was his opportunity. As a bonus, it was also something he could do for Josh and Taylor. "If you're considering having an engagement party and need neutral ground, feel free to use this space. We're not officially opening to the public until the spring, so it's available anytime."

"Really?" Josh took another look around. "That's a great idea. But if you're siding with us in this mess, it's going to make you some enemies."

Ian pushed down his anxiety. "I know, and I'll need to run this offer by Micah to get his approval, but I'd rather side with the love crowd than keep kissing the asses of the haters. I made the mistake of not choosing love once. I need to correct it."

"I'M STILL MAD at you, FYI," Maggie said, leaning over the table at the Espresso Express. "You know how much I read, and you never told me you write books."

Kelsey broke off a piece of the chocolate lava cake they were sharing. "It was nothing personal."

"Oh, I understand your reasons for keeping quiet. But books!" Maggie smacked Kelsey's fork away as she dug into the cake too. "Has anything truly terrible happened yet?"

Kelsey shook her head, washing down the overly rich cake with her caffè mocha. She'd filled Maggie in on her reasons for keeping her profession a secret, but as far as she could tell, her secret (that was no longer secret) had yet to spread beyond the few people she'd told. Maggie was the first who didn't count as family, since Kelsey was considering Peter to be as good as a Porter, given his engagement to Kevin. Regardless, if the news did begin to spread, it wasn't half as juicy as the news that her cousin was marrying a Lipin.

Kelsey had been as surprised as anyone when she'd heard about Josh and Taylor this morning. Not that she hadn't seen it coming eventually, but it was a brash move, and although Josh hadn't outright said so, she suspected the timing had been partly for her sake.

She liked to tell Josh it was a good thing he hadn't grown up in Helen. He was too damn nice.

"How was your date last night?" Kelsey asked. She was glad to see Maggie happy, and if her friend happened to have heard any news about Ian, well, it wouldn't be unfortunate if she shared.

"Fun. We played a lot of pool." Maggie narrowed her eyes. "Are you okay to be asking?"

"I'm fine. Why?"

Maggie shrugged and sipped her coffee. "Micah said Ian was not fine, and I don't want to talk about my love life if you're hurting."

Kelsey smiled, although the news about Ian didn't bring her the joy she wished it did. "Better than fine. If Ian is not fine, I'm extra fine."

"Uh-huh."

Was everyone capable of seeing through her ruses these days? Did letting on that she wrote romance mean people had started to assume she had a heart?

A text from Josh arrived, and Kelsey used the excuse to drop the subject, deciding she'd been wrong to think she wanted to hear about Ian. Unfortunately, if she'd wanted to put him out of her mind entirely, Josh's message had the opposite effect.

"What?" She nearly knocked over her mug and had to read the text a second time. "Josh sent me a save-the-date message for an engagement party."

"Why is that shocking?"

"It's not. It's the location. He's having it at the brewery."

"Ooh." Maggie lifted her own mug before Kelsey's flailing caused an accident. "That's a cool idea."

Cool was not the word that had popped into Kelsey's head. "Ian's going to piss off everyone if he lets them use the brewery."

"Not everyone," Maggie said. "If everyone was pissed off, there'd be no party."

Kelsey jabbed her fork into the cake, unsure whether her friend was being deliberately obtuse or if she really wasn't getting it. "Ian was stressed about losing the Lipins' business. It's why . . ." She trailed off, unable to form the words *he dumped me* without gagging on them. "I would have expected him to have been kissing up to the Lipins all this time. Making sure they know we're no longer together. But if he's letting Josh and Taylor use the brewery, it'll be for nothing. They'll be furious all over again."

Maggie's brow wrinkled. "True. Or maybe he tried ingratiating himself with the Lipins again and it didn't work, so he figured why not help your cousin?"

That was a possibility, but Kelsey didn't want to believe it. Ian had kicked her out of his life because his work was more important than she was. After doing that, how dare he not take every opportunity to put the brewery first? How dare he quit trying?

Unless he'd never been that invested in her in the first place.

Kelsey took a big sip of her drink, using it to swallow down a fresh wave of tears. She hadn't cried over Ian in days. There was no way she was getting sucked back into this pit of dejection, especially not in public.

Shifting focus, she shoved her phone aside. "I can't believe Josh would want to have the party at the brewery after what I went through with Ian. It's rude."

Never mind that her cousin was helping her. Kelsey would take anger—even unjustifiable anger—over more pain. She was sure Josh would understand.

28

THERE WAS NO amount of sugar that could heal the wounds Josh's text had reopened, although Kelsey had tried. After parting ways with Maggie, she'd bought herself a half dozen cupcakes to take home as a metaphorical bandage. If she didn't watch it, this broken heart was going to start taking a toll on her waistline, and she loathed clothes shopping, so that would be unfortunate. But hey, she could always take the dogs for another walk before dinner.

Feeling somewhat cheered up by her plan, Kelsey bounded up the path to her front door, doing her best not to jostle the cupcakes. She didn't notice that there was a paper bag sitting on her stoop until she almost kicked it over. It looked vaguely bottle-shaped, but that told her nothing, and she didn't trust it. Unlabeled, mysterious packages were reminiscent of Porter and Lipin childish pranks, so she temporarily left it alone.

"What is going on in here?" Kelsey shoved the door closed behind her, taking in the living room and the three excited dogs who immediately started barking. She was usually pretty chill about letting them on the furniture, and they normally didn't abuse that privilege, but today there were pillows scattered all over the floor and an overturned chair in the corner.

Her first thought—that someone had broken in—was quickly dismissed. The dogs were happy excited, tails wagging fiercely. As Kelsey set down the cupcake box in the kitchen, she looked for any signs that someone else had been in the house, but there were none. Kevin had a key in case of emergencies, but he wouldn't have used it without telling her, and nothing appeared out of place besides the furniture.

"Why?" she asked the dogs.

Only Juliet acted a bit remorseful. She hung her head and stretched out on the floor as though she could make herself disappear. Romeo and Puck chose to follow Kelsey around as she picked up their mess, acting like they'd done nothing wrong.

Kelsey remembered the mysterious bag as she tossed the last pillow on the sofa, and she glanced at the huskies. "Is this because someone left something on the step?" The dogs would have had a clear view of anyone approaching the door.

That Juliet and Puck were happy excited could mean anything. They were as thrilled for the mail carrier as they were for Josh or a total stranger. Romeo, on the other hand, narrowed down the options considerably. Whoever it had been, it was someone the husky liked, and that was not a long list.

Kelsey knelt in front of him and cupped his face. "Who?"

Romeo barked. It was probably a name, and so it was too bad she didn't speak dog.

"Not helpful." She opened the door and contemplated

the bag. It definitely resembled a bottle, and there was no stench emanating from it, so it was unlikely someone had left her a bag of shit.

Gingerly, Kelsey pulled it open. Inside was, in fact, a bottle, as well as an envelope. With a glance up and down the street, she snatched the bag and took it into the kitchen. There was nothing written on the envelope, so she retrieved the bottle next, which appeared to contain beer. A piece of paper was taped to it.

THE KELSEY PORTER
A LITTLE BITTER, A LOT OF SWEET.
SERVE COLD, FEEL WARM.

It took her a second to get it, but although she didn't drink the stuff, she did know that a porter was a type of beer. She'd just never made the connection between it and her last name before.

There was only one person this could be from. No wonder her dogs had gone wild. They must have been missing Ian, and then they'd seen him drop this off.

Kelsey collapsed into a chair and tore open the envelope with shaky fingers. Not that she cared what was in it. Not that anything Ian had to say would make any difference.

Unlike the label on the beer bottle, the letter was handwritten.

Dear Kelsey,

I wonder if you're even going to read this, but I have to have hope. I don't know where that leaves me in comparison to Captain Wentworth and his much beloved half hope/half agony words. I'm

*more of a miserable schmuck these days, to be
perfectly honest. Still, I've been reading that copy
of* Persuasion *you pushed on me, and following
Wentworth's example didn't seem like the worst
idea. It worked for him. It even worked for Darcy.
(See, I told you I was paying attention for all five
hours of* Pride and Prejudice.*) Anyway, I can hope
this might work for me too.*

*Speaking of hope, I hope you can read my
writing. I'm not sure when the last time I tried
writing something this long by hand was . . .*

*So, to get to the point, I'm sorry. So very sorry.
There's no way around it—I messed up badly.
When I heard the news about more businesses
canceling their orders with the brewery, I
panicked. And like people do when they panic, I
overreacted, and I hurt you in the process.*

*When I told you I'd moved on from what my
father did, I think I was trying to mislead us both.
But you were right, and I'm not as over his words
as I wish I was. I've spent most of my life
determined to prove my father wrong. I told you he
thought I'd never be successful. Never amount to
anything. I thought proving him wrong meant I
had to beat him at the only game that mattered to
him—business. Therefore any threat to the
brewery became a threat to my self-esteem and
everything I've built my life around for the last
nearly twenty years. But all that's made me do is
turn into him. I put work before people. Before
love.*

Before you.

*It's not concern about the brewery that's made
me miserable over the last couple of weeks. It's*

been missing you. You see, putting work before people has always been easy for me. It was never even an issue before, because I never cared about anyone enough to see what a mistake it was. But I knew you were trouble from the moment you first stepped foot in the brewery. I knew I should have stayed away, but I couldn't. You made me like you despite the SHS. Then you made me love you despite my every intention to not get close. You were the first woman who ever tempted me enough to break my no-relationships rule.

So now I understand failure for real. It's not about whether the brewery does well, or if it even exists in another year. Losing you would be the true failure.

I love you, Kelsey. And I'm sorry. I can't promise I won't make more mistakes, but if you'll give me a second chance, I can promise I won't make this *mistake again.*

Love,
Ian

p.s. If you won't think of me, think of all the dogs I'm not petting because I need more dog therapy.

p.p.s. Okay, we both know I don't need more dog therapy, so think of your dogs. I actually miss them too. Who knew that would be possible?

p.p.p.s. Do you think Wentworth's agony referred to his hand cramping up? Mine hurts almost as much as the rest of me.

"Oh God, you're such a dork." Kelsey clamped a hand over her mouth and squeezed her eyes shut. No surprise, her hand was getting wet. There were tears streaming down her cheeks. Damn him. She'd said she wasn't going to cry over him again, yet here she was.

This was the problem when you let someone break through your defenses. You could never rebuild them as strong as they'd been the first time. They would know you, and therefore know how to knock the walls down—faster and easier the second time, as evidenced by Ian writing her a letter. A letter! Yup, she'd let him get to know her too well.

"You're an insufferable jackass." Kelsey sniffed, and the dogs came over to lie at her feet and lick her hands.

What was she supposed to do? It wasn't that she didn't believe Ian's sincerity. She did. In fact, she thought she finally understood his motivation for allowing Josh and Taylor to hold their engagement party at the brewery. It wasn't that he'd given up trying to win back the Lipins' business. He was trying to show her that it didn't matter to him. That it was the people who did. Love and relationships came first.

Kelsey blinked, unable to stop more tears. She could sympathize with Ian's situation. She knew all too well the ability of someone else's words and behaviors to play havoc with your better sense and emotions. If Anthony wasn't proof of that, her own family surely was. In her own way, she'd grown up completely used to toxic behaviors. Her inability to trust had roots far deeper than anything Anthony had done, and she was only starting to see how much she'd misjudged people.

But second chances, even those asked for in handwritten letters, were dangerous. Ian might have been miserable these past several days, but she had been too. Kelsey wasn't sure she could subject herself to the possibility of going through this pain again.

Kelsey wasn't aware of how long she sat at the table, reading and rereading Ian's letter, but shadows moved across the kitchen with the sun's lowering angle. It was only pounding on the door that snapped her out of it. She hadn't locked it, and Kevin sauntered in before she could get up.

"Does privacy mean nothing to you?" she asked, furiously scrubbing away her dried tears with her shirt sleeve.

"What's the point? You're like my other half." He took off his shoes and lavished attention on her very-happy-to-see-him dogs.

Pulling herself more together, Kelsey stood. She should probably feed those dogs. The pre-dinner walk she'd been planning to take them on didn't appear to be happening. "Better not tell Peter that."

Kevin started to say something else, then took a good look at her and frowned. "What happened? Who do I need to beat up?"

"Ugh, what is it with you and Nate offering to beat people up for me? Do you think I'm helpless because I'm the girl? I'm perfectly capable of destroying my enemies on my own."

"You're the one looking destroyed."

She must not have done a good job with the tears. Kelsey scowled. "It's nothing."

"If you say so." Kevin picked up the bottle from Ian. "Is this nothing too?"

She snatched the letter away before her nosy twin could get his hands on everything. "No, that's called beer."

"A Kelsey porter. Cute. Wait. Is this from Ian?" When

she didn't answer, Kevin nodded to himself. "That's why you're upset."

"I'm not upset."

"Oh, please."

"Bite me." She turned her back on him and began getting out the dog food. "Where's the puppy?" If Kevin had come over to annoy her, the least he could have done was bring her a puppy to play with.

"Probably napping," her brother said. "It's a hard life chasing your tail until you collapse from exhaustion. So come on, stop lying so badly and tell me what's going on with Ian giving you beer that you won't drink."

"Hey, I'll try it." Maybe. It would have been more fun trying it with him around.

Kevin crossed his arms and stared her down.

Kelsey groaned. "He apologized. He wants me to give him a second chance. Here." She thrust the letter at her brother, because talking was getting difficult. Her throat felt like it was closing up.

She hoped Ian wouldn't mind Kevin reading it. Her brother had been through hell with their own family for getting engaged to Peter. He could relate to parental drama.

"That's actually sweet," Kevin said. "Dorky, but sweet. No wonder you like him."

Kelsey whined and set the letter back on the table.

"What are you going to do?"

"I don't know." Merely thinking about the decision made her ill. So much for her determination to not care what Ian had to say.

"Do you love him?"

"Yes." She whispered the word so as not to give the confession too much power over herself.

"Then I think you have your answer."

Kelsey snapped her head up. "It's not that simple. He hurt me. What if it happens again? I'm tired of being hurt."

Her brother looked heavenward as though she were being absurd. "Hurt happens. People screw up. Ian screwed up; you'll screw up too someday if you get back together. If you love someone and they love you, you work through the screwups together. Love requires taking risks."

Kelsey pressed her lips together in frustration. For once, she did not have a witty comeback for her brother. Kevin might as well have picked up one of her books. Those were the sort of lines she'd put in someone's mouth. Hell, she'd once used similar lines on Josh.

There was no advice more annoying than the advice you'd given others being thrown back at you.

"Look," Kevin went on, frustratingly sensible. "If you need me to make a different argument, consider this one. People will go to all kinds of ridiculous lengths to protect their dreams. For Ian, that explains his panicked reaction about the brewery. For you, it was not telling anyone— including your favorite brother—about your real career."

Wow. Kevin had just punched her and he didn't even know it. When she'd told her twin about her writing, she'd omitted the part about what Ian had said to her. So here was Kevin independently tossing out the same truth bomb as Ian. She supposed she shouldn't be surprised. Josh was too nice to let on if she'd hurt him. Nate was too calm, and Maggie wasn't family. But Kevin had given her plenty of grief when she'd confessed her secret to him.

"Since when are you my favorite brother?" Kelsey crossed her arms because it was the least defensive thing she wanted to do.

Kevin flipped her off. "My point is, your inability to trust me hurt too, you know. Ian isn't the only one who acted irrationally regarding his job."

"I'm aware. I've been fixing that mistake."

"Yes, and it's about time." Kevin picked up the beer bottle again, looking like he really wanted to open it. "But if you want even more advice—"

"No. No more advice."

He talked over her. "If you want even more advice, make Ian squirm for a while before you accept his apology. You have a rep to uphold."

"Okay, that I agree with." She snatched the beer bottle away, a new realization dawning on her. "Exactly, I have a rep. Ian and the brewery have been paying a price because of the feud. Whether it was Dad being pissed off because the guys were trying to stay out of it and he thought they owed him or it was the Lipins being pissed off because Ian and I were dating, most—maybe all—of our problems are because of the damn feud."

"So?" The huskies had finished dinner and wanted to play, so Kevin picked up the ropes and led them into the living room.

"So I'm going to make sure this shit doesn't get between us ever again. Dad wanted me to be his little warrior?" Kelsey sneered. "He's going to get that. He wanted me to date Ian to help ensure the family's legacy? He's going to get that too."

Even more than opening up to her family and Maggie, this plan made Kelsey feel better. More like normal. Her father was right about one thing—she had always been a fighter.

But until now, she'd been a fighter without a fight, and Kelsey was realizing why. It was because she'd never been motivated to fight for herself. When it was about her, she avoided conflict. That was why she'd kept her pen name a secret; it had been easier. But this time the town had come for the the people she loved, and that meant it was time to uphold her reputation, bare her claws, and create some legacy.

29

⋇————————⋇

KELSEY WAITED UNTIL Tuesday. It wasn't so much that she wanted Ian to squirm for an extra twenty-four hours, although she kind of did. But by waiting until Tuesday, she could put her plan into action in person.

In person struck her as key. She might not look intimidating, but if she wanted to start asserting her influence, she had to make it clear that her appearance was meaningless. It didn't matter how short or cherubic she looked. This angel came carrying a flaming sword.

Sadly, one that was only metaphorical. Literally, Kelsey came carrying the beer from Ian.

Frankie's Fish Café was a Helen institution that dated back over a decade before she was born. Loved by locals and tourists alike, it was one of the handful of restaurants in town that stayed open year-round. Tuesday during lunch, Kelsey knew the current Frank would be there.

Frank Porter was one of her father's cousins, and he'd been among the first of the Porter business owners to cancel their orders with Northern Charm Brewing after her father had thrown a hissy fit. He had influence—perhaps not as much as her father, but plenty as the second-generation owner of Frankie's.

Somewhere in the research she'd done for her book series, Kelsey had read that in nature, predators hunted the weak because they were easier to kill. She didn't have time for that. If this was one of her stories, she was one alpha challenging another alpha. Win, and she got control of the pack.

Noon at the restaurant was pretty quiet midweek in early October. Kelsey took a seat at the bar and waited for the bartender to find Frank. Her father's cousin emerged from a back room a minute later, clearly surprised to see her.

There was additional symbolic value in approaching Frank rather than any of her other, more distant, relatives. Despite only being cousins, Frank and her father looked a lot alike. Her father was shorter and sported less of a gut, but the resemblance was uncanny. Personality-wise, Frank had always seemed more laid back and friendly, but that might have been because he hadn't needed to parent her. He could be the genial not-uncle. Regardless, talking to him felt an awful lot like talking to her father.

"Kels, what can I do for you?" Frank leaned over the bar.

Kelsey pushed the unopened beer toward him. "You can reinstate your order with the brewery. Look at that."

The bottle didn't have the official Northern Charm label, but Ian had included the brewery name and logo on it.

Frank chuckled. "You convinced them to name a beer after you, huh?"

"I didn't have to convince anyone. I don't even drink beer. My point in showing you this is to remind you that the brewery is on our side. They support *me*." She pointed to her chest for emphasis. "Supporting me means supporting the family. There's no beer named after a Lipin."

"Ah, Kels." Frank rubbed his whiskers. "You know it's not that simple."

"Actually, it is. The brewery has been doing business with both our family and the Lipins, like many of the unique businesses in this town. Also, the brewery is on track to be extremely successful. The way I see it, our family can either share in that success, or we can watch as the Lipins form an exclusive relationship with them."

Kelsey had heard from Maggie, who'd heard from Micah, that the Bay Song Inn was holding to their promotional deal with the brewery. With Lydia Lipin on their side, Kelsey expected other Lipin businesses would slowly get back on board. Assuming they hadn't already done so after learning that Ian had dumped her, that was.

"The brewery is an up-and-coming business in this town that's bound to draw good press and lots of tourist money," Kelsey continued. "Do you want to be left behind?"

Frank sighed. "I don't disagree, but your father—"

"My father forgets that I'm dating Ian." Which would be news to Ian at this point (never mind the Lipins), but she'd address that next. What was important here was that Frank was willing to think like a business owner and not a feud soldier. Or rather, she needed him to think like both. Only this time, instead of taking orders from her father the general, she needed to convince Frank to take *suggestions* from her.

Kelsey leaned closer and lowered her voice dramatically to drive home what she considered to be the killer attack. "If the brewery isn't successful enough to stay open, Theresa Lipin and the Save Helen Society win. They'll have had a taste of victory, driving out a new business that could have benefited this town. They won't stop there. If anything, they'll become bolder. The mayor's anti-development policy moves forward, and the people living here suffer economically. The Lipins win; we lose."

The words left a bitter taste on her tongue, given her real opinion about how much development Helen deserved, but for Ian's sake, they were worth it. Besides, like she'd admitted to him weeks ago—it wasn't as if the brewery was another chain store or franchise destroying the local families. The town really was likely to benefit from their presence.

"That's a good point too." Frank was back at rubbing his chin, and Kelsey was pretty sure she had him.

"My dad isn't infallible, and he doesn't run the family. You should feel free to do what you think is best for the restaurant, and you can do it knowing it sticks a knife into the Lipins' plans."

Okay, that might have been laying it on a bit thick, considering she was tired of the feud, but she wasn't above doing what had to be done.

Frank shook his head, a bemused smile on his face, and Kelsey got the sense he was seeing her for possibly the first time. She was no longer Wallace's cute little girl. She was his goddamn legacy, and if this was what it took to get some semblance of peace around this place, then so be it.

Especially if that peace was going to benefit Ian.

WITH A START, Ian realized he'd been staring at a wall for who knew how long. It had been two days since he'd left the beer and a letter for Kelsey. Two days, and he hadn't gotten so much as a text acknowledging that she'd received them. Probably she didn't have his number anymore. But if that was true, then how would he know she'd gotten them? Someone could have stolen the bag off her front step.

For the hundredth time, Ian debated texting her. Just to ask— Did you get it? If she had, he'd leave it at that. There was his answer.

For the hundredth time, he dismissed this idea as too needy. And anyway, if she had gotten his letter and wasn't going to accept his apology, did he want to know? He could live in hope—cruel, agonizing hope—for a couple more days this way. He could tell himself she hadn't rejected his apology; she simply hadn't seen it.

Or what if his apology hadn't been enough? He was the one who'd told her that no one should be under any obligation to accept an apology, particularly if the person in the wrong had made no effort to correct their mistake. Ian had hoped offering up the brewery to Josh and Taylor would be evidence that he was trying to do the right thing, but Kelsey could have a different opinion.

He had to get up and move. He was in no state to work.

Micah found him pacing the brewery's back room when he returned with lunch. "Hard at work, are you?"

"I'm thinking."

"About Kelsey or about beer?"

Ian shot him a disgruntled glance.

"About Kelsey, I see." Micah held up a bag with fish tacos. "Might as well eat, then. You've probably paced and sweated away breakfast."

Micah wasn't wrong, but he hadn't had much of an appetite for a while.

Ian followed his friend into the tasting room, where they could sit, eat, and presumably talk about something other than his misery. Work would be good. If he couldn't concentrate on his own, maybe Micah could force him to.

Micah had no sooner set the bag on the bar, though, before his phone rang. "That's interesting."

Ian didn't have a chance to ask what it was before Micah answered, so he started going through the food.

"Yeah, I think we can do that." Micah turned to Ian and made a hand gesture that Ian couldn't translate. "I'll have to double-check, but I can get back to you today. Obviously we started lining up other buyers."

Ian sat up straighter. "What was that?" he asked after his friend hung up.

"That was Frank Porter asking if we could un-cancel his purchase order for the café." Micah pulled one of the packages of tacos closer. "Says he realized he acted too hastily and hopes we can continue working together."

"That's . . ." Ian faltered, searching for the right word. *Odd? Encouraging?* He had no idea.

"My feelings exactly," Micah said. "But I'll take it. Speaking of which, we need to make sure we can fulfill the order, and if not, start negotiating a new one."

Ian nodded, his thoughts racing. He could look up that information, but his brain was too busy making leaps of logic. Could Kelsey have had something to do with this? That sounded like wishful thinking, and yet there had to be some reason behind the sudden reversal of their biggest Porter family contract.

In a daze, he unwrapped his fish taco and proceeded to stare at it until someone knocked on the brewery's main door. Since he couldn't seem to focus enough to eat, he left Micah at the bar to answer it.

Kelsey stood on the steps, her ponytail whipping about in the chilly wind. Ian immediately glanced toward her feet, looking for the dogs, but they weren't there. He wasn't having a flashback to the day they met. She was actually here, for real.

His heart skipped a beat as his wishful thinking no longer seemed so wishful. Then again, there was an arrogant tilt in her chin and a challenge in her blue eyes. His heart might be getting ahead of reality. But she was still here, still the same mess of contradictions—hard and soft, sweet and bitter—that he'd come to love.

"We need to talk." Kelsey stuck her hands on her hips.

Talk, yes. That was a positive sign. Only Ian's tongue felt heavy and useless, and all he wanted to do was drop to his knees and apologize.

Maybe not in front of Micah though.

Ian stepped outside, heedless of the cold seeping through his flannel, and shut the door behind him. "Kelsey."

"Stop." She held up a hand. "Did Frank call you?"

He nodded, and she cut him off a second time.

"That's because I can help you. I'm not sure I should help you, but I can. And you never gave me the chance. We never got to try acting like a team."

"I know, and I'm sorry." He did collapse to the steps. It wasn't quite to his knees, but the pressure of standing—or maybe it was the weight of his guilt for hurting her—was too much, and he dropped to an awkward crouch by her feet. "I panicked, and I messed up."

"Yes, you did." Kelsey sighed and bent down to kiss the top of his head. "But as it's been pointed out to me recently, I wasn't exactly in a position where I could judge you too harshly for it. I don't know if I'd have even told you about my job by now if you hadn't found out yourself. And, well, I know a thing or two about having your head messed with. It's never as easy to let go as we think it should be. Basically, I'm saying I forgive you."

It was a good thing he was already practically kissing the concrete, because the ground was swaying. Ian closed his eyes, overwhelmed by the tide of emotions crashing over him. "I shouldn't have said what I did about your writing. Our situations aren't the same, and it wasn't fair."

"No, they're not, but you weren't wrong. Turns out people *were* hurt that I'd been lying to them." Kelsey sounded mildly surprised by that. "But if you want to grovel a bit more while you're down there, I won't say no to it."

Some of Ian's relief escaped him in a laugh. He wrapped his arms around Kelsey's legs and pressed kisses to her knees.

She laughed as she wobbled. "Never mind. As amusing as this is, maybe it's not a great idea."

Probably not when it came to stability, but now that he was holding her, Ian didn't want to let her go to stand up. "I guess we can resume this position later. I've read enough of your books to know you appreciate a good grovel, and I can do this better if you're naked."

"I'm holding you to that."

As if he'd renege on that sort of promise.

Ian blinked, trying to ignore the mist in his eyes, and stood. Kelsey looked wobbly all over, smiling but also with some definite wetness clouding her eyes. Damn this Helen weather. It wasn't even raining today.

"Kelsey." He traced his thumb over her cheek, as though his heart was struggling to catch up with the fact that she was truly in front of him.

"Shut up and kiss me."

"You're so demanding." But he did as asked, gleefully and greedily, relishing the luck that had brought her to knock on his door. A first time, and this second time.

There would never be a third time, because from now on, that door would always be open to her.

Kelsey's hands curled around his shirt, driving home how cold the air was, but he couldn't let go.

"You like me demanding," she said at last before kissing his chin.

"No. I love everything about you."

She closed her eyes, her smile actually making her look angelic in that moment. Not that he'd ever tell her that. "I love you, too, but especially your letter writing skills."

Ian pulled her closer. "Would your love for me diminish if I told you I typed up a draft so I could plan out what to say?"

"I'll overlook it. Does your love of everything about me include my dogs?"

He laughed and grabbed her mouth with his. "I wasn't lying when I said I missed them. Are they here?"

He was a little sorry he'd asked when Kelsey pulled away, but she tugged him over to her SUV, where the dogs were waiting. "I think they missed you too."

Romeo started barking his head off before Kelsey could even open the door, and she let the huskies out into the empty parking lot. Immediately, they started jumping all over him, licking his face and hands, vying for his attention. How he'd gotten to the point where their excitement brought a smile to his face, Ian wasn't sure. It all seemed like it had happened so quickly. From the moment Kelsey had scowled and snarked her way into his life, nothing had been the same. And he couldn't be happier for it.

This town might have issues, but it also had some wonder in it, and he no longer worried about his sister possibly joining him up here and being miserable. But he didn't need her to join him, either, if she chose not to. He was finding his own pack.

"The dogs are part of our team, right?" Ian asked.

"Absolutely. You can't have me without them." She made an apologetic face. "You also can't have me without the feud."

That much was clear. "You're worth it. I ran to the other side of the continent to get away from some of my family. It didn't work out like I'd intended, and I ended up running from you. I'm done running. I'm here for you, regardless of family or work or whatever life throws at us next. Like I told Josh the other day, I've picked a side—and it's not going to be your family or the Lipins. It's going to be the side of doing things for love, and we'll deal with the consequences."

"Good." Kelsey grabbed his hands away from the dogs, who were circling the two of them. "I've been running, too, in my own way. Running and hiding. But I'm done with that. From now on, we're fighting together."

"Promise." He yanked her closer and kissed her again. If this was fighting, he could get used to it.

"You write really nice letters, and you kiss really well," Kelsey said, burying her face against him. "I'm going to expect lots of both to keep morale up."

"Consider it done." Although the thought of writing more by hand made him wince, he'd do it if it made her happy. "You know what else I do really well?"

"Actually, why yes. I do." She slid her hands into his waistband.

Ian's body stirred. The rush of blood dulled the chill against his skin. "Well, thank you, but I was actually thinking—brew beer. Did you try the one I gave you?"

"Nope. I thought I'd save it and try it when you were around."

"I like that plan. I like *both* plans." He caught her hands as her fingers rubbed his stomach. Hopefully Micah could check whatever supply numbers were needed to give to Frank. He was clearly not going back to work today. "The beer can wait though. As promised, from now on, you will always be my first priority."

30

THE ENGAGEMENT PARTY for Josh and Taylor was, by Helen standards, a raging success. Of course, for that to be true, it only required that no blood was spilled. Still, Kelsey was feeling pretty good about it as she watched members of both families cautiously circle one another and the food like two wolf packs, uncertain about this whole idea of sharing a meal.

There was a warm, content feeling in her chest that made it easy for her to be on her best behavior. It could be from seeing her cousin happy, or it could be the possibility of peace due to her generation of Porters and Lipins being more levelheaded than their forebears. Most likely, though, it was due to the past month's freedom. Freedom from worrying about her secret being revealed. Freedom from feeling guilty about what the feud did to innocent outsiders. And freedom to simply be with Ian. To be able to enjoy his company without creating elaborate excuses for their time together or why she got all giddy when he kissed her.

She didn't even mind when Josh teased her about losing her edge. She *had* lost her edge, and she didn't miss it. Ian calmed her prickly thoughts and occupied her sharp tongue with far more pleasurable activities than trash-talking. At least he did in private, or the relative privacy of someplace like this party where she could afford to let her walls down. She hadn't spent years perfecting her drop-dead scowl to abandon it after a month of relationship bliss, after all. Life in Helen remained tumultuous, to put it nicely, and Kelsey remained on alert for the occasions when she had to kick some ass. That was just no longer her default state of mind.

"Happy?" The reason for this unexpected change in her life slipped his arms around her from behind, and Kelsey settled herself against Ian.

Officially, her stance would remain that she could take or leave tall men since almost everyone was taller than her, but there was definitely pleasure in being held by a guy whose body seemed capable of containing her own.

"I am." She wiggled against him, knowing the effect it would have. Predictably, Ian's grip on her stiffened.

It was a small group that had gathered, but they were the important ones—Josh and Taylor, naturally, Taylor's sister Lydia, Kevin and Peter, Micah and Maggie, and a few other friends of the future bride and groom. A couple of the more courageous cousins on both sides had stopped by, too, and although he hadn't attended, Frank had helped out with the catering. Even Nate had called earlier to offer his congratulations.

"Are you trying to tempt me?" Ian whispered in her ear.

"Always. Is it working?"

"Always." He kissed the ear he'd been whispering in, causing shivers to run down her neck. "But patience. We shouldn't be sneaking out to have sex by the brew tanks."

Sex by the brew tanks. There was an idea. "It might help me develop more positive associations with beer."

She'd tried the one Ian had made for her, and while it was drinkable, her taste buds weren't excited about quaffing an entire glass's worth. So for now, she was content to sip small amounts of the various beers he suggested, and they were slowly growing on her.

Ian smacked her ass, discreetly, but it was enough to make her determined to have revenge later. "I'm winning you over without any underhanded tricks. Admit it."

She grinned. He was, but the idea was now set in her head. "Fine. Sex by the brew tanks can wait until after the party."

"There are a lot of tanks. Just so you know."

Kelsey raised an eyebrow at him. "Is that a problem?"

"Nope. But when I say *tanks*, you should know I'm referring to them as individual locations. In fact, I'll be starting a new beer soon. So once we make it through these batches, we'll have to start all over again."

"This sounds like a plan that could take some time."

He kissed her neck, tickling her and pulling her close. "A very long, never-ending time, I hope."

ACKNOWLEDGMENTS

Thank you to my wonderful agent, Rebecca Strauss, who throughout this process has been part agent, part brainstormer extraordinaire, and occasional therapist. I couldn't have done this without you.

Thank you to my fantastic editor and pun-master, Sarah Blumenstock, for getting this story and for the amazing notes that helped me take it to the next level. And also thanks to Natalie Sellers, Stephanie Felty, Martha Cipolla, Farjana Yasmin, Rita Frangie, and the entire Berkley team working behind the scenes who bring these books to life.

Writing is a solitary endeavor, but publishing is an experience that requires lots of support. Thanks to my online writing friends and to my writing groups—the Purgies, the Y-Nots, and the Berkletes debut crew—for the insights, the laughs, the commiseration, and the occasional poop joke (not naming names, but she knows who she is).

And last but never least, thank you to my husband and my family for always being there.

Don't miss

LOVE AND
LET BARK

Coming Fall 2021 from Jove!

IT HAD BEEN a long day even before her refrigerator died. Lydia glared at the errant appliance as she refilled her cat's water dish, and water spilled over the sides. Because of course it did.

Cursing to herself, Lydia set the dish down and dried her hands on her flannel pajama pants. Luckily, she wasn't much of a cook, so a dead fridge was more of an inconvenience than a tragedy. The few items she kept in it had been moved to the inn's kitchen, and that was where they'd stay until a new one was delivered. The rest of the day's troubles had been far more annoying, culminating in a section of guests' rooms where the heat had gone out.

She'd been able to move the guests into vacant rooms with working heaters, but although they'd been in good spirits about it, such a problem did nothing for the hotel's normally stellar reputation. On top of it, Lydia had to get someone to come out to fix the issue. The Bay Song was small enough that there was only one dedicated maintenance worker, and he typically contracted out HVAC issues. Since Ralph was out sick, Lydia had to deal with the contractors herself, and they'd treated her call with suspicion. Was she sure the heat wasn't working? Had she just done something silly like forget to bump up the thermostat? After she'd snapped at the man on the phone that having ovaries did not lower someone's IQ, he'd apologized, but still. She had not been in a mood for dealing with a dead fridge after work.

For that, however, there was wine. When Lydia had taken her few staples (mostly cheese) down to the inn kitchen, she'd left a bottle of pinot grigio to chill on the tiny deck outside her door. Living in the apartment above the inn's main building had the occasional drawback—namely, work never really went away—but at times it was awfully convenient as well.

Yawning, she retrieved a wineglass and pondered what to watch on TV while she pretended the day hadn't happened. It had to be mindless and low stress. That made a reality show a good bet.

"So what should it be, Merlot?" Lydia called over her shoulder to her cat. "*The Great British Baking Show* or *Queer Eye*?"

Merlot, who was getting up there in age and was no less crabby for it, jumped off his favorite windowsill and took up residence on the sofa. Lydia supposed that was the best she could hope for as an answer. She loved the tabby dearly, but he'd never been much of a conversationalist.

"You're right," she said to herself. "*The Baking Show*'s stakes are too high for my blood pressure. *Queer Eye* it is."

Merlot blinked at her, which seemed like proof of agreement.

Lord, she was becoming pathetic. Lydia suspected all people talked to their pets like this, but the fact that Merlot was the only constant male companion in her life was another story. To be fair, he set a high bar. He kept his messes confined to the litter box, didn't hog the blankets, and if he had unwanted opinions about her appearance or homemaking skills, he kept them to himself. She couldn't very well expect the average human male to compete, and she'd pretty much given up hope of finding one who could. Cody might make for an interesting diversion while he was around, but Lydia wasn't overly optimistic about his chances.

She grabbed the giant cardigan she kept by the door before opening it to get the wine. The sweater had belonged to her grandfather, and she'd inherited it along with the apartment. It was old, green, and becoming pocked with holes, but it reminded Lydia of its former owner, as well as being soft and warm. Evenings like this, cozy was far more important than stylish.

A cold wind blew her hair back. It was a rare mostly clear evening. The ever-present dimness of winter had become full dark hours ago, but moonlight filled the sky, and the inn's lights illuminated the paths below her. During the light hours, if she squinted, she might be able to make out the bay and the lines and lines of boats in the harbor. But at night, all she could see were dark trees swaying in the breeze.

She'd left the wine bottle right by the door so she wouldn't have to put on shoes to grab it, but as Lydia reached over, a scuttling sound drew her attention. Hand on the bottle's neck, she searched for the source but saw nothing. It was probably a bird or a squirrel in the trees. Unless it got inside the inn somehow—and God forbid, she'd have enough to deal with today—Lydia paid it no more heed.

Merlot, on the other hand, was extremely interested. Before Lydia could shut the door, he shot past her, a streak of orange fur disappearing down the wooden stairwell to the ground.

Shit. Lydia almost screamed out the word in frustration. Merlot getting out was exactly what she needed to end a wonderful day.

"Merlot!" She called after him once, then twice, but didn't bother a third time. It wasn't like he ever came when called. "Damn it."

She knew exactly where the furball had gone. Winding paths threaded through the trees around the inn, and on one of them between the inn and the Tavern was a metal bench. For some reason, Merlot liked to curl up on it after he got bored chasing whatever prey he found. Not that Lydia ever intentionally let him outside, mind. Merlot might fancy himself the big, bad predator, but he was a tiny snack for too many creatures in the area.

Muttering under her breath, she stuck her bare feet in fleece boots, wrapped the cardigan tighter around herself, and trudged out. One downside to her male companion being a cat and not a human was that she'd feel guilty shutting the door on him and locking him out overnight.

The evening air was biting, yet on the warmer side for late January. It got plenty cold in Helen, but the climate was a far cry from places like Fairbanks, where her maternal grandparents lived. She didn't want to be outside long without a coat, but as long as she kept moving, frostbite wasn't an immediate concern.

"Merlot!" Although futile, Lydia couldn't help but continue to call out his name as she traipsed down the steps. At least it was winter and she was unlikely to run into any guests going for a late evening stroll around the hotel grounds, seeing her dressed in her frumpy finest.

Lydia picked up her pace, hoping to get to Merlot faster and to ward off the chill. Gravel and dried leaves crunched under her feet, but the path was dry. Remnants of the last snow lingered in the brush, too covered in dirt to glisten in the lamplight. She made the turn through the trees, expecting to find her beloved cat sitting on the bench, probably proud of himself for sneaking out, and found something startling instead—a man, bending over her cat, while two dogs chased their tails in circles around his legs.

Not just dogs actually. Puppies. And not just any breed of puppies. Husky puppies.

Lydia tensed. Huskies were a popular breed, but in Helen, huskies usually meant their owner was a Porter. The joke around town was that all combined, the Porters owned enough huskies to field multiple Iditarod sled teams. Lydia didn't get the obsession, but then Lipins were cat people. Why, she couldn't say anymore than she could understand the link between Porters and huskies. Supposedly, the feud had something to do with it. If the tales were to be believed, one of her ancestors had tried stealing some Porter's sled dog. But that sounded like nonsense.

Regardless, happy, cute puppies—and they were cute; she could acknowledge that despite her genes—were not the problem. The problem was that someone, possibly an enemy, was walking his dogs on her property and picking up her cat. And Merlot, the traitor, was allowing it. Lydia wasn't sure which part of this entire adventure was more surprising.

This section of path was dimly lit, and the man's face was cast in shadow as he coaxed Merlot into his arms, but he was broad beneath his coat, and tall. Sturdy boots poked out from a pair of weathered jeans, and he wore a knit cap on his head that matched her cardigan, in terms of having seen better days. He also appeared to have a sling on his left arm, not that he was letting that get in the way of cat-napping her purring fluffypants.

The puppies had noticed her and were straining toward her in excitement, but the guy ignored their barking while maintaining his hold on the leashes. Lydia couldn't hear him, but she was pretty sure he was whispering to Merlot to get him to behave.

Surprise had rendered Lydia temporarily speechless, but she should say something to the cat-whisperer before he absconded with her only male companion. "Hey! That's my cat."

What it lacked in eloquence, it made up for in directness. Nothing more should be expected of a woman wrapped in an old cardigan and wearing pajama pants in subfreezing weather. Especially not when she'd had a long day.

"Oh, good. Then let me hand him back to you. I was afraid he'd run off and freeze out here overnight." The cat-napper-whisperer straightened with Merlot in his arms, and turned.

For a second time, surprise left Lydia gaping. "Nate?"

So it *was* a Porter on the hotel property. Lydia hadn't seen Nate up close in over a decade, but some people couldn't be forgotten. In fact, being unable to forget Nate had been a persistent problem in her life. She thought about him way too much and had inevitably compared every guy she dated to him. Or if not to him exactly, then to an idealized memory of him. It was easy to put someone you'd lost contact with on a pedestal, and even easier to use that memory as a way to dismiss others for not living up to an unobtainable standard.

Seeing Nate, however, made it clear that not everything she'd chosen to focus on about him had been idealized. He'd aged, certainly, but in a way that only made him more appealing. Though his heavy coat hid everything below the neck, his jaw line had somehow become stronger, and his eyes remained the same smoky blue—a trait shared by most Porters. Teenage Lydia had always thought he was cute, and adult Lydia saw no reason to revise that opinion, although she might choose a different descriptor. *Ruggedly handsome* would do.

Acknowledging this caused a butterfly to flap its wings in her gut, and she didn't like that at all.

"Lydia." Nate's eyes opened wide, and he almost dropped her cat. Swearing, he readjusted his grip and winced as the movement probably hurt the arm in the sling.

"Yeah, hi." She pulled her cardigan more tightly around herself. Strangely, she was no longer feeling as cold, but she'd become super aware of her disheveled state. "I'll take him."

"You'll take? Oh." Nate shook himself and placed Merlot in her outstretched arms.

Puppies nipped at her ankles, but Nate's face was so close that Lydia scarcely noticed. There was a day's worth of stubble on his cheeks, and he smelled like . . . Well, she didn't know what, but it was musky and warm, and that damned butterfly was spawning an army of followers. She should have chosen to focus on the puppies instead.

Lydia snuggled Merlot close to her chest, both for warmth and for the way his body covered some of her fashion sins. "Thanks. He used to be such a skittish kitten, but he lost his fear of death a few years ago, and now he loves to escape."

"No problem." Nate took a large step backward, nearly tripping over his dogs. "Feel free to make your own joke about firefighters rescuing cats."

She hadn't forgotten Nate was a firefighter, but recalling it did nothing to quell the butterfly infestation. The demands of his job probably entailed that his coat was hiding a body every bit as appealing as his face.

Lydia smiled, thankful her cheeks already felt flushed from the cold. "Does the job explain your arm?"

Again, Nate seemed startled by her question. "No, actually. Nothing so interesting. That was a car accident."

"Sorry."

He shrugged with one arm. "I got off lightly, all things considered."

Merlot dug a claw into Lydia's chest, and she tried to gently remove it without drawing attention to her boobs. "Are you staying with your parents?"

The question she really wanted to ask was why he was walking his puppies around her hotel, but that seemed confrontational, and Lydia was not confrontational. Particularly when her body had abandoned her better sense. She had her cat. She was cold and underdressed. And yet instead of running back to her apartment, she was trying to prolong this conversation.

If she and Nate were two other people reconnecting after years apart, she'd think nothing of exchanging phone numbers and planning to meet up while he was in town. But they were not two other people, and that was undoubtedly why they'd lost touch to begin with. So talking to Nate while she had the chance, even if it was in the cold and dark, was the only sensible solution. When they'd gotten together secretly in high school, they'd always had to be sneaky. Nothing had changed since then.

Well, some things had changed. Nate was even more attractive now than he'd been then. That stubble on his jaw had her licking the back of her teeth since she couldn't lick *it*.

Lord, she was definitely pathetic. She was literally freezing her fingers off so she could soak up the sight of the man who'd once fueled her fantasies.

The way Nate laughed at her question gave Lydia her

answer before he responded. "No, much to my mother's dismay. My family owns those rental cabins down the road. Most are empty for the winter, so I'm staying in one of them. There's only so much family I can take, you know, and my mother stayed with me for the week right after the accident, so it's been a lot already." He shut his mouth abruptly, as if shocked by the torrent of words that had poured out.

Lydia bit her lip to keep from laughing. From Nate, it had been quite a speech. "I know those cabins."

Ugh. Brilliant response. Of course she knew those cabins. That Nate was staying in one of them kind of explained why he might be walking his dogs around the hotel, but not entirely. She'd assume it was because of the path lights. It would be quite dark in the trees; not an ideal location to be walking a couple of energetic puppies.

She started to ask about the dogs, but Merlot chose that moment to dig his other claw into her arm, and the poor cardigan did not provide much armor against that sort of assault. Her cat had to be cold. For that matter, so was she, and Lydia shivered.

"I've kept you," Nate said. "Sorry."

"No, it's okay."

"You're not even wearing a jacket. Here." He pulled his hat off and fitted it over her head. Once more, his nearness set Lydia's nerves on high alert. His hand was gentle, tugging the hat down over her hair and ears, and Lydia closed her eyes. If she hadn't been holding Merlot, she told herself she'd have protested. But she was, and Lydia didn't know if she was lying to herself. There was something so familiar about the way Nate wanted to take care of her, but she had to remember this was just Nate. He wanted to take care of everyone he met. It had nothing to do with any residual feelings or attraction he might have to her. And that was for the best.

Still, the heat from Nate's body seemed to wrap around her like a blanket, and the chill resettled under her clothes as he stepped away too quickly. "Thanks again."

Nate smiled. "No problem. Now get inside before you get any colder. Your cheeks are bright red."

Her nose probably was, too, but Nate was too kind to mention it.

One of the puppies raised its fluffy head at that moment and barked into the trees, and Nate sighed. "I hope I tired these guys out enough that they might let me sleep. Good night, Lydia. It was nice to run into you."

"Yeah, you too." She nuzzled her chin against Merlot's fur as Nate turned to leave.

A few minutes later, Lydia shut her apartment door with little memory of how she got back. An ungrateful Merlot swatted her with his tail before reclaiming his spot on the couch, but she stood by the door a moment longer, clutching the wine but no longer feeling the need to drink any. Her head felt light enough.

"This is absurd." Lydia shook herself, trying to toss off the adrenaline rush. It was only the cold having this effect on her. Once she warmed up, her nerves would settle. She'd realize running into Nate had not been such a significant event, but rather something inevitable given the size of the town, and not at all meaningful. She'd been flustered from surprise and nothing more.

Which didn't explain why she sniffed his hat when she removed it, hoping to catch a trace of him in its wool fibers.

Fine. She apparently found him attractive. Whatever. He had been attractive then, and he was attractive now. Plenty of men were attractive. That was also not significant.

Lightheaded or not, she should probably have that glass of wine anyway.

WELL, SHIT. THAT had not gone the way Nate had imagined it would.

Back at the cabin, he let the little monsters off their leashes, and took some comfort that the long, late walk seemed to have done the trick where they were concerned. They dashed about the downstairs before collapsing on the rug by the wood stove. It figured that they'd probably sleep tonight while he'd lie awake thinking about Lydia.

He'd been back in town for two days and was still unsure of how to approach her. Running into her while walking his dogs, however, had not been part of any of the plans he'd concocted and dismissed. The idea to walk the puppies around the hotel paths had undoubtedly been because Lydia was on his mind, but they were also well lit and so they'd seemed ideal. Since most people didn't go for random nighttime walks in an Alaskan winter, and Lydia wouldn't have dogs to make the behavior less random but more of a necessity, Nate had assumed he wouldn't disturb anyone.

Technically the hotel paths were private property, and Lydia had every right to kick him off them, but Nate hadn't worried about that. And if another staff person saw him, it was unlikely he'd be recognized at this point. He could just play lost and confused, like any number of tourists. He was almost surprised that Lydia *had* recognized him.

She, on the other hand, hadn't changed a bit. Her face had matured, as presumably had the rest of her. Though he couldn't tell, he'd no doubt be thinking about it later. Either way, she remained the most beautiful woman he'd ever seen. Her dark hair and eyes had set off the flush of cold on her pale cheeks, turning her into a creature out of a fairy tale as she stood among the dim trees—equal parts sweet princess and seductive witch. Just the memory of her grateful smile as she took her cat from him had his mouth going dry.

He'd rambled. Actually rambled in front of her. Christ.

It was fair to say his plan to get closure by showing himself that he was over Lydia Lipin had been a failure in every conceivable way.

Also, he needed to stop reading those damn paranormal romance novels Kelsey wrote because those stories were obviously affecting his brain.

Nate hung up the leashes on hooks by the door, and placed his coat next to them. Reaching for his hat, he recalled that he'd handed it over to Lydia along with the wayward cat. He supposed that gave him an excuse to track her down again, so that was something. He wasn't devious enough to have given it to her on purpose, but he wasn't above using any opportunities that came his way. At the time, though, she'd just looked so cold. He'd have given her his coat, too, if getting it on and off with his sling hadn't been such a pain.

"You're such a dumbass," he muttered to himself, and the confession was punctuated by puppy snores.

Nate hadn't considered that visiting Helen and tracking down Lydia would be a risk, but it wouldn't be the first time he'd misjudged a situation. At least this risk didn't endanger more than his emotions. He would have just preferred to realize he was risking more than his family's overbearing attentions by coming home.

While the puppies snoozed, he adjusted his sling and made himself a cup of mint tea in the cabin's tiny kitchen. The tea would warm him up, then he'd go up to the loft where his bed was and watch something suitably loud and obnoxious on Netflix. Something that would keep his mind off Lydia.

But he didn't make it past the tea steeping before his thoughts returned to her because the reminders were everywhere. Even the cabin's dark wood-paneled walls reminded him of a lean-to on one of the nearby trails. During the summer after graduation, he and Lydia had hiked out there a couple times since they couldn't hang out together where they'd be seen. She'd liked to sketch the trees, the fallen leaves, the pine cones—anything she could find on the ground. The father of one of Nate's friends had made and sold wood carvings to tourists, and he'd taught Nate enough to make him curious to try it. So he'd sit out there next to Lydia, occasionally shaving a tree branch but mostly watching her.

The way her deft fingers danced over the paper.

The way her brow furrowed in concentration as she struggled to capture something.

The adorable sigh of discontent she made when she became frustrated with her fingers' inability to capture whatever greatness lurked in her head.

Even the so-called worst of her drawings amazed Nate. He'd compliment her skill—and mean it—and he'd show her his abysmal attempts at wood carving, and she'd laugh and tell him he simply needed more practice. But he'd never told her that the only reason he bothered was because it gave him something to do while he sneaked glances at her. Because he'd wanted to spend as much time with her as possible that summer before she left for college. Because he'd just won her over after all those years, and he didn't know how to keep her thanks to circumstances beyond their control.

There had probably been less pine in the woods than there was in his heart.

His chest constricted with the memory, and Nate poked himself in the ribs. They were feeling much better, but were still sore enough that the pain could cut through his mental bullshit.

Yup, he'd really done a great job of screwing himself over by coming home, if Memory Lane was the road he was headed down.

Nate dumped his tea bag in the trash, and gingerly carried his mug up the creaky steps to the loft. By the stove, Dolly rolled over in her sleep, but the monsters remained conked out. No way would he be so lucky.

It was just nostalgia coupled with a strong physical attraction, he told himself. Their body chemistry hadn't changed, but why would it have? No question everything else about them *had* changed, and that was important to remember. When he got his hat back, those changes would become clearer. He'd make sure of it. He'd grill Lydia on the last ten years if needed. And once he realized how different they'd become and that she was no longer his vision of the perfect girl, the physical attraction would relent.

Past would give way to present, and eventually he'd be able to leave the past behind.

Ready to find
your next great read?

Let us help.

Visit prh.com/nextread

Penguin
Random
House